FURY
A Sci-Fi Alien Romance

Hattie Jacks

Copyright © 2022 by Hattie Jacks

All rights reserved.

No part of this book may be reproduced in any form or by any electronic or mechanical means, including information storage and retrieval systems, without written permission from the author, except for the use of brief quotations in a book review.

Cover by Kasmit

Editing: Epona Author Solutions

Proofing: Polaris Editing

 Created with Vellum

Lauren

"Hey, you!" the big green lizard creature shouts at me.

The words are partially garbled by sharp teeth and a heavy accent. But then, these are aliens. I'm on an alien planet, and somehow—they haven't bothered to explain the process—I can understand them.

"Yes, you!" it repeats. This one is male, over six feet tall. It carries a long silver tube which lights up at the end and burns. Don't ask me how I know.

I point to myself. "Me?"

'Hey, you' indeed! It's come to this, abducted by aliens and I go from 'Professor' to 'hey, you' overnight.

"Come here, female," it snarls.

Oh, yes. And 'female' is the other generous nickname bestowed on me by my new alien friends. I walk slowly to where he is standing. Attracting the attention of the lizard aliens, who call themselves 'Drahon', is never a good thing. Or so I've found out in the time I've been their captive.

"Clean this up." He points at a pile of what can only be dung.

"Really?" I stare at him, which is a mistake. Questioning him at all is a mistake. He wields his stun tube, and the light glows.

"What the zark else are you here for, female?" He spits, towering over me in an attempt to intimidate, his hand around my neck, pinning me against the wall.

I shrink away from the light. They only had to touch me with one of those things once, and I understood the hideous pain it created once it hit my skin.

I shouldn't even be out in the compound on the alien planet, where two moons always hang in the sky and their twin suns seem a long way away. Dust drifts where it hits the high walls, intended presumably to keep in all their prisoners. I was only using a short cut I discovered from one side of the interconnected domes to the other, better to speed up the drudge work I now do.

I might be the only human captive of these lizard aliens, but I'm not their only prisoner.

Which is presumably where the dung comes in.

I spot an implement nearby that could be a shovel and hurry over to collect it. The last thing I want is for the Drahon to question why I'm out here in the first place. We get precious little food or rest as it is. Any punishment will result in those limited privileges taken away from me.

"So, where do you want me to put this?" I ask the Drahon who hovers over me disconcertingly. I swing around with the shovel full of evil smelling stuff, and he takes a step back with what seems to be a look of horror on his weird lizard face.

"Over there!" He points to a hole in the ground. "Quickly," he adds.

I deliberate whether I can manage to 'fall over' and get some of it on him but decide such a small victory would probably not be worth the punishment.

Because when it comes to pain, I'm pretty weak. Something the Drahon had found out quickly when I'd first arrived. They haven't even bothered collaring me; I'm that easy to control. Doesn't stop my mouth running away with me on occasion, with inevitable consequences.

"That's enough, female. Get back inside," the Drahon snarls at me as I dispose of the last shovel full.

"No, really, it was my pleasure," I mutter under my breath as I dump the shovel and have to go back the way I came.

All of which means I'm now late to clear up after the midday meal. There will be consequences.

I hate what I've become. It's a far cry from my job as a senior locum lecturer in ancient studies, most recently at a prestigious university in the North of England. I might not have been a professor exactly, but it had been a dream of mine to get to that level one day. The job wasn't great. A constant fight for funding with the university board which contained my ex, Mark, the senior professor in History and the man I'd caught fucking his secretary just before we were supposed to go to my mother's funeral.

But shitty though my situation was, I didn't shovel dung or clear up after a myriad of lizard aliens in my day to day life. I wasn't constantly threatened with pain, or worse. The one saving grace is apparently the only reason I've not been sold for 'pleasure,' as the Drahon put it, is because I'm considered too puny to survive the sexual attentions of other aliens.

I'd hardly consider myself 'puny,' certainly by human standards. I'm taller than average with a generous amount up top, down below, and everywhere else. Even the significant diet since I've been here hasn't reduced me that much. I suppose I should be grateful for small mercies, especially given the types of aliens I've seen since I've been at the Drahon's mercy.

Yep, if aliens that look like massive walking monitor lizards weren't bad enough, there are *things* with tentacles, claws, more than two eyes, snapping sharp teeth, and all manner of unearthly things.

"Lauren?" a low voice calls to me out of a dark corner. "Where have you been?"

A small body steps out of the shadows.

"I tried to take the shortcut and got caught. Sorry, Nari," I say to the little lizard alien.

She's smaller than the Drahon and claims she's a different species, something called a Kijg. Her skin changes color with her mood, unlike the Drahon. Presently, she's a deep purple, which means she's worried.

"You're late." Her black eyes dart from side to side. "I did what I could, but she noticed."

"Don't worry, I'll deal with *her*," I reply with a boldness that belies the quaking terror within.

Every day I wake up in this hideous new existence, I wish I'd not gone star gazing that night. Out in rural Northumberland, up near the Scottish Borders, where the skies were dark and clear. Where we were excavating some Roman remains. If I'd not left the camp to look for the aurora the weather forecast had said would be in the night sky, the aliens never would have found me.

Instead, I'd be back in the ruins of my existence, hating my ex, hating his new partner, and fighting to have my contract renewed.

It's funny how a crappy life can suddenly seem so much better when viewed through the lens of alien abduction.

Instead, I'm about to go toe-to-toe with the nastiest creature this side of Alpha Centauri, or wherever the hell I am. If I thought dealing with academia and betrayal was bad, they have nothing on Yuliat, the Drahon boss.

"Where is the human?" Her shrill voice rings out farther down the corridor.

There's something about me being human that pisses her

off. I can't put my finger on it, but somehow, I can't help but emphasize how human I am when I'm around her. Because I want to piss her off more. It's as if I can't help myself.

"I'm here." I push Nari behind me. It's not her fault I'm late, and I don't want her punished. "I got asked to clear up some shit outside. We're going to start clearing up in here now."

Yuliat stomps through from the canteen. Nari tells me she used to be a high-powered scientist, with friends in high places. What she's doing here is anyone's guess. Although in the main, it appears all she wants to do is make my life a misery.

Fortunately, not only am I already miserable, there's not anywhere to go when I'm already at the bottom, so her attempts generally fail. Which usually pisses her off even more.

My shoulder is grabbed by a three-fingered, clawed hand as Yuliat leans into me, her eyes glittering nastily as her lips hitch in a grimace that I believe passes for a smile among the Drahon.

"You won't be doing any more cleaning today, human."

"I won't? You are most kind, Yuliat," I reply, knowing that sarcasm is entirely lost on aliens, but it makes me feel better.

"No, you've got a special assignment," she says, leaning closer, almost conspiratorially.

Oh, shit. That is not going to be good. At all.

"I don't mind cleaning the canteen," I garble out. "I can do some feed rounds as well," I add, meaning the other prisoners, some of whom have disgusting eating habits, and most of whom have sharp edges and short tempers.

Occasionally, the Drahon bring them out into the compound and make them fight each other. It's never pretty.

But I'd do anything to avoid doing something 'special.' It's likely to result in bodily injury.

"No." Yuliat looks me up and down. "You're perfect for

this assignment. You'll be tending to the Gryn until he recovers."

There's a sharp intake from Nari behind me.

"What's a Gryn?" I ask, and I wish I hadn't because Yuliat's grimace widens.

"You'll find out soon enough." She laughs, increasing her grip on my shoulder and propelling me in front of her towards the prisoner's cells.

Jay

I ATTEMPT TO GROWL OUT A WARNING AT THE approaching Drahon male, but my lungs don't want to comply.

"Wake up, Gryn. You're being moved," he snarls at me.

"Vrex off!" I snarl back, swiping out at him. Anything to keep the disgusting creatures off me. Their scent alone fills my mouth with bile. It takes a huge amount of effort, but I unfurl my wings and attempt to make myself look as big as possible.

"Zarking Gryn. I hate them," the guard shouts over his shoulder at his friend. They always come in pairs as a bare minimum. Since yesterday, there haven't been less than four. "All feathers and nasty tempers."

"Like you can talk, Drahon scum." I spit at him as my breath wheezes, and every single part of me hurts like a bastid. "Can't say it's been sweetness and light for me either."

He slams me in the side of my head with the less painful end of his stun stick, and I fall back onto the floor.

"Hold this piece of trash down," he calls over his shoulder. "Yuliat wants to see him."

There's some grumbling because I've probably managed

to mark every single Drahon in this place with my claws at least once. But I'm pretty badly banged up, and it only takes three to subdue me.

Some time ago—I'm not entirely sure how long, given everything that's happened since—I stupidly allowed myself to get caught by the Drahon while trying to free my commander from their clutches.

Instead of staying with my unit, I charged ahead of my fellow warriors, so vrexing sure of myself, so vrexing clever. All that had happened was I ended up trapped in an escape pod with the Drahon after they set the auto-destruct on their ship.

Even now, the idiocy of that move burns within me. Because, by now, I'm probably light years from Ustokos and my unit. All I want is to get back home. I want to know if my unit is alive or if the blast I saw as we ascended into space killed them all.

If they're dead, that's on me. The thought fills my mind in every waking moment. It haunts my dreams.

"What's Yuliat want with him?" A Drahon male kneels on my chest, making breathing harder and more painful. "He's zarking untrainable. She won't be able to sell him."

The Drahon have plans for me, or so I've been told. But, to my amusement, it's not been working out for them. The control collar they fitted might shock me, but I don't comply. They repeatedly try to goad me into fighting, but I won't, no matter what they do.

Because I have to get back to my unit. I have to get back to Ustokos and make sure I didn't kill them all. Getting back is all I can think about.

So for the last seven turns, I'd been observing. Keeping up enough resistance to the Drahon so they don't work out what I was doing, but I was working out their weaknesses, their routines.

It was more than enough knowledge for me to escape.

And that's what I did. Yesterday.

My problem was I didn't know there was some sort of energy field over the compound. Once I got outside, it seemed easy enough to fly away. Instead, I flew head first into something that disabled me. I hit the ground hard enough to do some damage to my ribs and shoulder, and what's worse is I've injured my left wing. Something I can't let the Drahon know.

A Gryn warrior has always been ready for the fight, but injured and alone? I'm angrier than I've ever been, despite my flesh being weak. Once I'm back to strength, the Drahon will pay for what they've done.

"Get the vrex off me!" I squirm under my captors.

"Want to fight, Gryn?" The guard laughs at me. "I'll fight you and I'll win."

"That sounds like your style, taking on an injured warrior," I reply, unsheathing my claws.

He pulls out one of his stun sticks, the white light glowing at the end, and shoves it into my injured ribs. Unable to help myself, I let out a howl of agony, white sheeting my vision.

"Stop that!" a higher pitched voice rings out in my tiny cell. "We need this one alive and well if we're to meet our quota."

I look up from my position on the floor to see a female Drahon. She's slender like most of the Drahon, possibly feminine, but then she's the only female I've seen so far. She is slightly taller than the males and wears a long coat over their usual uniform of a single one-piece white suit.

"Nothing we do makes him comply. This one's been free far too long. He's useless to us if he can't be trained," the Drahon not currently kneeling on a body part says.

"And we need to recoup the costs of the ship you lost." She stabs a green finger at him. "This is all we've got. We don't have to say he's trained. There are buyers for Gryn regardless. They're rare enough."

She kneels next to me and runs something over me which beeps, and she frowns.

"I prefer my Gryn compliant, though. But a shot of this," she pulls a silver injector from the pocket of her coat, "should cure his rebellious nature for the time being." Yuliat grins at me, or at least she bares her teeth.

She goes back to studying the small pad in her hand.

"What did you let him do to himself?" She glares at the guard standing at the door. "He's going to need some time to heal and, while he's under the influence, a nursemaid."

"He did that to himself because he zarking escaped. Put two of my cohort in the infirmary, even in that state," the male snaps, and one of the other Drahon holding me down thumps me in my ribs. I grunt.

"He's worthless if you kill him, understand?" Yuliat fires out. "And your cohort need more weapons and armor if they can be beaten by a Gryn warrior in this state."

"Where do you want me to put him? He can't stay in here," the male says. "He smashes himself to pieces, even in *this state*."

"He's going to be just fine." Yuliat presses the injector into my neck. I feel a cool sensation against my skin as it hisses the narcotic into my veins.

"That stuff should do the trick, but in any case, put him in room four. Maybe with a bit of pampering and the right incentives, he might see the sense in complying." She takes my chin in her hand, turning my heavy head to face her.

"See? They're such darlings when they're like this. All soft and dreamy." She croons horribly.

I try to pull my chin from her grip, but I can't. Everything is weak. The female Drahon swims in my vision, and I feel nauseous.

Then I feel good.
Really good.

Lauren

Yuliat digs her claws in as she drags me through the large central chamber into the prisoners' quarters. It's not like we're not all prisoners here, but the Drahon have their own area, away from the other aliens. Nari and I are the only ones allowed to go between the two, providing we have a mop and bucket in hand.

Yes, aliens do have mops and buckets. You'd have thought they would have robots for cleaning, but Nari says they are expensive and break. Apparently, that means we're marginally better because we're less breakable than machines. Brilliant.

All the same, although I might have volunteered for feeding duty, I've only done it once and never again. Even the Drahon guard agreed that it probably wasn't safe for me, given that I had been nearly eaten by an alien looking like a cross between a squid and a lion, and not the way around you might imagine.

That is the line. The Drahon can't be arsed to fix a robot, but they don't want their drudges eaten, just yet.

So this 'Gryn' that Yuliat seems so fired up about fills my stomach with ice. It's bad enough being around the Drahon. I definitely don't want to get up close and personal with any more aliens, especially after I've just had to shovel a whole load of alien shit.

We reach the cells, and Yuliat takes a turn to the right, not where I was expecting. This is a part of the alien compound that is usually kept locked.

"The Gryn," I hesitate over the pronunciation, "is down here?"

"The visitors' suites can be kept locked the same as the rest of the facility, and this Gryn needs some careful handling. He's valuable, and he's already gotten himself damaged once." She halts next to a door. "If you do a good job in taking care of him, I'll be in your debt."

Her nasty little eyes and sharp pointed teeth tell me a different tale. That if I don't do as I'm told, I may just become a snack for one of the other creatures they keep here.

"I'm not sure I'm the best person for this job." I try to work out if there's anywhere I can run to as Yuliat snaps a thin black band on my wrist.

"You are," she says emphatically. "This circlet will get you access in and out of his quarters. It is keyed to your DNA, and only you can use it, providing your heart still beats. I suggest you tell him this as soon as you can, to avoid him tearing your arm off." She makes a sound that can only be a snigger. "He's had some preliminary treatment, but I expect, with your help, he'll make a rapid recovery. Won't he?"

She stares down at me, her expression entirely dead, before she grabs my wrist and slams it on a black pad next to the door, which slides open, making me jump.

"He'll have meals prepared for him by the canteen. You are to fetch them, make sure he eats, and provide him with whatever else he needs."

There's something about the emphasis on 'whatever else' that I don't like, but given this is clearly the assignment from hell, I'm not going to antagonize Yuliat any more. Or she might put the squid-lion in with us too.

I risk a peep through the door. There's a short corridor that leads to a small open pool, the type the Drahon favor for bathing, and, through an archway, I see a large bed.

It's pretty opulent for a prisoner. It's also not the sort of place you keep something violent. Or tentacley. It's too nice. This Gryn must be important to the Drahon because they don't do anything good for anyone.

Not without a reason, and usually, that reason has to benefit them.

"Where is he?" I ask, given that the suite seems empty.

Yuliat gives me a push into the room. "Wait," she tells me with a snarl, her indulgence of me at an end.

I stumble inside as the door closes. Every atom of my body screams at me to run. But where would I go? I straighten out the short shift dress every drudge in the place has to wear. Gray, made of a strange slippery material, it has a thin belt to cinch it up and one patch pocket on the front where I keep all my possessions.

There are not many.

My stomach churns as I wait, seconds turning into minutes as I wonder exactly what sort of alien is going to come through that door. The Drahon are as cruel and unpleasant as they are green and scaly. Whatever is going on doesn't bode well for me or the alien Yuliat has decided to dump in my dubious care.

I jump again as the door slides open suddenly. A large Drahon male shoulders himself through it, he's carrying something...

Feathery.

As he makes it through with some difficulty, it's clear that there is someone slung between him and another Drahon, and this someone is...enormous.

The male they carry, and I'm in no doubt from the rippling abs that this is a male, is at least a head taller than the Drahon and wide, too. His musculature is something most human bodybuilders would die for. But it's not his muscles that have me spellbound.

He has wings. Huge, slate gray and white wings, like an alien angel, only very alien, because from what I can see, he also has a set of fearsome claws protruding from the ends of his fingers.

A wicked alien angel then.

For a second, he hangs between the two Drahon, then his head lifts, and a pair of the most gorgeous dark eyes peer drowsily in my direction.

"Stand up, you zarker!" The first Drahon guard lifts the Gryn's arm over his head and shakes him roughly.

He groans but manages to stay upright.

"He's all yours, female." The second guard flickers out his tongue at me, a disgusting habit of the Drahon when they're trying to work out your emotions. "He's a little worse for wear at the moment, but that should work in your favor. He'll comply with whatever you want him to do."

He plants a hand in between the Gryn's wings and shoves him forward. The male stumbles and puts out his hand to take hold of the wall, looking for all the world like a drunk on a stag night, providing the dress code was 'wing man.' He clutches at his abdomen, where I see a riot of bruising.

"Any trouble, well, you're on your own." The first Drahon cackles as they back out of the room and the door slams shut.

The Gryn doesn't move. His eyes are closed, his head bowed, and his breathing ragged. He mutters something to himself, something incomprehensible. Now I get the chance to have a good look at him. He's covered in injuries, some older, some more recent. He's also filthy, streaked with blood, dirt, and god knows what. His short dark brown hair is mussed, sticking up at all angles. Around his left bicep is a golden metal band, which shines through the filth.

He is absolutely ripped, though, with abs a girl could get lost in. For an alien, he's pretty damn fine.

"Er..." I'm not entirely sure how to address an alien angel who makes my stomach go stupidly gooey. "Sir, would you like to take a bath?"

Worst. Chat-up line. Ever.

He lifts his head painfully and sniffs the air. Then he puts one foot in front of the other with infinite care and staggers slowly towards the pool.

"Shit!" I hurry after him, not wanting my new charge to fall in head first and drown himself, as I suspect Yuliat might see that as a failure on my part. "Wait, let me help you."

The alien angel ignores me and wades into the shallow section, slowly getting deeper, until he's up to his waist. I hop from foot to foot with concern. I should stop him or do something. I'm just not sure what I should do. He has to be close to seven feet tall, and I'm pretty sure he could eviscerate me with those vicious looking claws.

Evil alien angel.

He groans again, then drops one wing into the water. With a sudden violent movement, he beats out, spraying the entire room with water and soaking me. Immediately, he dips the other wing below the surface but lifts that one gingerly out of the water without a splash.

"Hey!" I call out, but it's too late. I'm hit in the face with another deluge that sends me running to the other side of the room.

Not that it matters. I'm already soaked, and he doesn't care one way or the other.

Then he drops beneath the surface and doesn't come up.

Jay

There are so many good scents. So many. I blow out a breath and close my eyes. I'm so vrexing drunk, it's like being dunked in a barrel of my favorite var beer.

I could be back at the lair, back on Ustokos with my brother warriors calling to me. Talking with me about our latest mission, joking, messing around…

Everything hurts. All I want is a bath and a preen. I feel good, drunk maybe, still good, but at some point, I'm going to have to sober up and get cleaned up or Commander Strykr will be displeased.

"Sorry, Commander," I mutter, my lips not wanting to comply with the words.

Cleaned up! That has to be what's familiar. It takes some effort on my part, but I focus ahead of me and see the water.

It's hard going, which is wrong. Even when I'm this drunk, I can fly and fight. I should look for Ayar. He's always ready to spar. Part of me wants a fight.

I groan as I enter the water. It feels incredible, like I haven't bathed in a long time. There's another familiar scent which calms me. It makes me believe I can have a bath in safety. Water sluices over my feathers, over my skin, and it's great. More than great. I could just fall asleep and dream away my pain.

"For fuck's sake." I'm being hauled out of the water. "What do you think you are doing?" The voice interrupts my wet, happy thoughts.

It drags me back to the surface where hate fills my veins. I've been tranqued. I can feel the narcotic running through me. It's making me weak and pathetic.

"Get off me!" I growl at my, as yet unseen, assailant. "If you know what's good for you."

"I wasn't going to let you drown, but fine, if you think you're in any condition to be left alone, I'll drop you back in," the voice grumbles at me.

I twist my head to see what dares speak to a Gryn warrior in that manner. My vision finally focuses.

It's a human female. Small, like they all are. This one has long hair, and the color shifts as it moves, somewhere between brown and gold. Crystal gray eyes flash beautifully. She looks wet. And angry.

Something I can relate to.

"I can look after myself," I snarl. This has to be a Drahon trick; the female probably isn't even human.

The Drahon are always trying to trick me, promising to send me home, claiming they have my commander ready to reclaim me. It's all lies. The Drahon are the more slippery versions of their cold-blooded cousins from Ustokos, the Kijg. And everyone knows you never trust a Kijg.

So I'm not trusting this female. The Drahon want my compliance, and they are not going to get it, no matter what they do.

Or what they offer.

I attempt to wrench myself out of the water, but it's clear I can't. The warmth has helped with some of my injuries, but my ribs still crunch, and whatever I've done to my left wing, it's excruciating. I hiss under my breath.

"You can't just lie there. Come on." The female puts an arm under my neck and levers me into a sitting position.

"Don't touch me."

"Okay, fine, get up on your own." She stands back, and my tranqued vision blurs.

Why is she doing that? Presumably so I can't see she's not human. Vrexing Drahon.

With some difficulty, I flip myself over onto my hands and knees. Water runs off my feathers and onto the floor. I flick out my right wing, shaking off the water, and the female squeals.

I laugh. That'll teach the dirty Drahon to play tricks on me.

I put considerable effort into slowly standing. Once up, the room spins, and I stumble over to a doorway, hanging on for dear life. I'm sure if I go down on the floor again, I won't get up.

Through the alcove is a large bed. Much bigger than my ledge in the barracks, it's more like a nest. My heart does a funny flip in my chest, aching, with a longing I don't understand.

I don't want to understand. I want to escape the Drahon and get back to my unit. Without them, I'm just a merc. A Gryn warrior without purpose. I am nothing.

But I do want that bed. It looks very comfortable. I'm tired and I hurt. No part of my tranqued body wants to properly obey my command, and I stagger forward until I fall face first into my nest.

"Fuck, they did a job on you, didn't they?"

Vrex it! The female is still hanging around. She sits beside me on the bed, folding back my good wing and inspecting my side.

"Vrex off!" I say, my voice half-muffled by the bedding. "I don't need any help. I just want to sleep."

Lithe fingers trip through my feathers, over my shoulder and up into my hair. I should tell her to go away again. I should use my claws on her, my teeth, anything to get this harridan to leave me alone. I don't want to be touched by anyone.

And especially her. Vrexing female!

Her touch is light, pleasant even. After a bath, what a Gryn warrior most wants is a preen. She's preening me, and I groan out loud. I should fight her. I have to fight them all.

Vrexing Drahon and their tricks!

"Do you want him to get better or not?" an angry voice shouts, and it makes my head ache.

I peel open my eyes to see the female standing at the end of the bed and find I'm somehow on my back, propped up on pillows, my breathing easier.

I must have fallen asleep. Even so, I'm still tranqued to the eyeballs, my limbs not wanting to respond.

The female has her hands on her hips, but her slave shift is semi-translucent with water, the outline of her buttocks clearly visible. Two Drahon males stand in front of her. One holds a laser pistol lazily, the other has his arms folded over his chest.

She seems tiny in comparison.

"Because if you do, you'll let me go get something to treat his wounds and leave him be," the female fires out.

"He's a zarking Gryn warrior. He'll kill us all if he gets half a chance," the larger of the two Drahon guards replies, jerking his laser pistol at me.

"If I don't treat his wounds, they might get infected, and he'll die. Is that what you want? Is that what Yuliat wants?" The little human female vibrates with anger. "Well, do you?"

The guards drop their weapons and look at each other, clearly debating what to do.

"Yuliat will not be happy if he dies."

"I'll be zarking happy. He properly cut me up last time he tried to escape," the guard without a pistol huffs.

"I'd do it again," I snarl out, attempting to get up.

And failing.

All I have between me and the Drahon is this scrap of a female, who for some reason, appears to be fighting in my corner.

Vrexing Drahon tricks!

Lauren

My new alien is as grumpy as fuck. He's also drugged to the eyeballs, hardly able to string a sentence together, and then when he does, his words are slurred.

Having soaked me to the skin, he fell asleep on the bed as I attempted to check his injuries. It's possible he looked worse once he had finished bathing, partially because all the dirt was cleaned off, and I see the bruising bloomed over most of his torso, but also because the warm water reopened many of his crusted over wounds.

Having snarled/slurred at me when awake, his face when asleep is devastatingly handsome. All high cheekbones, strong aquiline nose, and a bottom lip that protrudes just a little as if wanting to be kissed. Which is a stupid sentiment.

I'm definitely not kissing an alien.

I squeeze my eyes closed and try not to think about finding my ex, Mark, his face suctioned on hers in a slobbery kiss. Although that wasn't all he was doing with his secretary. My stomach still rolls at the memory.

Nope, no kissing of aliens or otherwise, but I do need to make sure this one is kept alive, and once he's on his front, his breathing gets worse and worse. Presumably, some of that bruising relates to a broken rib or two. With some considerable effort, because the wings have a life of their own, I get him turned over, and he begins to breathe easier.

His wings are something else. Soft, steely feathers, most of them taller than I am, are glossy, glinting in the light. The wing he managed to shake out over me, soaking me to the skin again, is in better condition than the other one. It has a nasty injury just where it bends, feathers matted with blood and the ones underneath streaked with pink where the water sluiced the blood away.

Overall, they might have heavily sedated this alien angel, but it doesn't look to me like he's that much of a threat, anyway. Far too much of a pretty boy.

Except for the claws, of course. Onyx black, viciously sharp, and retractable like a cat's. I can imagine they would do a lot of damage.

I know Nari has a small first aid kit in the alcove where we sleep. Presumably, Yuliat doesn't think any of the Gryn's injuries are life threatening, but he can't continue bleeding everywhere. Which means I need to find a way to treat him, avoid infection, and get him better. Then he's not my responsibility anymore.

Fucking hell, I can hardly care for myself, let alone an enormous alien male like this one. I'm putting all my effort into surviving the next twenty-four hours, not getting beaten up by the Drahon, and finding enough food not to starve.

Which meant I had to run the gauntlet of the Drahon guards posted outside of the cell/suite my alien is being kept in, and they barreled in, presumably to gloat.

They are not happy with their lot and not prepared to accept that the alien angel is injured enough to need more treatment.

But I know the Drahon enough. These two are just bullies

looking for a reason to do some damage, and the injured Gryn is fair game.

Which means I need to be wily and invoke the name of almighty Yuliat.

"Yuliat will not be happy if he dies."

"I'll be zarking happy. He properly cut me up last time he tried to escape," the guard without a pistol huffs.

"I'd do it again," a deep, velvet voice slurs from behind us.

My alien flaps on the bed, attempting to get up.

"See what I mean?"

"No!" I put my arms out to stop the pair from advancing. "You know you're both a match for him in his current condition. Just leave him alone, and let me treat him, or I'll have to tell Yuliat you stopped me."

It's my last ditch attempt, and I hope my idiot alien has half a brain cell left to keep quiet. I risk a look over my shoulder. He's stopped trying to get up, one arm clutched over his abdomen, his dark eyes dull with pain.

"I can't be bothered dealing with the Gryn today. Let the female do what she wants to do. It'll keep him busy," the Drahon with the gun says to the other one with a distinct leer at me. "The Gryn love a female. And their anatomy? *Very* interesting."

Fucking Drahon. If they can make a situation worse, they will. Now I really don't know what to make of my alien.

The two guards file out, slowly, and as soon as I can, I hurry out and back to my quarters.

"Lauren? Why are you wet?" Nari stands up from her bed, which is on the opposite wall from mine in our tiny alcove. "Are you okay? Did the Gryn hurt you?" She's staring at me.

When I look down, not only am I still soaked, but I'm covered in his blood.

"It's fine, Nari. He's heavily drugged, and this is his

blood." I indicate the streaks of red on my clothes. "I need something to treat him with. Can I borrow your kit?"

"You want to treat the Gryn?" Nari flushes orange, her eyes widening.

"I don't..." The words stick in my throat as I try to process them. "I don't think he's that dangerous. He's just hurt and maybe scared like us."

"The Gryn are not scared of anything. They were protectors and warriors on Ustokos."

"Ustokos?"

"That's where the Gryn come from, their planet." Nari dips her head, her skin changing to a light blue. "And mine."

"So, you've met them before?" I ask.

"Not met them. Not really. I saw their patrols when I was a youngling. Many Gryn, all in the air." She lowers her voice. "They are dangerous, vicious warriors, Lauren. You must take care."

"This one isn't in any fit state to be dangerous or vicious," I tell her. "He's wasted."

Nari retrieves the pouch containing the medical kit from under her bed. "The Gryn like to party. I wouldn't be so sure that he's not a risk just because he's sedated," she replies. "They're predators, pure and simple. They couldn't indulge their instincts on Ustokos because it was ruled over by a sentient AI system called Proto. Some of us, some of the Gryn, managed to evade the robot systems and live freely, or as freely as we could. But it kept the Gryn busy."

She hands over the kit but holds onto it for a short while.

"Just be careful, okay? Gryn warriors are unpredictable," she says, her black eyes full of concern.

Now I have *questions*. Many, many questions about him, about Ustokos. None of which I'm going to get answers to because I have Yuliat on my back. Because if I thought my life couldn't get any more shitty than being abducted by aliens, playing nurse with a predator half the galaxy fears has just ramped it up to shit-tastic.

"I'll be careful, I promise," I say to Nari, and she lets go of the kit.

"You'd better. I don't know what I'd do without you," she says, her skin turning pink, almost like mine.

"You'd be just fine without me, and you know it. Yuliat won't do anything to you." I give her a big smile. "I'd better go."

Giving Nari's cool, three-fingered hand a squeeze, I hurry back to the canteen where I'm given a tray laden with food for the Gryn.

Yuliat really does want him up and about.

The two guards are missing when I reach the cell/suite, and I let myself in. Fortunately, my charge has not drowned himself in the pool, and as I turn the corner into the bedroom, he's where I left him. Asleep.

I put down the tray and turn back to him. His eyes are open and his expression a little clearer.

"I just want to help you." I hold up the first aid kit. "Fix you up a bit. Can I do that?"

He winces as he shifts position on the bed. "Why?"

"Because I've been told to," I answer, honestly. "If I don't, the Drahon will probably kill me or something." I sigh. To think I used to be anxious about the constant threat of death.

He mutters something under his breath.

"What was that?" I ask in my best teacher's voice.

"Nothing. If you're here under sufferance, you may as well do what you have to." He relaxes, sprawled over the bed. He's wearing nothing but a pair of tight-fitting shorts, and the words of the Drahon guard come back to haunt me. *"Their anatomy. Very interesting."*

I take a step towards him. "The Drahon are just outside, though, so don't try anything," I lie.

He snorts and looks away from me as if I've disappointed him.

Next to the bed, I unpack the kit and start on his wounds. Nari has a pot of healing gel and a strange implement that can be used to seal shut the slightly larger cuts. Both of which I'm familiar with because the Drahon took a while to work out how badly they could treat me and not cause injury. Slowly, I work my way over the Gryn until I've managed to get most of his injuries seen to, except the one on his wing.

I look up from my work to his face. It seems like he's fallen asleep again.

"I'm going to have to get on the bed to treat your wing. Please don't hurt me," I say quietly.

He opens his eyes. I thought they were completely black, but close up, I see a dark brown iris surrounding a pinprick pupil.

"I wouldn't hurt you," he says, his deep, velvet voice wrapping around me like silk.

I kneel next to him. He's holding his injured wing stiffly. "I'll be as gentle as I can," I tell him.

Spreading the feathers, I see the cut on his wing looks like it's gone down to the bone. I swallow hard as I feel bile rising. I am so far out of my comfort zone, it's not even funny.

"Is it bad?" he asks, his liquid eyes suddenly clear again.

"It's not good." I gulp down a breath. "Let me see what I can do."

Jay

I'M NOT SURE IF THE TRANQ IS WEARING OFF, BUT the female does certainly appear to be human now that I can see straighter. There's a strong smell of food in the room, but it doesn't disguise her.

It's a familiar scent, and that can't be possible. I've met human females before, but not her. She's new to me.

Which means this has to be something Yuliat wants me to think. She wants me to trust this female.

That is not going to happen.

I watch as she works on my wing, closing my eyes against the pain as she seals the wound shut. Then she covers it with the cool gel she used on the rest of me, and it feels much better. I even feel like smiling, but I don't.

"Would you like something to eat?" she asks, wiping her hands on a rag. "There's some food over there." She points to a small table across from me. It holds a tray groaning with meat, most likely tranqued.

"You'd like that, wouldn't you?" I snarl at her.

She recoils. "I...I'd like you to eat something, if that's what you mean."

The food smells good. I am hungry.

"No." I fold my arms over my chest, noting the pain in my ribs is better.

"Oh," she says, carefully reaching onto the bed to put all of her medical supplies back in their pouch.

"It's tranqued."

"I don't think it is," she replies.

"You would say that." I narrow my eyes at her.

I still feel impossibly light-headed. Whatever Yuliat dosed me with, it's taking a long time to leave my system. The last thing I want, if I'm going to escape again, is to get another dose. Which means I'm going to have to play this carefully.

"Suit yourself." She shrugs. "If you're not going to eat it, do you object to me having some?"

"Do what you want," I growl and have a pang of regret when her eyes widen with fear.

I don't want this female afraid of me, although I'm not sure why. If only I could think clearly. But the scents in this room are overwhelming, and I'm incredibly hot.

"I'm Lauren Ellis," she says, walking over to the food. "Everyone calls me Lauren."

"Lauren." I roll her name around on my tongue. It feels right, but then I am vrexed.

She's cramming the meat into her mouth like it's going to be taken away from her, as well as slipping some into the pocket on the front of her still damp dress.

Maybe it isn't tranqued after all. Maybe Yuliat prefers the direct approach to subduing her Gryn.

With some effort, I lever myself up from the bed and stumble over to the food.

"Slow down. You'll choke," I say, and Lauren jumps away from me, a lump of meat dropping from her hand. "Don't you get fed?"

"Yes, sometimes." Lauren looks guilty.

Vrex the Drahon, they're trying to make me feel sorry for this scrap of a female. They want me to trust her.

"Well, then." I take a step back.

The food does look good, and my stomach growls. But I'm not going to break that easily. My captors can put me in a comfortable nest, with a bathing pool and a female and food, but a Gryn warrior knows when he's being played.

I make my way stiffly back to the bed and sit down. I have to work out a way of escape, of getting back to my planet and my unit.

But the ache in my ribs and the pain spearing through my wing means I'm not going anywhere. I just have to hope that the female hasn't done anything to make my injuries worse. In the meantime, if I avoid getting tranqued again, I'm sure I can succeed next time.

"You do know you're speaking out loud, don't you?" I look up to see Lauren standing next to me. "I really don't think you should be trying to escape." She lowers her voice. "Not yet, anyway."

If there was ever a reason to distrust this female, the fact that she's allowing me to consider an escape has to mean the Drahon are behind her being with me.

"What I choose to do is none of your business, female," I spit out at her.

"Fair enough." She holds up her hand, a small roll of some sort held in it. "I've made you a sandwich. Given I'm not snoring on the floor, I thought you might decide the food is safe enough to eat."

I stare at her. She's brazen, I'll give her that. But when it comes to subterfuge, I learned from the best that the Gryn have to offer, our senior spymaster, Ryak. Two can play at this game.

"Maybe, as long as you're my taster, maybe I'll have something to eat." I give her the benefit of my best smile.

She takes a step back and holds out the food.

"I'm not on the menu," she stutters out.

Looks like my smile didn't work, which leaves me at somewhat of a loss. I might have met human females, but they were always the mates of my fellow warriors. I've never been around one on my own.

In fact, I try not to be around any female on my own. They're dangerous. And complicated. And unknown.

But I'm not about to let her get the better of me. I snatch at the roll, snagging it with my claws as she gasps out loud. I shove it into my mouth and luxuriate in the flavor that explodes over my tongue.

"I'm Jay, Warrior in the Legion of the Gryn," I say, with my mouth still full. "I do hope we can get better acquainted."

Lauren

He chews the food, huffing like a drunkard, so obviously still sedated. That much was clear from the way he was muttering to himself about escaping. And that smile he just gave me.

It was all teeth. White, sharp teeth.

But he's told me his name, and it seems like he's going to trust me, for the time being, which will make my job a hell of a lot easier.

Thirty-year-old university lecturers are not cut out to be nursemaids, but relating to people—okay, aliens—I can do. I've spent enough time helping students and dealing with difficult senior professors to be attuned to the needs of someone.

But patching up a massive alien angel can now go on my list of jobs I never thought I'd have the guts to do. Or never expected to do. But I'd rather not stay as an alien cleaner and nurse to a stubborn, grumpy, and, frankly, still wasted alien angel.

I have my reasons. Men, males, are not on my radar.

Jay, like any drunk, seems to be enjoying his sandwich. It's gone in a couple of bites, and he licks unsteadily at his clawed fingers in such a way I fear for his tongue.

"Do you want anything else to eat?" I ask him, conscious that he probably should be resting, given that most of his left side is a nasty shade of dark purple, which can't be his natural color.

He also has the oddest skin over his shoulders. It feels like old leather, soft and supple, but also tough, like it has a job to do. So, he's humanoid and alien all wrapped up in a package that is probably more human than alien.

Does that mean I like him? *Reasons, Lauren. Don't forget the reasons.*

"No more food," Jay growls at me, even as he eyes the tray behind me.

Stupid, stubborn alien.

"Okay." I take hold of his arm, and he flinches, dark eyes staring at where I'm touching him. "I need to change this bed. It's covered in your...well, everything. You can't sleep on it. Sit over there."

I point to a corner. I'd prefer him sat down so he can't fall over and hurt himself more.

"Vrex you, female," he snarls, swaying to his feet.

"Stay there then." I swiftly strip off the bed coverings and carry them out into the corridor.

When I get back, he's face down on the bare foam which passes for a mattress, snoring.

"Oh, dear god, give me strength!" I've no idea what Yuliat will say, but there's no way I'm going to be able to make the bed with him in it.

I carefully tuck a wing under him and roll him onto his good side. Yet again, I'm struck by how handsome his face is as he sleeps.

Yeah, alien handsome, Lauren. Don't you forget it.

Because the one thing I need in my seriously fucked up life is to have any sort of relationship with an alien. My love life on Earth was a disaster area, and my heart has taken a beating it doesn't need again. Men, males, they just betray. Make you feel like you're the one in the wrong. All because you 'don't understand my needs.'

There's no way I'm going through all that again. Whatever I'm feeling for Jay, it doesn't mean anything. Not to him and not to me.

I pat his wing, the feathers silky under my touch, and return to the pile of sheets in the hall. The door chimes quietly as I press my bracelet against the black pad next to the door, and it slides open.

"That Gryn is a fast worker, isn't he?" My new Drahon nemesis steps in front of me. "Already made a mess of those sheets and maybe your hot little cunt too?" He sneers out a laugh.

"Surprised he didn't split this female in two. Who'd have thought they were compatible?" his smaller friend adds.

"Fuck off." I realize I've said the words out loud. "I mean, I need to get to the laundry, and I have other work to do," I add hastily.

"You're not going anywhere, female."

"I have to..."

The soiled sheets are torn from my hands with a ripping sound, and the large Drahon guard is in my face.

"You stay with the Gryn. Those were Yuliat's orders. You feed him, you treat him, and you stay with him."

"My other duties..."

"You can return to them once the Gryn is comfortable."

"But..." I flail around for an excuse, a reason not to have to go back into the room with the enormous grumpy predator. "There's only one bed."

"I'm sure he'll share." The Drahon grins at me, or grimaces, it's difficult to tell without lips.

He grabs my arm roughly, spinning me around as I cry out in pain. I shouldn't let them know they hurt me, but this time, my reaction is one of surprise. "Back you go."

He slams the wrist with my bracelet against the panel, and the door opens again. I'm shoved back into the suite/cell, door swishing shut behind me.

In the quiet, I shiver. My shift hasn't dried much since Jay, warrior of the Legion of the Gryn, soaked me. Now there is no bedding, nothing I can use to get dry.

Having inspected every single inch of the suite, it's very clear that, unless I want to sleep on the floor, the only option I have is to share with the massive alien, currently snoring happily to himself and taking up most of the bed.

I pick at the remaining food. Somehow, I've lost my appetite, now I've been locked in with him. As I can't get any of the food to Nari, the joy of getting hold of additional rations has waned.

My new alien friend shifts on the bed, grumbling in his slumber, his claws stretching out and retracting, his good wing flapping slightly.

"I really hope that the only thing you do in your sleep is snore," I mutter at him as I walk around the bed and slide on the side as far away from him, as possible. Given that he's doing a really good impression of a starfish, that doesn't leave me with much room, even on a bed this big.

Tucking my arm under my head as a pillow, I lie on my side, facing him. Watching as his chest moves up and down rhythmically. Wondering about how we both came to be here, at the mercy of the Drahon.

He is a huge predator, all claws, suspicion, and anger, but he's also a perfect predator. From his silky steel feathers and his muscular form to his ability to heal.

He might be drugged, but he could have ripped my head off. And he hasn't.

With that comforting thought, I close my eyes, hoping that sleep might take me.

And that Jay stays sedated for the time being.

Jay

The scent filling my nostrils is utterly enticing and familiar. Shame my head is still full of fog. I might have slept like the dead, but it's done little to clear the narcotic from my system.

This is the Drahons' doing. I'm supposed to be disoriented; it's a way of breaking me. I won't break, no matter what they do.

Although, that scent is particularly enticing after my sleep. I raise my head to check my surroundings. I remain in the strange room where I was brought. I'm not bound, and my wounds feel considerably better. On my left is what's left of the food I refused and on my right…

Is a sleeping human female!

I shuffle away from her, over to the other side of the bed. She shouldn't be here. Not with me, on my own.

Her long, golden-brown hair spills over her shoulder, her head resting on her hands. Close up, she is very beautiful. Dark eyelashes on her skin, spread with little brown dots. Lips pursed, she is still. Very still. Maybe too still? Shouldn't she be breathing?

With an effort because my limbs, ribs, and left wing ache, I turn on my side and reach for her. Just as I'm about to touch, her eyes spring open, and she lets out a short scream, scrambling away and falling off the side of the bed.

If I could move fast, like normal, I'd have caught her in an instant, but nothing wants to work. Not my mind, not my wings, or anything. Instead, I employ an ungainly scramble towards where she has fallen, only to see her spring to her feet.

"Friend, not food!" she says rapidly.

"I wasn't..." I lift my hand to run it through my hair in exasperation. "I wouldn't...*eat* you! What sort of warrior do you think I am?"

"I don't know. You're an alien, with claws," she replies, taking another step away from me, staring pointedly at my hands.

I sheathe my claws. My control over them is compromised at the moment, and I can't say I'd blame her for keeping her distance.

What am I thinking? She is the same female from yesterday placed here to tempt me with drugged food and bathing.

"Why are you here, anyway?" I fire at her. "Surely, you have other duties to the Drahon?"

Her eyes dart over to the food. "I did have other duties, but apparently, I'm supposed to stay here with you, catering to your every whim."

"Vrexing Drahon!" I swear. "They think this is going to make me comply?" I wrench myself off the bed, staggering into the corridor. "Do you think I'm going to do your bidding?" I roar.

Anger swells inside me, anger at myself for stupidly following my nose on that ship, seeking out something...I don't know what. Anger at getting caught, at allowing my unit to be killed.

Anger I want to take out on something.

A door at the end of the corridor slides open, and to my deep joy, a pair of Drahon enter. Before they move any farther, I charge at them, good wing propelling me forward until I barrel into both, knocking them flat. The doorway empty, I'm already out and running. Somewhere, somehow, I will be free, even as the alarm blares.

"Jay!" A voice behind me calls out my name. I check over my shoulder. It's the human female. She picks her way over the fallen Drahon. "Don't do this. They'll just punish you."

I laugh out loud. Like I care. With a snarl, I turn away from her. I will be the one doing the punishing, I can promise her that.

A cohort of Drahon round the corner, blocking my exit. Or at least that's what they think. Claws extended, I growl. My wing better not fail me now.

With two strokes, I launch myself towards them even as something hard and sharp hits me in my shoulder. Nothing should penetrate my skin there, but this thing does.

Time seems to slow. Instead of heading towards the Drahon, I'm going down towards the floor, and I can't stop myself. Everything is warped.

And everything goes black.

"Vrex!" I lever myself upright or try to.

Something cool is placed on my forehead. "Don't try to move. Not yet. I told you there would be a punishment."

I'm back on the bed, this time both hands are fastened to the wall behind me. The human is gently wiping a cool, damp cloth over my face.

"Lauren?" Her name comes back to me. Human females like being called by their names, I remember.

"Please, just stay still. Let me clean you up." Her voice is soft, calming.

It shouldn't be. I should be raging, but that scent, her scent. I know I've smelled it before.

"I had to try."

"You shouldn't. The Drahon have very limited patience." She wipes the cloth down my chest, swiping it over my abdomen and only just skirting the waistband of my pants.

My cocks spring up. Not just wanting attention, they are painfully hard. Wanting her.

"Please?" I don't want to beg, not if she is in league with the Drahon. It'll only make them redouble their efforts to get me to comply. "Not there," I finish.

Lauren looks down at my crotch, where my arousal is extremely evident.

"Shit!" She pulls her hand away rapidly. "Shit!" she repeats the human swear word.

I try to think about zeroing my laser rifle. I try to think about flying competitions with my brother warriors. I try to think about anything other than where her hands have just been.

"Can I have some water?" I ask. It's all I can do to get her gaze from me, the one that's serving only to inflame things, not cool them.

"Yes, yes! Of course!" Lauren jumps up eagerly and runs out of the room.

I squeeze my eyes closed, rolling my neck. I've been tranqued again, but this time, it's not as bad. I can sort of think straight. I can sort of get things under control, or at least half under control.

"Here." Lauren is back, holding a cup up to my lips. I drink deeply. Until I remember about the risk of narcotics in the food.

For a second, I think of spitting, but Lauren is right in front of me. I hesitate, then swallow.

"Is that okay? Do you want more?" she asks, bright gray eyes studying my face. "I promise it's not drugged." She takes a mouthful from the same cup.

I nod, and she lets me drink again.

"Any chance you can let me out of these restraints?" I ask her.

"After what you did this morning? You're lucky they brought you back here at all." Lauren bustles away, coming back with a small jar of something clear. She opens it and dips in her fingers. "And you're lucky you're still in one piece. You must be valuable to them."

She starts to dab the clear gel on my skin. I've got a whole load of new scrapes, presumably from where I crashed and burned earlier.

"The Drahon sell Gryn warriors as slaves. They sell humans, too," I tell her.

"Apparently, I'm not worth selling," she replies as she concentrates on her work.

"Not from what I've heard," I reply. "You're just as valuable as me."

She laughs, the sound hollow. "I've never been worth that much to anyone. That's my lot in life." She stands, reaching up to the shoulder of my wing. "You've reopened this wound. I'm going to have to try to close it."

"Do what you must, but I will try to escape again. You need to know that. I will get back to my unit and to my planet."

"That's your choice." She picks out the wound closing instrument from the pouch and holds it up to my wing. I feel a searing heat, and then she's slathering gel over the area. "But I'd rather not be the one patching you up every time you try."

She runs her hands up my bound arms, like she's checking

them over, her ample chest pressing against mine. She leans into me farther, lips brushing my skin, and again, parts of my anatomy go wild.

"I got the tranquilizer dart out. It hadn't discharged all its contents. But Yuliat doesn't know. Can you still pretend that you're drugged for me? I might be able to get them to release you if they think you're not a threat."

She withdraws immediately, and if it wasn't for the intoxication of her scent, I'd be able to speak. My head swims, not from the narcotic or lack of it, but because I know where I scented her before.

Lauren was on the ship with me when I was taken. She was there.

And there's a good reason I charged ahead of my fellow warriors.

When I scented her, I knew.

Lauren is my mate.

Lauren

Jay's eyelids start to droop as I finish cleaning him up. I try not to think about the bulge that appeared in his shorts earlier.

It looks like he has more human anatomy than I was expecting. Anatomy which responds in a similar way, too. But anatomy which is much, much larger than any I've seen before.

And I shouldn't be thinking about alien anatomy, at all. *Behave, Lauren! He's in your care and nothing else.*

Because all he wants to do is escape. I couldn't help but admire how he downed the two Drahon and was prepared to face another dozen without any fear. If Yuliat hadn't gotten him with the tranquilizer dart, maybe he might have made it.

Instead, he's back in my unspectacular care, and this time, he's chained up. That hasn't exactly helped my plan.

After the Drahon had dragged him back into the suite, I got the opportunity to pull to the dart before Yuliat saw. She then berated me for nearly half an hour until I pointed out if all her guards couldn't stop the massive warrior, how was I supposed to do the same? At which point, she gave me a very knowing smile.

Gryn are compatible with humans, apparently. He might start to like me after a while, she said.

I understood what she wanted me to do, and I want no part of it. I'm done with men. They are untrustworthy, dangerous, and should be banned.

Does this man ban extend to aliens? I study Jay's handsome, relaxed face. It should. Being as alien gorgeous as he is, it has to be illegal somewhere.

And yet, Jay, despite his injuries, isn't going to accept his fate. This huge brute of an alien fought and fought. He's still fighting now.

I should have fought more. I shouldn't have passively accepted my ex cheating on me was my fault, like he said. Because I was too caught up in my mother's sudden cancer diagnosis and death because I had no one but her. And then I had no one at all. Maybe I didn't need to fight to save the relationship, but I could have been stronger. I could have told myself it wasn't my fault. I could have been more like Jay.

We're both prisoners, but he has a chance. He's big and strong. If I can help him control himself, he might just manage to get free.

"Asleep again?" I tut out loud. "Lazy Gryn." I look up at his face, and he's opened one eye. It glitters briefly with mirth before he closes it again, relaxing himself on the bed.

I clear up my medical supplies and head back out of the suite where the Drahon are on guard. My nemesis from earlier sports a fetching bandage over his shoulder. I hide a smirk.

"Where are you going?"

"I'm going to get food for the Gryn for when he wakes up."

The guard huffs at me, but it's not like he can argue. Jay

made a bit of a mess of them both, and Yuliat wasn't interested. That's how I know he's valuable to them.

And how I know I'm expendable.

I hurry to the canteen to collect the food. When I arrive, nothing's ready.

"Get whatever you want. I don't have time to deal with the whims of prisoners," the Drahon cook yells at me.

At least I can be certain the food isn't drugged if I've picked it myself. Maybe I can convince Jay this time. I load up a tray with similar items to last time, assuming that they are all things he can eat. What that means is there's a lot of meat. I guess a warrior of his size needs protein.

Back at the suite, I find Jay still on the bed, only now he's not bound to the wall anymore.

"Hey," I whisper, prodding him gently in his abdomen.

"Mmph?" He jerks awake. "Lauren?" My name rumbles on his lips and a frankly surprising burn of desire runs down my spine.

"How are you feeling? Who released you?" I ask, busying myself with the food and ignoring the completely inappropriate wetness gathering between my thighs.

"Oh, Yuliat came in and made one of the guards do it. She seemed to want to check me over. She took some blood, look." He points at a puncture wound on his arm.

"Did she give you anything?"

Jay yawns widely. "No." He snuggles back onto the bed.

"Are you sure?"

"I'm feeling more awake now, since you..."

I'm across to him in seconds, hand clamped over his mouth. "Quiet. If Yuliat finds out what I did..."

I realize immediately what I've done and spring away from him. He eyes me carefully, and I don't blame him for being suspicious.

"I didn't tell her," he says, quietly. "I'm not that stupid."

"I brought some food for you." I retrieve the tray and dump it on the bed. "Hand-picked. By me," I emphasize.

"Why are you doing this for me?" he asks, narrowing his eyes, even as a clawed hand creeps towards the tray of food.

"Why wouldn't I do this for you? Wouldn't you help me if you could?" I ask.

So far, he's either been as grumpy as hell, drugged to hell, or asleep. So, to some extent, I'd like to know the answer.

"Gryn are honorable males." He attempts to straighten himself up, wincing as he does so. "We are protectors. Of course I'd protect my mate...my female...a female." He stumbles over the words. "As long as that female was honorable in return," he finishes.

Perhaps honesty is the best policy, now my alien is finally awake and seems to have all his faculties.

"Look, if I don't take care of you, the Drahon are going to do something nasty to me. What's worse is they'll also probably do something equally as unpleasant to my friend, Nari. I'm not about to let that happen to anyone I know, so I'm here, with you, making sure you're fed and your injuries are treated. I'm sorry if you think there's something wrong with that, but it's about survival, not about you."

I fold my arms and look down pointedly at the tray. All of Jay's feathers prick up over his wings as he studies me. Then they slick down again when there's a noise out in the corridor. He turns with a growl.

"Don't!" I exclaim, and, without thinking, I put my hand out to grab his wing, my fingers going deep into his feathers. He spins back to me, grabbing hold of my wrists and pulling me into him. Holding us together.

He smells like spices. Warm, toasty with a hint of leather. Hard muscle undulating under me as he breathes raggedly. I feel something stirring in the depths of my core. Something I've not felt for a long time. A pinch of desire.

Desire for him? Not possible. Men...males...they can't be trusted.

This predator can't be trusted.

Footsteps sound in the outer part of the suite.

"Don't let them see you like this," I say hoarsely.

"Vrex!" He drops me and flops back onto the bed, doing a very good impression of a heavily sedated male. Although the snores might be a bit theatrical.

"Ah, you're caring for him," Yuliat says. She has a small, rectangular object in her hand. I've seen them before. They're like a sort of tablet.

Before I can move, she grabs hold of me and slams my hand on the side of the device. I feel a sharp prick in the palm and immediately pull away.

"What the hell...?" I forget myself, swearing out loud.

It would normally be enough for a punishment, such as time spent clearing up after the other species. Ones not as easy on the eye as Jay.

Fortunately, Yuliat ignores me, her beady eyes on the tablet for a long while until she looks up with a flicker of her blue tongue.

"You're doing a great job. Make sure you get food for yourself whilst you are aiding the Gryn."

"Er...okay," I reply.

"He'll have slept off that dose in a few hours, then you can keep him *company*, can't you?"

I do not like the look in her eye. She spins on her heel, and I massage my stabbed hand as she exits.

Jay opens one eye and stares at me.

"She's gone. You can have something to eat now," I tell him.

This time, he doesn't need asking twice.

Jay

I'm trying not to let Lauren see me watching her. She's my mate. I'm not sure how I know, but I know.

The thing is, she could also be a Drahon spy. They might have done something to me that would make me believe she's my mate.

But then how can I explain I sensed her when I was on Ustokos and again on the Drahon ship? Fate is never wrong, that's what our Prime, Jyr, has always told us. He insists that our goddess, Nisis, knows what a warrior needs and provides it.

Which means I've found my mate, and I need to protect her.

But that residual concern sits in my stomach alongside the enormous meal I've just consumed. I was so sure she was working for the Drahon. But my head is clearing for the first time since my ill-fated escape attempt, my stomach is full, and my injuries tended to.

If she's just pretending to care, she's doing a good job.

But then what do I know about females?

I dredge my memory for times spent with the human females on Ustokos. My female sits on the end of the bed, chewing at her finger ends with her back to me. If I was back in the eyrie, I'd be making a nest for her.

Females like a pretty nest.

I look around at the room. It's mostly bare, but the bed has a silvery covering I could use, along with a couple of strange looking lumpy things. None of these are the furs I would prefer to use in my nest, but I have to start somewhere.

I pull at the covering, and it rips with satisfying ease under my claws.

"What the fuck are you doing?" She spins around, pulling the covering out of my hands.

"I want to make a nest for you."

"What?" She stares at me like I've grown an extra pair of wings. "No!"

"No?"

How would she possibly know about nesting? Unless the Drahon have told her. My old suspicions return. All of this is incredibly confusing. Any female would love a nest. This female should be no different.

"You can't go ripping up the bedding. It's all we have." She inspects the tear and glares at me through the hole.

"We?"

"Apparently, you can't be left to your own devices, and I need to stay with you until you are healed. You may not have noticed, given your recent...condition...but there's only one bed."

That hadn't escaped my notice, nor that she was sleeping next to me when I woke. None of this makes sense, and my head is beginning to ache, along with the rest of me.

"If you don't want my nest, presumably you can find somewhere to sleep," I grump at her, unable to help myself.

Lauren rolls her eyes. "Could you nest without shredding the soft furnishings, perhaps?"

I look at what's available. The two squashy lumps. I pick one up in between my claws, put it back down in a different position, then push it around a little until I'm satisfied it looks right. Then I look up at her for her approval.

"That's perfect, just perfect," she says, her mouth pursed up strangely.

I'm not sure I can believe her, but then, can I believe anything? My instincts are all skewed. What I need to be doing is working out a way of escape. Only then am I going to know if she is my mate and can be trusted.

I think.

Shifting back onto the bed, I extend my injured wing carefully to inspect the damage. It's painfully sore, and any sort of flight will be nearly impossible until the skin knits back together some more. The last escape attempt was poorly thought out, and being vrexed isn't an excuse.

"Can I take a bath?" I ask Lauren, hopefully.

"If you're careful." She's been watching me, the silver covering clutched in one hand. "I'd prefer it if you didn't undo all my good work."

"I wouldn't dream of it. Not this time." I get to my feet, finding that the ground seems a long way away. I sway a little before my legs decide to hold.

"By that, I mean you're not to get so over enthusiastic this time," Lauren adds.

"Enthusiastic?"

"You soaked me."

I vaguely remember taking a bath. Like a youngling, making sure all my feathers were properly under the water, like we were taught by the seniors in the lair.

I vaguely remember Lauren being wet too, her little shift

clinging to her curves. That causes my cocks to jerk awake. Again.

Another trick? I can't be entirely sure, not yet.

"You don't have to join me. Stay dry this time." I can't help a smile hitching the corners of my mouth. It makes me think of times bathing with my fellow warriors back on Ustokos. Ayar in particular was always very messy, and he would do anything to avoid a bath.

I slowly make my way through to the bathing pool. My slow progress due to every single part of me hurting is additionally hampered by my failure to get my cocks under control. Lauren hovers behind me.

"I mean it. I don't need help." I look over my shoulder.

I don't want her to see my arousal. Even thinking about zeroing laser sights isn't working this time, not with her scent in my nostrils.

For all I know, this is exactly the reaction the Drahon are looking for.

"I'm just checking," she says, folding her arms over her chest. "Making sure you don't fall face first and drown yourself."

I reach the pool and wade in as quickly as I can until I can immerse myself in the water, propping my wings out on the side. My left wing is incredibly stiff and painful as I lift it, hissing at the pain.

"Do you need some more healing gel?" Lauren is crouching next to me, inspecting the damage.

"I just need time. Gryn are fast healers."

She ignores me. Pulling out the pot from the pocket on the front of her shift, she dips in her fingers and slathers the area with the gel. It gets in my feathers and feels sticky. I frown.

"The sooner you're healed, the sooner we can get out of here," she whispers in my ear, her hair tickling my shoulder.

Unbidden, my cocks jerk even higher at her proximity and her words.

If this isn't a Drahon trick, then I really don't know what I should be doing next.

Lauren

Mr. Grumpy-wings seems settled in his bath. He's not happy the gel has gotten on his feathers, but he'll have to suck it up. His wound is red and raw after his failed escape attempt, and it's clear from the way he's holding his entire wing it's painful.

He's still suffering from the effects of whatever the Drahon gave him; although, as I got the dart out quickly, he doesn't seem as out of it this time. His eyes have gained a fierce intelligence as opposed to a feral rage or a sedated droop.

The rage remains as an undercurrent, but his talk of 'nesting' threw me. Maybe that's what winged aliens do as a comfort thing? However, his use of his claws to destroy the blanket was clear evidence he's perfectly designed as a predator.

And yet, there's something about him I can't shake. A twinkle in his eye, the way his mouth crinkled upwards when he thought about having a bath. There's something almost *sweet* about this monster.

It's crystalized my plan. Jay could break me and Nari out, if I can persuade her to come.

I've not had any hope since I arrived here, but Jay has given me hope. He's strong enough to defeat the Drahon, and given enough of an advantage, he could do it, I'm sure.

I just have to work out a plan and keep the Drahon at bay in the meantime.

Jay lets out a low groan, and I realize I've been running my fingers through the short silky feathers on the edge of his wing while I've been thinking.

"Shit!" I withdraw my hand, thinking I must have been hurting him.

Jay blinks languid, dark eyes at me. A level of calmness I haven't seen in him before. I'm mesmerized.

"It's fine. You can touch," he says quietly.

"I...need to clear up in the bedroom." I stumble over the words. I stand and back away.

His eyes don't leave me. Not for a second.

As soon as I'm out of his sight, I breathe in deeply. This is so wrong. The Drahon will use this against us, both of us.

Whatever 'this' is.

I need to get a grip. All I have to do is get him well, and we might be able to get out of here. I can't play in to Yuliat's plans. And I'm sure she has plans. The Drahon might be a different species, but I learned early on how to read them in order to avoid the worst of any punishments handed out.

Which means we have to be one step ahead of her.

I gather up the tray and head out of the suite. The Drahon guards sneer at me as I leave. I duck my head down and hurry away, hoping that they don't decide to goad Jay into anything stupid while I'm gone.

"Lauren." Nari embraces me when I arrive back in our alcove.

"The Gryn didn't eat me." I smile at her. "He's not dangerous, Nari. Not to me or anyone who isn't Drahon."

"Are you sure?"

"Well, I'm stuck with him until he's healed enough to be sold, so I guess I'll find out soon enough." I lower my voice. "I think he might be our key to getting out of here."

Nari checks outside of the alcove before turning back to me. "An escape? It's suicide, Lauren."

"I don't think so. Jay is strong. He just doesn't know this place like we do." I sit down on my thin bed. "He took on six Drahon, Nari, and if Yuliat hadn't shot him with the tranquilizer, he might have even made it."

Nari sits down next to me, taking my hands in her own three fingered ones, her skin a pale mauve. "I don't want you getting hurt. Not by him or Yuliat."

My stomach clenches. I can't remember a time anyone actually cared about me.

Properly cared, not because they wanted something from me—a better grade, a better position, a convenient woman with a similar social standing to present to colleagues. Nari just cares.

I look into her black eyes. I don't think Kijg can produce tears, but what's there is definite worry.

"Jay won't hurt us. Can't say the same for Yuliat, but I know her type. She'd crawl over the bodies of the others to get her own way. She's the one we have to watch."

"The Gryn are unpredictable." Nari clutches at my hands and cocks her head to one side in the way she does when she's thinking. "But they are supposed to be honorable."

"Here." I let go of her to delve in my pocket, bringing out a roll filled with meat. "There's another benefit of me being with him. I get all the food I like."

Nari laughs, a short choking sound. She takes the food reverentially. "I guess looking after the Gryn does have some benefits." She takes a bite and then puts the food to one side for later. "Just as long as you know what you're doing."

I haven't a fucking clue, but it probably makes sense not to communicate that to Nari.

"I have to get back. I'm supposed to be in there with him all the time, unless I'm getting food or medical supplies." I take her hand again, finding comfort in her warmth.

I gather up a couple of blankets, given that Jay has shredded the only one we had, and then I hurry back out into the compound, towards the suite where Jay is being held.

The Drahon are clearly not prepared to leave him unguarded, and there are two fat lizards lounging outside as I approach. I hold up my bracelet to the pad, and they both watch me with interest.

The door slides open, and a loud growl sounds from inside, causing both to scramble upright, pulling out their laser guns.

"Hey! Wait! He's not supposed to be harmed!" I step into the doorway, holding up my hands, as if I can stop them.

One guard looks at the other. Then he gives me a shove, and I fall backwards through the door as the pair of them laugh at me, and the door slides shut.

"Vrex!" A velvety voice just over my left shoulder makes me jump. "Are you okay?"

Crouched down, Jay holds his abdomen but puts out an arm to help me. He straightens up, movements jagged and his wing still drooping, taking me with him.

I rub at my bottom.

"I'm fine. The Drahon are dicks."

"Dicks?" Jay inclines his head, dark eyes searching my face with a quizzical look.

I wonder if the word doesn't translate. After all, I woke up on the Drahon ship being able to understand their language, so whatever was done to my brain, I have no control over.

"Yeah, cocks, wankers, arseholes. Not-very-nice lizards. If

they can push someone smaller than themselves around, they will."

Jay bristles, his feathers lifting as he draws himself up to his full height, muscles rippling.

He is most definitely not the sort of creature the Drahon can push around.

"You should know. You're the one working with them to spy on me, to get me to comply," he says.

"Hell no!" I pull away from him. "What makes you think that?"

Jay

I dozed off in the bath. The narcotics remain in my veins. With each hour that passes, I'm feeling more alert, but it's taking forever to rid my system of the dratted stuff. Vrexing Drahon!

Part of me remains highly suspicious of Lauren. She wasn't there when I woke up, and with each passing minute she was absent, it felt like an itch I couldn't scratch.

I wanted her near me, so I could keep an eye on her, make sure that my mate is not working with the Drahon.

Because if she is...

Lauren stares up at me as I rise to my full height, bright gray eyes blinking at me. She rubs her ample behind, and I long to grab it, to feel her skin under my fingers.

"I am not working with the Drahon," she says through gritted teeth. "I am certainly not their spy. I've got no desire to do anything to help them." She puts her hands on her hips. "I'm going to give you the benefit of the doubt because you're injured and not quite in your right mind, but I've not done anything at all to make you think I'm working for them, have I?"

She's right. As if to remind me of how vrexed up I am, my head spins, and I sway on the spot.

"The Drahon are without honor," I say/slur. "A species of slavers is always without honor." I snarl at the door and hope the guards can hear me.

When I saw one of them behind her, it made me want to rip out his throat, despite my injuries. The mere fact he has touched her at all means I will kill him.

Lauren gathers up the additional bed coverings she dropped when she was pushed to the floor, muttering to herself about me thinking she's a spy. I'm disappointed there are no furs among what she has brought, but I'm hoping she'll like what I've done with our nest.

"What. The. Fuck." Lauren stops dead as she enters the bedroom.

I stand behind her proudly. The silvery covering made ideal nesting material. I have strung it over the bed, and a slight breeze from somewhere makes the thin strips flutter like feathers. It turned out that the strange squashy lumps were full of a downy, fur-like material, and I've been able to spread it out like a proper nest.

"Our nest, my mate."

She turns, her mouth open, and I wrap my arms around her. Lauren freezes. I can almost feel her vibrating against me, she is that immovable.

"Jay, no. You can't do this. We can't do this. If the Drahon think...*anything*...is going on, they'll use it against either you or me."

She wrestles herself free and immediately starts dismantling my nest.

"Females need a nest. If you are staying in here with me, I have to nest," I explain, plaintively. "It's what Gryn males do."

Lauren stuffs the last of the white fur back into the bag it came in and then throws the coverings she brought with her onto the bed. "Please, Jay, just lie down and sleep it off, will you?" She sighs.

She still thinks I'm in the grip of the narcotic.

With a growl, I stomp over to the bed but think better of my temper when my footsteps fire pain through me. I crawl onto it and settle myself into the bedding she has brought. I have to admit it's comfortable.

"I guess I really need to know more about you." She stands at the foot of the bed, arms folded. "If you're going to pull this sort of stunt, and if you're going to accuse me of being a spy."

Perhaps, just perhaps, I might have gotten things wrong. Maybe she really isn't working with the Drahon. Why else would she reject my nest? They would want her to do whatever I wanted her to do.

I settle myself on the bed, stretching out my injured wing to inspect it, claws worrying at the crusting around the wound.

"I am a Gryn warrior. I'm part of an elite unit on my planet. There's not much more you need to know."

"Stop picking at it." She's on the bed beside me, slapping my hand away.

"Only if you stay with me." I grin at her, eager to see what she says.

"I don't have any option." Her fingers trip through my feathers as she inspects the area around my injury. "Yuliat's made it pretty clear I have to stay with you while you're recovering." Her eyes meet mine. "That doesn't mean I don't want to stay, but you have to understand that Yuliat is a slippery, evil bitch."

I rumble out a laugh. "You don't need to tell me about her. She's been attempting to gain my compliance since I got here."

Lauren looks me up and down. "How's that working out for her?"

"I'd say we're about even."

She snorts out a laugh and covers her mouth with her hand.

"Why are you here, Lauren?" I ask, wanting her to stay close to me, maybe even preen me a little more. I shift my wing, and she's drawn to it again, tracing her hands through my feathers.

"Wrong place, wrong time, I suppose. I didn't even believe in aliens until, well, I ended up here." She gets herself comfortable sitting next to me. "Normally, alien abductions happen to other humans, on the other side of my planet, a place called America. Because aliens are apparently fussy like that." She looks at me from under her eyelashes. "But lucky old me, I get to be the first alien abductee from the United Kingdom."

The fiasco of my nest is forgotten. Lauren is as much a prisoner as I am. Why I even thought she was working with them is simply the effect of the narcotics.

I feel like a complete idiot.

"How about you? How did a great Gryn warrior like you end up in the hands of the Drahon?"

"I made a mistake." I look away from her. It pains me more than my injuries to say such a thing out loud. "And my fellow warriors paid for it, maybe with their lives."

I ball my hands up into fists, not caring that my claws spear my palms. The narcotics had, at least, made that pain easier to bear. With a clearer head, I know what I've done, and it destroys me.

I don't deserve a mate. Not after my failure. My duty has to be to escape, to destroy this base and free all the prisoners, including Lauren. After that, I need to get home.

And face my prime and my commander, if he still lives, to accept my fate.

Lauren

Jay has gone into brooding mode. He stares at the wall for a while and eventually closes his eyes. Given that he's nearly naked, I cover him with one of the blankets as much as I can. Having gently reapplied the healing gel to the injury on his wing, I settle myself down on the bed, putting as much distance between us as I can.

I don't want the Drahon getting the wrong idea. Jay might be a magnificent specimen of a male, but until I know what Yuliat has planned for us, it's best we pretend not to be friends.

When he's not being feral or grumpy, Jay is amusing. I've got so many questions for him, about his planet and his species. Can they actually fly? What is his planet like? Does he like me?

Er, scratch that last question. Just because this drugged male has had a couple of boners in my presence doesn't mean anything. Men the world over get hard all the time for no reason. Plus, Jay will have a gorgeous tall, winged lady Gryn back at home and half a dozen little cherub Gryn fluttering around. Because men always keep secrets and can't be trusted.

Keep telling yourself that, Lauren.

Good grief! As if my life couldn't get more complicated than being abducted by aliens, now I have to catch *feelings* for one.

I'm watching him again as he sleeps. Relaxed, like a big cat, all softness until something edible crosses its path. Then it will be all movement, claws, and teeth. Flesh being rendered from bone.

Cute until he kills.

Yet another spectacular thought to sleep on.

Jay's breathing deepens, and I hope that the last of the sedation will be out of his system by tomorrow. The Drahon want him, which means any window for escape is going to be short—sometime between when he is actually well enough and when they think he is.

Timing is going to be everything.

"Get up!" Something sharp prods me in my foot.

Yuliat stands at the foot of the bed, staring at us both. She isn't happy.

Not that she ever is.

"Go and get the Gryn some food, then report to me," she fires at me.

I look over at Jay. A Drahon guard stands over him, laser gun pointed at his chest.

I slide off the bed, attempting to shake off sleep and the dream I was having, where a big, winged warrior had me caged under his feathers, his mouth on mine.

Jay squirms on the bed, ruffling up the blanket.

"Don't move, Gryn," the guard snarls.

"Go on. Go!" Yuliat shouts at me.

Her ire and change of mind are nothing new. I troop out

of the suite and head through to the canteen, where there is a tray loaded for me. I return to the suite, and my way is barred by a large Drahon guard.

"I'm bringing food for the Gryn warrior." I try to sidestep him.

"He's not your concern anymore."

I take a step back, shaking my head, not entirely sure I've heard him correctly. "I'm supposed to be providing him with food and medical assistance. Yuliat specifically chose me."

"You are to go back to your other duties, female," he snarls, snatching the tray from me. "Yuliat will deal with you later."

None of that sounds good. But what's worse is the way my chest aches. Like indigestion, only worse, deeper as if my soul is aching too. The guard slams the tray into the side of my head, sending me reeling. "Zark off." He spits.

I clutch at my head and stumble away. This time of day, I'd normally be cleaning out the area near the cells, so with my head and chest equally painful, I make my way back down the corridor. Inside our alcove, there's no sign of Nari, but her bucket and mop have gone, so she's presumably working elsewhere.

Grabbing my cleaning implements, I fill my bucket with water and add the slippery liquid that acts as soap before heading back to the cells.

The smell coming from the darkened corridor where the other creatures are kept is particularly rank today. There are also no Drahon about, which has to be a blessing. I can get on with my mopping without being shouted at for a change.

As I slop the water and soap on the floor, I try to use the boring work to take my mind off Jay. We might have been somewhat personal over the last few days, but I can't get attached. That would be foolish. Perhaps he was my only chance at escape, but where would we go? How would I get back to Earth?

As much as that seems to be my only choice, I've no idea if it's even possible. Dreams of escape, with Jay, especially with Jay, are just the dreams of an alien abductee with a mop in her hand and the smell of alien shit in her nostrils. Pretty pointless. Me and an alien? An alien and me? Sounds like a recipe for disaster.

And I'm all about the relationship disaster.

My mop slurps from side to side as I work my way over the floor, heading down the corridor to the cells and dragging my bucket with me.

Usually, the lights come on when I start to work in this area. It's not great when this happens as it sets off the occupants of the cells, some of whom make very unpleasant noises. Some throw themselves at the cell doors, which I hate.

I'd definitely prefer to be back nursing a grumpy alien warrior who thought I was a spy for the Drahon. That's laughable. I can't even tell a little white lie without blushing.

In the dark, down the corridor, something moves.

Scratch that. Something slithers. It hisses.

One of the creatures is loose.

I start to slowly back away. Claws clack on the metal floor.

A set of tentacles slides towards me.

"Oh, holy shit!" I scream as the squid/lion thing looms at me, its front half the mass of tentacles, backed up by a lion like rear. I hurl the mop at it, followed by the bucket, both of which it bats away easily. There's nothing left for me. I have to run.

Turning, I slip on the wet floor, try to recover, but my second step has me going down again. I feel something wrap around my ankle, pulling me with suckers that rip at my skin.

I take a breath to scream again, but something lands on my

back, forcing all the air out of my lungs. Something horribly sharp sinks into my shoulder.

A deep, feral growl rends the air.

This is it.

This time is my last.

I'm dead.

Jay

Yuliat didn't seem interested in me after she sent Lauren away. I was half expecting a fight, but instead, once Lauren had gone, she left along with the guard.

Some time later, he was back with food.

"Where's the female?"

He looks me up and down with a sneer on his lips. "You didn't seem that interested in her. She's been reassigned."

Damn the Drahon to the Goddess!

They wanted us to mate. It has to be Yuliat's plan. Which makes me feel pretty stupid, given that until yesterday, I had thought that Lauren was in league with them.

I know little of females. Sure, I've met the seniors' human mates, but every warrior knows you don't approach another warrior's mate, not if you value your wings. Otherwise my interaction with the females of other species on Ustokos has been limited to fending off their strange advances.

My fellow warriors tease me with suggestions that the feline females that inhabit our planet, the Mochi, find mating with a strong Gryn warrior attractive.

Not something I've ever wanted to find out.

But Gryn are compatible with human females, the one thing I do know. Little younglings appear on a regular basis from our seniors' nests.

My mind wanders for a short while, steeped in pleasant thoughts of Lauren, her belly rounded with my youngling, gently preening my feathers as I pleasure her.

Clearly, that's not going to happen. Not while we're at the mercy of the Drahon. The last thing I want is for Yuliat to have any inkling that Lauren is my mate. That is going to spell disaster for us both.

Providing she is my mate. I frown at the tray of food brought in for me. Why isn't she here? Another Drahon trick? They spent a lot of time and effort putting us together, but now, I don't get to have her?

Maybe they want to drug me again? I think I'm finally narcotic free since I awakened. My injuries seem better and my head clearer. Which is why I need to be careful, not only of the food but to ensure the Drahon don't get any further leverage.

Except my feathers prickle with something. Not an itch—the bathing has helped enormously with the filth that had accumulated on them. It's something else, something I've never experienced before. I can't stay still any longer. I heave myself to my feet and begin to pace. At first in the bedroom, then out to the corridor. The more I pace, the worse the feeling gets.

I have to get out. Not just escape. Out of this cell. I stalk up to the door. There are no handles, nothing to indicate it can be opened from the inside except a black shiny square, similar to ones I've seen on Ustokos in the lairs where the tech is ancient Gryn.

I tap the square with my knuckle.

Nothing happens.

My feathers prick up uncomfortably, and it's then I hear the scream.

Lauren!

My claws slam into the black square, and I rip out the innards of the locking mechanism. The door slides open, and a Drahon gapes at me.

One swift punch in the face, and he's lying prone on the floor, just as the scream comes again.

The entire Drahon compound is seemingly deserted save for that one guard. I don't have time to think any more about it. I know that scream came from Lauren, and I spring down the corridor, scenting the air. My blood rushes through me, filling my muscles and dampening down the pain.

She is mine. To protect, to claim, and to mate.

Vrex the Drahon!

There is silence, and my senses go into overdrive as I stalk my way forward, my left wing trailing. It doesn't matter. The only thing that matters is Lauren. I have to find her.

To my left is a dark corridor, and immediately, I can scent her. Her usual delicious scent is tinged with the tang of something bitter. Her fear.

With a snarl, I leap into the dark, my eyes adjusting instantly. I see her prone form outlined on the floor.

She isn't moving.

I'm beside her in a snap, hands hovering over her. She's streaked with blood from wounds on her wrists and ankles. Her eyes are closed, and I'm not sure if she lives.

"Lauren?" I breathe her name, hoping beyond hope I get a reply, or movement, or...anything.

If she is gone, I may as well give myself up to the Drahon. A fated mate is not something that the Goddess gives lightly, and I have failed her as surely as I failed my unit.

"Please, Lauren?" I touch her on her forehead, trailing my knuckle down her face, one that looks like it's made from stone.

Her eyelids flicker, and she sucks in a breath.

"Don't move. You're injured," I say. A pair of terrified gray eyes stare up at me, not quite seeing. "It's me. It's Jay, my *eregri*. Lie still."

"I'm okay." Her words are a bare whisper. "I think."

She is very clearly not okay, not from the damage done to her beautiful skin. I feel the rage rising within me. It's hot and pure, an anger made from molten metal.

"Who did this to you?"

Lauren

"Who did this to you?" The dark voice echos in my head.

I can't see. I'm not entirely sure, but I think the voice is Jay's.

It can't be him. He's locked in the suite.

"The squid-lion thing." I can barely get the words out. My throat stings, and I attempt to wipe over my face to clear my vision, but I can't move my arms.

"Gryn!" Another voice, louder. Too loud.

A sizzling sound, warmth removed, shouting, fighting. Movement. I'm scooped up and pressed against something hard.

Something that smells really good. Like coffee and cinnamon as you walk into a café. Tears spring to my eyes at the scent, familiar, comforting, and a million miles away. Why did it have to be like this? It's not like my life on Earth was a bed of roses, but I don't want to die on an alien planet either.

I wanted to have a job I loved, a man who loved me and didn't cheat on me. I wanted kids, a home. Stability. Instead, I got the politics of academia, an ex who was a complete bastard and ruined me for anyone else, a rented flat, and a barren womb by the time I was thirty.

A sob escapes my lips. I've never felt sorry for myself, but I hurt. I'm abducted, and I think I'm going to die.

For once in my fucking life, I deserve to cry tears for myself, not for anyone else.

Someone brushes a hand over my hair, a word is whispered in my ear. A word I don't understand but is filled with meaning.

"*Eregri.*"

Then it's all gone. And I am alone.

"WATER," I CROAK, MY CRACKED LIPS SPLITTING AS I put my hand up to my face, trying to work out if I dislike the darkness or the fire in my throat.

My eyes are bandaged.

"Wait, Lauren." It's Nari.

A cup is pressed to my mouth, and I gulp down the water while she hisses at me to take it easy.

"Why can't I see?" My voice trembles, despite myself.

"You were stung." The deep male voice rumbles through me.

I realize that, although I'm lying down, I'm not on a bed.

I'm on something hard. Something that moves under me. I'm covered with soft, scented feathers.

With some effort, I put my hands up to my face and push at the bandages.

"No, Lauren. Leave them on. You need to allow your eyes time to recover," Nari says, but I ignore her. I want to see what I'm lying on.

The bandage comes off, and I blink, squeezing my eyes

closed and opening them to a blur. Slowly, my vision clears. I'm not in our alcove. It looks like I'm back in the suite.

The one I was sharing, reluctantly, with a seven-foot predator.

I drop my hand down and touch skin.

Not my skin.

"Lauren," Jay rasps.

With every ounce of strength I have, I twist to work out exactly what is going on. I'm cradled against the enormous male, one of his wings draped over me. An arm encircles my waist. The one saving grace of this situation is that someone has finally found Jay some pants.

"What stung me?" I ask as he studies me, his dark eyes impenetrable. "How did I get here?"

"It won't do it again." Jay hitches up his lips to reveal sharp canines in a grimace.

"The Xople," Nari says. Her eyes flick to Jay and back to me. "It escaped. It came for you."

"The squid-lion?" I had no idea it had a name. I squirm against Jay. "Where is it?"

"In pieces." He growls. "You are to rest. Nothing else will happen to you, providing you stay with me." He takes in a long, deep breath. "You will stay with me."

His words have a finality to them.

"It's what the Drahon want," Jay says. "That Xople couldn't get out on its own. Yuliat made sure it would and that you would be working near the cells."

"I don't understand," Nari says. "Why would they not just," she swallows, "kill her."

"Because they want me to take you as my mate." Jay levels his dark gaze on me. "They want me to breed with you." Jay sighs deeply, and I can't deny he feels good under me, even as I shiver at the word 'breed.' "I'd be worth more as a breeding male and you…"

He lifts a clawed hand, tracing it gently over my cheek as I hold my breath.

"You'd be worth more with my youngling in your belly."

"Oh, dear god." I gasp. "I thought Yuliat had a plan for us. I just assumed she wanted to make you want me." It's my turn to swallow. "So she could use me as a reward or something."

My face flames when I say the words out loud. It's not like I'm a stranger to sex, but talking about breeding with an enormous alien who I'm well aware has been aroused around me…

Awkward.

Although, he was also not quite in his right mind, so maybe he's not interested in that when he's sober. Wouldn't be the first time.

"Mating is only a reward when it's freely given," Jay rumbles beneath me. "I do not mate what I do not want."

Oh, shit.

Instead of making me feel better, I now feel worse. Does this mean he isn't interested?

And why do I care?

"You know what this means, don't you?" Jay bends his head and sweeps my hair aside, nuzzling up to my neck and sending goosebumps running all over my body in the best possible way.

"No," I squeak.

"It means we have to escape. Together."

Jay

Like I was ever going to leave her behind. Lauren is my mate. Of that, I'm very, very sure now.

From the look in her eyes, I can tell she has questions, but those are going to have to wait. As soon as I found her, and the disgusting creature slid out of the shadows, it was obvious to me that this was a trap. Something designed to see if I would show my true nature.

If I thought the Kijg were slippery, they have nothing on the Drahon.

Because I fell right into their trap. Not only did I find my *eregri*, but also, I had no compunction in disposing of the foul thing that would dare to harm her.

Nor would I allow the Drahon anywhere near us as soon as Lauren was in my arms. I carefully transported her back to my cell and growled for medical assistance. I was sent the little Kijg female who said she knew Lauren.

All of it makes sense. They wanted to push us together, to see what I would do if my mate was in danger. They have taken advantage of my instincts, and I would curse myself, if I wasn't so glad Lauren is safe and in my arms.

"How are we going to do that?" She blinks up at me.

I want to bury myself in her intoxicating skin and hair. I want to lap over every single inch of her skin. She will never, ever be in danger again.

"My wing is more healed than they realize." I flex it gently. "If we can get outside, I can carry us out of here."

"Us? Me and Nari?" she asks. "She's a prisoner here, too."

I look at the Kijg female. She flushes a shade of orange.

"Yes, I can carry you both," I say, puffing up my chest and forgetting my injured ribs. They burn, and it's all I can do not to hiss out a breath of pain.

"There's one problem, Gryn." Nari swivels her head to stare at me. "The forcefield."

"Yeah." Lauren nods. "That is a problem."

It's not the only problem, but I can't admit that to her. As much as we need to get out of here, I don't want to risk her life with any plan that's not foolproof. The Drahon were willing to sacrifice the tentacled beast in order to get what they wanted; I've no doubt they will happily use or destroy whatever they see fit.

And that includes my *eregri*.

"It has to be controlled from somewhere," I flounder, not wanting to seem ignorant of tech, even though I am.

"If we could shut down the power somehow," Lauren says to the Kijg. "But how?"

"They have all sorts of protocols in place to stop the power going down," the female replies. "But there might be a way, if we can disrupt it."

I look between the two females, and I'm at a loss. They both look at me.

"The Gryn have been without tech for generations," Nari says, and I'm sure she would be smirking if the Kijg had lips. "This one will not be able to operate any."

"I know about tech," I reply, drawing myself up and

flaring my wings a little. "As long as I can point it and shoot it."

The Kijg snorts at me.

"Oh, great," Lauren huffs. "This is going *so* well. Two women slaves and one hulking alien angel who knows how to make things go bang."

"That's generally Vypr's department, but I have some experience in explosives too," I say with some pride.

"Okay, make that two women prisoners and a hulking alien angel who only sometimes makes things go bang." Lauren rolls her eyes at me.

"Two females, one of which needs to rest." I draw her back into my side.

"I'm supposed to be looking after you," she grumbles but doesn't resist.

"I'll see what I can find out about the forcefield," Nari says, gently stroking Lauren's hand. She gives me a sharp look, and I ignore her.

No Kijg is keeping me from my mate. She trots out of the bedroom, and I hear the door to the suite open, then close again behind her.

"Did the Drahon hurt you?" Lauren asks me, her voice sleepy. "For killing the squid-lion thing?"

"Nothing I couldn't handle," I reply. They tried, but without their narcotics, they know they're no match for me. "The thing is, we're going to have to convince them that something is going on between us. They might just leave us alone long enough to plan this escape."

"Spoken like a true male," Lauren says with a bark of laughter. "How about we keep them guessing instead? Perhaps they will wait and see if nature will take its course." She folds her arms and looks distinctly unconvinced at my suggestion.

As it turns out, I'm just as bad with females when I'm sober as when I'm vrexed out of my skull on Drahon narcotics. Not that I should be trying to convince Lauren to mate with me. Escape has to be our first priority.

"Can't blame a warrior for trying." I nuzzle at her neck.

"Jay? Really?" She gives me a stern look, but again, I notice she doesn't move away. Again.

"Get some rest, sweet mate. I will keep watch."

I wrap my wing around us both, making sure she's well covered. A small hand appears on the edge of my primary feathers, running over the shaft.

"Soft. Not like I expected it to be," she says with a gentle sigh.

"A warrior can have rough edges, but a pure heart." I settle back on the bed, to allow her some room under my wing. "I will never do anything you don't want me to do, regardless of what the Drahon want, my *eregri*."

"Eregry?" she asks, mangling the pronunciation with her gorgeous accent. "What does that mean?"

"*Eregri*," I correct her. "It means that you are my fated mate, my boundless flight," I blurt.

"Sounds serious." She yawns. "But we'd better not let the Drahon know."

She thinks I'm playing the part. I wish I were. As much as I know we have to get away from the Drahon, before either they get bored of trying to get me to mate with Lauren or they find a buyer for either of us, I know none of it will be safe for her, and all of it means I'd lose her.

If there was any other way, I'd take it in a heartbeat.

I cannot fail my *eregri* like I failed my unit. And that failure looms in my psyche like a black cloud.

Escape is everything.

Lauren

I nap for a while, and when I wake, Nari is back with a platter of food.

I completely agree with Jay about the escape. The last thing I want to be is a receptacle for an alien baby. Even though I did want children once, alien babies? That would be a nope.

Although…I can't deny that I am a little intrigued about the method of making babies with Jay.

Newly sober, squid-lion destroying Jay is hot. And I don't mean his temperature, which is most definitely warmer than a human's. Lying on him is like being on a muscular, cinnamon-scented hot water bottle.

A deliriously handsome warm beanbag of deliciousness.

Dear god! Has it really been so long since I had any action I'm thinking about Jay in these terms? He doesn't think of me in that way. He wants to escape, and he's willing to help me, which is nice.

Plus, Nari and I need his help to escape this hell hole, where bullies like the Drahon think they can do what they like to other species, including abducting, breeding, and torture.

"Are you okay, Lauren?" Nari asks me quietly as Jay rustles his way across the room with the care of a male who is still very sore. He approaches the food and makes an appreciative sound which does funny things to my stomach. "I've had a look around. The forcefield generator is fortified, and access to it is in one of the restricted areas. Are you really sure about this escape?"

"Jay's right," I say in a low voice. "We have to escape, all of us. The Drahon will eventually get their way, and it's not going to be pleasant."

"I don't know." Nari looks worried. "If we fail, there will be punishment."

I watch Jay, one wing drooping as he gathers up some pieces of meat onto a platter, snagging them with his enormous claws, and for every one piece he puts on the plate, he pops another in his mouth.

Such a greedy Gryn, and yet my stomach does a silly dip as I watch him enjoy his meal.

"If we stay, Nari, the Drahon will find ways of punishing us anyway. Look what they've done to Jay and to me already," I exhort her, still keeping my voice low. "We have to find a way of disabling the forcefield."

"Can the Gryn even fly?" Nari asks, her black eyes watching him. "He can fight, they all can. But against all the Drahon and their weapons? His flight is the only option."

I lie back on the bed, my head pounding with the effort of, well, everything.

"We have to try, Nari. One way or the other, Yuliat is going to get what she wants, and I'd rather not stay and wait for her next great plan. Next time, she could actually kill me, or you, or Jay."

Because as much as I shouldn't admit it, I like the big, winged, grumpy male. Far more than I should let on, certainly to him.

Probably to Nari, too. And definitely not to Yuliat, whatever the provocation.

Jay turns and carries the platter over to the bed, settling himself like a hen on eggs. He reaches out an arm and, clearly without any thought at all, drags me over beside him.

"My female needs food," Jay rumbles before I can protest.

With infinite care, he selects a piece of meat and offers it up to my lips.

I'm not going to lie — I'm so surprised by his behavior, I open my mouth, and he pops the morsel inside. He makes his appreciative sound again, halfway between a coo and a grunt. My stomach flip-flops.

"Jay!" I attempt to move, but I'm held fast. I also have a mouthful of meat.

"Good?" he asks me, his dark eyes tranquil.

"This is exactly what Yuliat wants," I hiss at him as I chew.

"I know. I thought we were pretending for the Drahon." His eyes glitter. "If she thinks we're getting along, she might just leave us alone."

"You mean fake it 'til we make it?"

"That's exactly what I mean." Jay does his nuzzle into my neck again.

I can't deny it feels good when he does that. Very good. He's warm, soft, and smells delicious.

Which remains completely wrong. *But oh-so-right.*

"I don't think we need to go mad, Jay," I say, but another piece of meat is pushed between my lips. "Aw! Come on!" I chew and swallow as quickly as I can, then lever myself away from him. "Don't Gryn believe in courtship? Don't you need to display to me or something?" I garble out, my brain not quite able to take in this new turn of events as I scramble over the other side of the bed.

He lounges on the bed. For a second, I see confusion flit over his face, then it sets with determination.

"I am your protector, Lauren. That is what Gryn do. It is what I will do. You are to be well fed and have anything you want," he says, looking somewhat self-satisfied.

"Oh yeah, and how do you propose to do that?"

He flares out a wing and extends the claws on one hand, huge vicious pieces of onyx curving like scimitars.

"I will ensure the Drahon treat you well, unless they want to find out how a mated Gryn male normally behaves." He growls from the very depth of his throat, eyes darkening with a repressed violence I have only seen once before.

When I woke in his arms, when he thought the Drahon had hurt me...when he thought I might not survive.

Jay isn't going to 'play' the part of a male interested in a mate because I think he might just be interested in me in that way far more than I realized.

He's acting on pure instinct, something the Drahon have pushed him into. I'm beginning to wonder if this idea of escaping with him is sensible. And, although I want out of the Drahons' clutches, it doesn't mean I want to fall into Jay's. He's a violent predator who will stop at nothing to get what he wants.

Even if, right at this moment, he looks like a satisfied cat who has got the cream. I can't let that fool me for an instant.

I need him to help us escape, and then we'll see who needs who.

Jay

I'm not sure if I'm doing a good job of convincing Lauren I'm a worthy male. Admittedly, my limited understanding of females means I thought all I needed to do was get her in my arms, and somehow that would lead to mating.

And mating leads to younglings.

When I really think about it, it gives me a headache.

I also ache somewhere else. Somewhere I'd like Lauren to pay some attention.

Problem is, she looks at me like I've grown an extra pair of wings, and she doesn't want me to feed her.

If I can't nest and I can't provide for her, what can I do? I'm stuck pretending to the Drahon I'm interested in mating, only it's not a pretense. I daren't risk Lauren being injured again, and I can't get out of the suite to look for a means of escape.

Feelings of utter failure haunt me. I am a Gryn warrior, and I am better than this. Not for the first time, I wish I was with my unit. Together, we were stronger. I could even ask my commander the best way to court a female.

The shoulder of my wing itches. I gently extend it to inspect the wound. The sooner it heals, the sooner I'll be able to fly.

Yes, I have been lying to my *eregri*, claiming I can fly. I already know I still cannot. The fight with the Xople opened the wound again, and the female Kijg had to fix it.

Flight still alludes me, and without it, I rely on my limited memory of the exterior of the Drahon base. Even without the forcefield, there are high walls which we have to scale.

I need to be able to fly as well as fight. I have to be able to protect her.

"If Yuliat is as tricky as the Kijg...no offense." I incline my head at Nari.

"None taken, we are tricky," she replies with a hint of amusement in her eyes.

"If Yuliat is as tricky, we need to be trickier. You are going to have to pretend, with me, something is happening between us," I tell Lauren, who is as far away from me on the bed as she can be without actually falling off the edge. "It doesn't need to be much," I say.

Any touch from her would be enough.

"I really don't know, Jay," she replies. "This seems like more than just a fake mating to you." Concern fills her eyes.

'Fake' is a word I already hate. But I don't hate her, not at all, so I push my anger down inside me.

"I can't fake my desire to protect you from any danger, my Lauren. I am an honorable male. If the Drahon dare to touch you, I will kill them," I growl at her. Her gray eyes widen. "But I am saying it will buy us time, if the Drahon think we're..."

"Getting on?"

It's hard not to smile, although I do my best.

"Yes, getting on. If we look like we're getting on, they might give us time."

Lauren drops her chin to her chest. This time, she's contemplating my suggestion rather than dismissing it.

Maybe feeding her was the right thing to do. Even if I can't make her a good nest, I can ensure she gets the choicest morsels and a bed of the softest furs.

She narrows her eyes at me. "And the mating—it's just pretend to you, Jay? Are you sure about that?"

I shrug, doing my level best to appear nonchalant. I spear another piece of food from the platter and eat it. "I can pretend if you can."

A smile steals over her face. "Well, there is a challenge. Can I pretend to like the clawed, grumpy alien angel?"

I frown at her. "Angel? What is that?"

"We don't have winged males on Earth, only in books. They are called angels," she explains.

I'm probably even more confused, but I want her to trust me and like me, so I nod instead. Being an angel doesn't sound like a bad thing.

"Are they warriors like me, your angels in books?"

Lauren's smile deepens, little marks appearing on either side of her mouth. Her eyes glitter with mirth, and she runs a hand down my good wing. "Yes, Jay. Some of them are warriors like you."

My heart fills with warmth. She knows a good warrior when she sees one.

Boots sound in the corridor outside, and in a move I wasn't expecting, Lauren leaps onto my lap, grinding her bottom against my crotch. She grabs one of my arms and pulls it over her body. Initially, I'm shocked at the suddenness of her movement, until I realize what she's doing.

Clever mate.

I hold up a morsel of food to her mouth, and she sucks at my fingers. My cocks immediately go into overdrive, pre-cum gushing from them. I'm singularly unable to control myself as her tongue licks over my claws.

"Lauren!" I breathe her name as a warning and as a desire.

"Shush!" she replies, snuggling herself against me and seemingly unaware of the destruction taking place in my increasingly tight pants.

"What do we have here? A Gryn warrior enjoying himself?" Yuliat steps into the room, and Lauren struggles against me, pulling away again, just as I was actually enjoying myself.

"Nothing is going on, Yuliat. I'm just looking after him like you asked," Lauren says hastily, smoothing down her clothing and shooting a glance at me.

"You seem to be doing a good job. He looks like a very relaxed warrior." Yuliat's voice drips with sarcasm as she levels her gaze at my crotch, which, even encased in the pants Nari brought for me, clearly reveals my arousal. "Very relaxed."

I will my cocks to behave and unfold myself from the bed, drawing to my full height, and attempt to set my wings to look like a warrior.

"My mate," I growl, "is not to be harmed."

Yuliat's tongue flickers out of her mouth, wet and interested. "Perfect, perfect," she mutters. "The human female will continue to tend to you, Gryn, despite your continued failure to comply with us." She folds her arms. "Even though you appear to have recovered enough to destroy a valuable Xople, I will give you the benefit of the doubt. You have three more turns together. Then you will be trained, one way or the other."

She looks between Lauren and me.

"If you choose not to be trained, then I will have to take matters with the human further." Her black eyes glimmer unpleasantly. "But if you copulate with the female, she will remain unharmed."

"What? No!" Lauren leaps off the bed. "You can't do that!"

"I can do what I want with my property," Yuliat snarls at her. "And don't forget, *human*, you are my property as much as the Gryn. If you want to continue to breathe, you might want to consider whether or not having his cocks inside you is a price worth paying."

Something has changed. I can almost scent it. Yuliat was prepared to allow things to take their course, but now she's putting a time frame on our 'activities.' It's not good, and it means we have to find a way out of this place sooner rather than later.

Because her plans for us have changed. She's no longer trying to be subtle.

I bristle at her.

"For all your honor, Gryn, you'll do what's right by your mate. If she is to survive, she needs your youngling in her belly. So, less nesting and more mating," the horrible Drahon female fires out as she grabs the little Kijg by her shoulder and throws her out of the room.

Lauren

"Fuck! This isn't good. It isn't good at all." I run my hand through my hair, which is sticky and itchy with some sort of substance, one I don't want to think about.

"We've got three turns to escape, my *eregri*," Jay replies.

I vaguely remember him using the term earlier when I was recovering from being nearly killed. I can't quite recall what it means. Probably 'little human,' knowing my luck.

"We'll need more than three days. Plus, if Yuliat wants us to…you know…she's hardly going to let us have a chance to plan anything."

Jay looks contemplative.

"Oh, no! We're not doing anything!" I back away from the bed. "Not one single thing."

I really cannot even give headspace to the fact that while I sat on Jay's lap and felt the monster bulge underneath me, parts of my anatomy responded. And my brain tried to work out why Yuliat used a plural when mentioning Jay's endowments earlier.

He's an alien.

An alien who is attracted to me? Maybe he responds like that to every female?

He didn't respond to Nari like that

I hate the voice in my head; it's invariably right. If I paid more attention to it, I might have left academia long before I was abducted. I'd have stood up to those other voices in my head that said no one wanted a fuddy-duddy professor who spent her time crawling in muddy trenches. Or listened to the one which said Mark was a lying scumbag after he claimed he was at a conference in Leeds, and I found the invoice from the hotel in London in his bag.

I'm not brave. At heart, I'm a coward because I can't face up to the truth until it's too late. I don't want to die here, at the hands of the Drahon, and yet I've let them manipulate me at every turn. I'm now in the one position I didn't want to be, not ever again. I'm facing down a male who I know will reject me.

With a heart that can't take rejection.

Which means I have to draw the line somewhere, and that's going to be doing the nasty with Jay. Easy on the eye, he may be. I even quite like his moody, broody glowers. I certainly like his cinnamon-scented feathers and how his skin is surprisingly silky soft. I definitely love the way he likes to bathe, even if it does mean I get soaked.

Jay doesn't want me any more than I want him. We're both being played where we should be finding a way out.

"I already told you, female," Jay says through gritted teeth, his hands balling into fists. "I will protect you, and I do not mate with the unwilling."

"Who do you mate with then?!" I fire back at him, my own temper getting the better of me.

Jay huffs out a vicious breath, his dark eyes locked on mine. "It doesn't matter. If you're not interested, it doesn't matter at all," he grinds out. "We need to work out a way out of here."

He uncurls his hands and pats the bed next to him. "And we may as well continue the pretense."

"Fuck you!"

I know he doesn't want me. All that stuff, rubbish about mating, about honor. My heart grows cold in my chest. For half a second, I thought he might say something, anything. Instead, he's proved what I always knew.

I'm not girlfriend material, I'm not baby making material, not even to an alien.

Jay doesn't move. Instead, he just stares at me, daring me to do something else.

"Fine." I sit back down on the bed.

"Closer."

"This is close enough."

"Fine," he repeats back to me as he settles himself into an insolent and comfortable position. "Tell me about the compound."

I SPEND THE NEXT HOUR TELLING JAY ALL ABOUT THE time I've spent with the Drahon since I awakened here. We discuss all the exits, all the guard rotas, the weapons I've seen them use.

"What is Earth like?" Jay asks me. "Is it a nice planet?"

"How do you know I'm from Earth?" I query.

"You're human. They are from Earth," he says, somewhat smugly, given I know so little about his species. "I've met human females before. We have seven in our lair. My senior commander is mated to one."

"There's so much wrong with that sentence, Jay, you have no idea." I laugh, but I'm intrigued he's met other humans.

What am I thinking? I'm ecstatic to find out there are other humans out in this galaxy, even though, at the same time, I wonder if they were taken from Earth by the Drahon like me.

"There is nothing wrong with finding your fated mate," he says seriously, dark eyes gazing at me in a way that sends a prickle over my skin. "Fate is never wrong."

"I'm not your mate, Jay," I say, quietly. "I'm not mating material."

I don't want rejection. I'm pathologically allergic to it.

"Then you've never been properly mated," he replies.

I shut my mouth with a snap. He inclines his head, his feathers raising slightly as he folds his arms over his chest.

"Earth is very nice," I garble out, unprepared and unable to respond to his challenge. "Green fields, blue skies, more food than you can shake a stick at. No Drahon to enslave you. We have our problems, but overall, I'd give it an eight out of ten."

I can't fall for him. I just can't. There's no such thing as fated mates for humans.

"What's your planet like?" I ask quickly.

"It's mostly a wasteland. We fought a war for generations against sentient AI that left us with ruins," Jay says. "But we won, eventually, and now we're rebuilding." He studies his claws and looks serious.

Serious Jay is cute.

"Well, that's something." I'm flailing to cover up what's going on in my head.

"I'd like to get back there," he adds, darkness stealing over his features. "Once we escape. I'll take you to meet the other humans, too."

"Has anything I've said been helpful?" I ask him, the turmoil in my head, of other humans, of fate and of mating, pushed the escape to the back of my mind.

"Everything you say is helpful, my Lauren," he rumbles and stretches out a wing. It shudders, and he quickly goes to pull it back.

"Is that hurting you?" I ask.

"No." He stares directly at me. "I always do that."

Stupid, stubborn alien angel.

"Let me check. If we're supposed to be escaping, then you need to be fit."

"Or what, we'll just have to stay here in this bed?" he asks, eyes twinkling.

I give him 'the look.' Jay holds up his hands in the universally accepted way of acknowledging defeat.

I should think so, stupid gorgeous alien angel.

My eyes alight on the pot of healing gel Nari left next to the bed. I hope the Drahon haven't punished her for helping me. I grab it before moving around to the sore wing side.

"Hold it out," I order as I stand over him.

"Yes, mistress." Jay grins at me, slowly opening up his wing. It stretches halfway across the room.

I run my fingers through the feathers on the edge of his wing, and Jay hums with pleasure.

"Seriously, Jay? No, bad boy!" I tell him, and the grin is back.

"The Gryn love to preen." He runs his claws through his feathers.

"You can preen later, once I've finished fixing you," I say firmly as I gently push back the little feathers surrounding the area where he was injured, blowing gently at the downy ones that hide the wound.

"I'd prefer to be preened by you, my *eregri*," Jay breathes.

I do my level best to ignore him as I slather on some gel and allow it to dry before brushing the feathers back. Pleased with my work, because up until a few days ago, treating someone's wounds was absolutely not in my lexicon, I run my fingers through his lovely, soft feathers. Something comforting about their silky feel.

It's only then I feel Jay's eyes on me.

"That's good." He smiles at me. "Thank you."

Jay

Lauren is an enigma I can't crack. She preens me but doesn't want to mate with me.

She'll sit on my lap and take food from my claws but doesn't want to mate me.

Maybe she knows? Maybe females can tell when a male is not a strong warrior? A warrior who should be able to protect her and has so far failed.

I have to prove to her what I am. I was an elite sniper for my unit. Give me a weapon, and I can hit anything at any distance. I am a Gryn, and we are protectors.

She looks down into my upturned face, her beautiful, pale eyes studying me. I want her more than anything, but until we escape, I can't possibly have her. Or even try.

Why does mating have to be so hard, anyway? I feel my feathers begin to prick in a precursor to the rouse that will follow.

Both Lauren and I have the sticky residue of the Xople on our skin. She has it in her hair. I can smell it, and it makes me sick to my stomach.

"Stand back," I tell her as I get up from the bed.

My feathers twirl as the rouse shakes through me, violent and at once, perfectly calming.

"What. The. Hell?" Lauren stares at me, at my wings, and back at me.

"It is time to bathe, sweet female. And you will accompany me."

"I don't think so!"

Swiftly, before she can protest further, I'm around the bed and have tipped her off her feet into my arms. In seconds, we're through to the bathing pool, and I'm wading with her into the water as she squeals at me to let her go.

"This is what mated pairs do, Lauren," I tell her emphatically. "And if we're to prove to Yuliat we are mated, while we make our plans, well, you get the picture."

"I'm going to get wet! Put me down!" She manages to get a blow into my thigh with her heel.

"Fine, but..."

"Fine, but I'm not getting my clothes wet. Neither should you."

She looks at her clothing and at her arms. "I guess I could do with a bath to get whatever the hell this stuff is off me."

Her fingers stick to her skin, lifting it up before she peels each surface apart. Lauren looks me up and down with an element of appraisal. "Are you sticky. too?"

"I got some of the Xople slime on me." I spread my good wing, showing her where the slime has matted my feathers.

"Okay." She elongates the word. "You turn that way, and I'll turn this." She makes a spinning motion with her long, slim finger. "No peeking."

"What's peeking?" I ask in all seriousness.

"It means looking. Don't look!" she replies with a laugh in her voice.

I wonder if this is what a mate needs—her partner to show her what he wants.

And I want her naked in this pool.

"Okay, you can take yours off too," Lauren calls out from behind me as I stare at the wall, not *peeking*.

I drop my trousers and kick off my boots, the ones Nari found and returned to me.

"Now you go in first," her sweet voice commands, and I wade into the pool until I'm able to duck under the water. "Don't look," she repeats.

I lift my wing as if I'm trying to keep it dry and risk a glance over my shoulder. Lauren is naked and unbelievably beautiful. Acres of pink skin, ripe, round breasts that are tipped with dusky nipples. Her body curves deliciously, and my cocks immediately respond.

She slips under the water and settles on the ledge. "You can look now."

I can look, but then she'll see my arousal and know what I've seen. Should a mate be embarrassed at his arousal in the presence of his female? I don't believe so, but then what would I know? All I know is that until I am buried in her body and have filled her womb, I am only half of what I could be.

"Beautiful." I can't help myself but breathe the word. Because she is.

"It's fine, Jay. You don't have to pretend around me," Lauren says, folding her arms over her chest. "I'm not all that."

It sounds like a challenge, and I've never shied away from a fight.

"If I say you're beautiful, then you are," I reply, attempting to sound emphatic.

I begin to sluice through my feathers. It's going to be hard enough flying with the injury to my wing. Having dirty feathers isn't going to help. Lauren watches me, her gray eyes not missing a thing.

Eventually, she ducks under the water for a short while. I

watch her pale form, shimmering below the surface. She's so close I could reach out and take her.

But mating has to be invited, I remind my aching cocks. And it seems like Lauren is a long way off from inviting me to mate with her.

Which makes me feel irrationally angry. I know it's because I can't make a proper nest and prove to her I'm a good, strong male. Killing the Xople which attacked her doesn't seem to have been as appreciated as I had expected.

Lauren surfaces, exploding out of the water, her hands running over her hair and her gorgeous breasts just breaking free of the liquid. Water beads on her skin. She opens her eyes to see me staring and ducks back down, eyeing me with interest once again.

I prop my wings out on the edge of the bath, allowing them time to dry.

"I should check your wound again," Lauren says. "Now you've got it wet."

"It won't be wet. My feathers are waterproof. I was taught by my seniors only to get my skin wet if my feathers were very dirty." I smile at the memory of all us younglings in the bath, messing around until we were shouted into silence by Myk, the lair blacksmith and, at that time, youngling wrangler.

"You weren't very dirty then?" A smile hitches the corners of Lauren's mouth.

"Not today," I reply in all seriousness.

Lauren

On the one hand, Jay behaves like a big, violent, and grumpy alien male. On the other hand, there is a naivety to him I can't quite pin down.

He broke out of the suite to kill the thing attacking me. He's all up for an escape and he has, so far, been completely *honorable*. And yet...he made that nest for us. He's clearly been aroused in my presence, and he wants to do the right thing.

He's a predator, pure and simple. From the onyx black of his huge claws, to the steely shafts of his wings and the acres of muscle he always has on display. He could rip me to shreds in the same way he disposed of the squid-lion. I'm not entirely sure what I feel about that. He killed it for me, to save me.

He's a killer.

Currently, Jay is looking anything but deadly. Instead, he's smug and comfortable in the bath, an alien spreading himself in a display of masculinity which my body, treacherously, responds to. But when I make a joke about being dirty, it seems to go right over his head.

But in the end, he's right. We have to at least put on some

sort of act to throw the Drahon while we work out if we can escape.

And if we can't...

I try not to think about it.

Okay, Lauren, let's pretend Jay is genuinely interested in you. Exude confidence. You are worth it.

I swirl over to where he's sat, and immediately, his demeanor changes. No longer smug, he looks a little uncomfortable.

"Relax," I purr. I actually purr! What the fuck? "I'm just checking your wing."

He likes a...what does he call it? A preen? I know he'll appreciate me ruffling through his feathers, and I can't deny I like it.

Dark eyes follow my every move. Molten chocolate, accompanied by the scent of spice that he seems to exude. I gently check his bad wing and find that he's right, the wound remains completely dry.

"Looking good," I breathe out. Maybe all prey feels this way in the presence of a predator.

Maybe I'm just a tiny mouse he wants to play with and devour.

My core clenches, which is entirely unnecessary.

"Is it?" Jay whispers in my ear. How did he get that close?

I turn, and we're face to face, almost touching, his handsome face millimeters from mine. A hand cups the back of my neck, and my breath is hot on his skin. A thick rod presses against my bare thigh.

"We shouldn't be doing this, Jay." I return the whisper. Pressing my hands to the bare flesh of his chest.

"I think we should," he replies.

Every atom of my being is screaming at me, and I tune it all out. My lips brush over his. Just an instant touch because we're so close. Electricity snaps at me.

Something shrieks. The sound is so loud it's painful, and I clap my hands over my ears.

"What the hell is that?" I yell.

Jay doesn't look perturbed in the least. "Sounds like an alarm," he replies.

"No shit! Why?"

"I suspect this might be our cue to escape," he says, spinning around and heaving himself out of the pool.

Water sluices off his wings and, as my breath stutters in my chest, his absolutely *gorgeous* bum.

It looks like it's carved from marble, and I can't stop looking at it, especially as he keeps his back to me while pulling on his pants.

"You need to get out." He turns to face me as I very nearly go under as parts of me fire into life I hadn't even remembered existed.

"Yes, I bum—I mean, I do." I swim to the side, and I'm about to tell him to turn around again, but he's already rustled off, water and feathers flying.

So much for electricity.

I've gotten it wrong again. He's just playing a part. Aren't all males playing a part? I've been caught out by a liar and a cheater before.

No wonder I'm alone at thirty. Why trust anyone?

With the alarms sounding, I don't have time to dry myself and instead pull on the awful shift and single pair of knickers which the Drahon saw fit to supply, just in time to see Nari hurrying towards me, Jay in tow.

"What's going on, Nari?" I ask as she grins from ear to ear.

"I found a way to disable the forcefield!" She laughs.

I look over at Jay, and he's not looking happy.

"She sabotaged it," he says.

"So? It's not like we're coming back."

"Can you not hear that?" he asks.

"Of course I can hear the alarm!" I fire back, still having to yell over the noise.

"It's not an alarm. It's a countdown. Your Kijg has tripped something that's going to make this entire place go up."

"Nari?" I turn back to her, and she wrings her three-fingered hands, her skin flushed a deep blue.

"The Gryn could be right," she concedes.

"I am right, and now we need to find some weapons and get the vrex out of here!" Jay grabs my arm, and we're out in the corridor before I know it.

Underneath the alarm/countdown, there are other noises, boots, shouts, and general panic.

"Why would the Drahon have a self-destruct on the compound?" I ask Nari as Jay continues to drag me down the corridor.

Nari shrugs at me.

"Because it's what the Drahon do," Jay answers, his jaw set hard. A darkness has descended over him, one I've seen before, when I woke on the floor outside the cellblock. "Anyway, it doesn't matter. How do we get out?"

As soon as he asks the question, a Drahon guard rounds the corner and stops dead. With a ferocious roar, Jay leaps at him. The guard looks surprised, begins to back away, but it's too late. Jay hits him with a sickening crack, and the guard goes down.

And stays down.

Jay grabs the laser gun, stun stick, and a couple of other items I don't recognize and then looks back at me.

"It's this way," I say, dully. I know that it's us or the Drahon, but Jay's display of violence has reminded me that he is a predator.

The predator.

And I'm about to put my life in his hands.

Jay

The Drahon male was just about to shoot my *eregri* when I hit him full force in the chest, knocking the weapon out of his hand. It skittered around the corner and away from where he hit the ground.

I retrieve the rest of his weapons, trying not to let the dark thoughts about the Drahon color my need to get my *eregri* and her friend to safety.

And yet, when I turn to collect her, her eyes are wide at the death of the guard. I need her to trust me, and I'm not sure she does. She's a diffcrent female from the confident one in the bath.

I grab at Lauren's hand again as we run across a large open area which is under cover of a large a dome. The countdown we can hear is exactly the same as the one on the Drahon ship.

The one that killed my unit.

I know we have some time but not much, and there's no way I'm making the same mistakes as last time. Lauren pulls me along, and we finally reach a door.

"Wait." I push her behind me as I put my wing to it. The door pops, and I spill out into the open air.

Laser bolts zip past me, and I retreat briefly, taking in the sandy-colored exterior walls that would be too high for anyone to scale but should be easy enough if you have a pair of functioning wings.

And no one firing laser bolts at you.

"What's going on?" Lauren asks.

"Hold on." I check over the weapon I took. It's not as accurate as my laser rifle, but it should be good enough to deal with the assailants outside. "I just have to deal with the Drahon, again."

They haven't exactly kept their positions secret, and three short blasts mean they won't be bothering us anymore.

"Come!" I call to Lauren and Nari, and they appear out of the doorway into the open area of the compound.

There's something familiar about the scent in the air, and for once, it's not my *eregri*. Although, if I could never scent anything ever again but her, I'd die a happy male. This is something else entirely.

"How do we know if the forcefield is deactivated?" Lauren asks Nari.

"Like this." I spring into the air, climbing upwards while scanning the ground below for Drahon. As expected, a volley of bolts spray in my direction, and I'm able to swiftly pick off the sources.

I climb higher and higher, not enjoying leaving Lauren on the ground, but once I'm up above the compound, it's clear the forcefield is no longer operative, and I dive back with all haste. My wing aches like vrex as I hit the floor. I'm guessing I have one more flight in me, and I'm going to have to make it a good one.

"Let's go." I beckon to the females, and they approach me. I snag my Lauren around the waist just as a further set of laser bolts ionize over our heads. "Quick!" I wave at the Kijg, and she jumps into my outstretched arm, her cold body slightly abhorrent as she winds herself around me. "Hold tight!"

It takes everything I have to lift off with both females. I was highly trained both to carry weapons and to carry another warrior if needed, but my enforced captivity and my injury is not going to make this easy. We lift away, and I make it over the compound walls but only just as several more laser bolts zip past us.

The Drahon are terrible shots, which is a good thing, given I can't fire back.

Nor can I gain any additional height. My wing is already failing me, and we have to get away from the compound. Underneath, the ground looks familiar, and it's only when I twist to look above me and see the twin moons I finally work out what has been preying on my mind since we got out into the compound.

This is Ustokos! I'm on my home planet. I haven't been spirited away to the Drahon home world as I thought I had been.

Which means I'm much closer to getting back to the eyrie and, what is even better, I may be able to strike back at the slaving scum who took me. The Gryn can blast their compound from the face of Ustokos, capture any stragglers, and make vrexing sure they don't take any more warriors or humans into captivity.

Just the thought of being able to exact revenge helps me lift just a little higher and fly a little farther until we're over a small dusty hillock. If I had to hazard a guess, I'd say we are on the borders of Kijg and Zio territory. I've never been this far out before, but the endless flow of dusty wasteland is what I've heard tales of.

It's not a place to get caught out.

And that's when my wing decides I can't fly any farther,

meaning we hit the ground with slightly more force than I intended. I release both females as I drop to my knees.

"Jay?" Lauren's sweet voice is in my ear.

"I'm okay. I'm fine, just give me a moment." I attempt to get the pain under control.

I'm supposed to be her protector, her warrior, her *mate*. Instead, I'm panting on the ground like a youngling after his first flight.

"We can't stay here, Gryn." This time, it's Nari.

"I know." I open my eyes. My left wing droops badly. "My wing is done. We're walking from here."

"Walking? Where?" Lauren's eyes are round as she takes in the wasteland. "What if the Drahon come for us?"

"They won't," I say, getting to my feet.

"How do you know?" she asks, hands on her hips.

"Because this is my planet, and if they wanted to take on the Legion of the Gryn, they would have done it by now," I reply. "Which gives us a distinct advantage over the Drahon."

Lauren steps closer to me and slowly runs her hand through my damaged wing. I hiss a little as she reaches the wound. It burns at me.

"We're going to need all the advantages we can get," she whispers, pale gray eyes bright as she looks up at me, concern written all over her face.

Lauren

Jay was, put simply, magnificent when he carried us out of the compound. I never thought I'd see those walls disappearing below us and to be in his arms as he flew. It was amazing.

Because I love flying, and it turns out, flying with Jay is incredible. But now that we're out, his wound is hot to the touch, and that last distance must have been excruciating for him, especially as he also had to carry me and Nari.

I don't know what to make of the revelation that we're on his home planet. It should be a good thing, but part of me feels uneasy. I think there's a lot that Jay isn't telling me.

However, as we're still not that far from the Drahon compound, we don't really have time to discuss the ins and outs of what happens next. I don't want to hang around to see if they come for us, and neither does Jay.

Although the dull thump of an explosion from behind us gives me a sense of satisfaction. I hope Yuliat was in there. Of all the Drahon, she's the one I'd least like to leave alive. Given that I consider myself a pacifist, she's definitely pissed me off.

Especially when I check over Jay. He's doing the whole 'I'm a vicious predator' thing (and he is, that's pretty well-established), but the way he's trailing his wing looks worse than ever, and there's a pinching around his mouth telling me he's in pain.

"Sounds like they're playing your tune." I give him a smile. "So, which way do we go?"

Jay looks at Nari. "This is Kijg territory, isn't it, female?" His voice is a low growl, and I find myself stepping in front of her.

Nari glances at me and nods.

"Did you know we were on Ustokos?" I ask her.

"No," she replies, emphatically shaking her head. "Until the forcefield was disabled, it was impossible to be sure where we were. I thought I'd been taken to the Drahon homeworld."

"Why were you a captive of the Drahon?" Jay narrows his eyes, stepping to one side to better look at Nari.

He's such a suspicious predator!

"The Kijg Council offered me up to the Drahon when I came of age. I had no choice but to be their servant, or my family would have suffered," Nari says, wringing her hands. "Now I know where I am, I can go back to my family. They will shield me from any further servitude."

My heart squeezes in my chest. The thought of going home to a family is one I wish I had. Both my parents are long gone, and I was an only child. My eternal search for someone to love me probably stems from the lonely days in the school holidays when my parents were at work and I had no one.

But of course, we all know how that search panned out.

A cheating ex, a heart which broke itself, self-doubt that crippled me.

At the same time, I don't know what being on Ustokos means for me. Nari's been a real friend, and, in the end, she was the brave one who got us out of the Drahons' clutches. But can I go with her? Will her family accept me if I do?

Jay huffs out an angry breath at her. "Kijg! Willing to sell their souls for coin and, it seems, their females too."

"Just because the Gryn lost all their females doesn't mean that every species values them the same," Nari says, sadly. "But I am Kijg, and not all Kijg behave badly. Some appreciate the protection the Gryn afforded us while Proto ruled."

A muscle ticks in Jay's jaw. For all his talk of mating, something is bothering him. Maybe I was right about a Mrs. Jay, maybe he lost her when his species lost their females, maybe he's still in love with her. My heart flip flops wildly, a physical pain spearing through my gut.

Why does that concern me so much?

"We need to move," Jay says eventually. He cocks his head to one side and looks up at the sky. It's milky, and the strange sight of two moons hanging low is something I can't get used to. It's wrong, and for some reason, it frightens me.

I'm not on Earth. I am on an alien planet. With aliens. What happens next will define me to the end of my days.

"We can go North. That way, we should pick up a Gryn patrol at some point," he says, breaking my spell. "Unless the Kijg knows where we are," he adds with a growl.

Such a grumpy predator.

"I'm from the southern lands. These are the waste seas. I've heard of them but never seen them. I guess there will be a settlement on the outskirts. I agree we should go North," Nari says, putting a finger on her chin, her skin a light pink, meaning she almost blends into the dusty soil.

"Waste seas." Jay snorts, looking around. "Suits this place." He reaches for my hand and takes it in his clawed one.

"We're away from the Drahon now, Jay. You don't have to pretend anymore," I say, although, stupid me, I don't remove my hand.

"You need protection, little human. Let me help you as you helped me," he says, his dark eyes trained on me, and a frisson of what we shared in the bath rolls through my body.

I have to put my trust in someone.

Does this mean I will trust him?

Jay

I have no idea where we are.

If what the female Kijg says is true and we are at the waste seas, we need to get off the shifting dust as soon as we can. Why the Drahon would build a base here is anyone's guess. It's a good place to hide anything you don't want seen, but the risk of losing it all is immense.

Now the sound of the explosion behind us takes on new meaning. If it destabilizes the area, we're vrexed. There's no way I'm flying anytime soon, and it means I can't help my *eregri*.

Yet again, I will have failed, and anger floods my veins.

But her hand is in mine, and I can almost forget the dead eyes of the Kijg looking at us.

Even if Lauren doesn't want to nest with me, I'll have these snatched moments, made all the sweeter because we are free, and like she says, we don't have to 'pretend' anymore.

I am not pretending. I am a worthy warrior for her attentions.

I attempt to keep a careful line skirting around the larger shifting dust dunes. It's not easy going, and my energy is already sapped from my injury. But there's no let up in my desire to protect my sweet mate.

Up ahead, I see movement. Five figures and a couple of maraha as beasts of burden.

"Kijg!" I hiss. "Vrex!" I'd hope we'd got farther, even find somewhere to camp for the night before we encountered any of the locals.

"It's okay, we've got Nari," Lauren whispers.

"They will be more afraid of you, Gryn, than you are of them," Nari says, matter-of-factly.

I pull myself to my full height and attempt to set my wings. Pain spears through me. Even injured, I am certainly imposing. Plus, I'm armed. My mate will require shelter, food, and water, and although I'm loathe to admit it, the local Kijg are going to be the best way of making sure she is provided for.

"Kijg!" I bellow out, and beside me, Lauren cringes. "What?" I ask her, confused by her attitude, which appears to be somewhere between horror and embarrassment.

Gryn warriors protecting their females are not embarrassing.

"Nothing, absolutely nothing," she replies, raising her eyebrows at me.

I guess she doesn't know how a Gryn is perceived on Ustokos. That we have respect and standing. That we're not all vrexed-up captives of another species, even if I was when she met me.

I stride towards the small group of five Kijg males. They stand their ground. I have an inkling of respect for them in their own territory, despite all of Ustokos owing the Gryn a debt of gratitude.

"Gryn?" one of them calls out, the boldest of them. "There are no patrols in this area."

"I'm not from a patrol." I bristle up my feathers and hope

they haven't noticed my lack of flight and my drooping wing that I'm unable to quite hide. "I'm here on a...mission."

"Ah, the Gryn and their found females," the Kijg says, peering behind me at Lauren.

I can't help myself. A growl rolls from my chest, and all the Kijg freeze. I fire out an arm and grab him by the throat.

"You do not even *look* at my mate. Is that understood?" I rasp, and he scrabbles uselessly at my claws.

"Ingt? Uncle? Is that you?" The Kijg female hurries past me, peering at the males.

"Nari?" A male, flushed orange with pleasure, sports a large fur around his shoulders which almost dwarfs him. "Little Nari? Is that you?"

She rushes into his arms, and I stare at them. I'm not sure I've ever seen Kijg touch each other before, let alone hug. It's enough to surprise me into dropping the choking Kijg back onto the ground, where he clutches at his throat and coughs.

"What are you doing here?" *Uncle* Ingt asks the female Kijg. "Your parents said you had gone with a Mochi caravan to seek your fortune."

Nari studies her feet. "That wasn't true, Uncle. The Council forced them to give me up to *them*."

I've never been great at reading Kijg, despite their colors changing depending on their mood, but the deep red this male turns is a pretty good indication that something isn't right.

"But this Gryn and my friend Lauren, they helped me escape," Nari says, one hand on his arm.

"For too long, they have been a blight on our lands." Ingt stares straight at me.

I put my hand on the laser pistol tucked in my pants, making sure the claws on my other hand are unsheathed, and prick up my feathers. If he wants Lauren, he'll have to go through me.

"The Gryn have always provided the Kijg with protection and respect," I say.

"If only the same could be said of the Council. They invite these Drahon creatures to our planet and allow them to do what they will." Ingt flushes scarlet.

Now I'm confused. "You know about the Drahon?" I pause as the realization hits. "And you chose not to tell us?"

"I always believed that was a Kijg matter, not for the Gryn." Ingt shakes his head.

"It's not now, not after they attempted to enslave a Gryn warrior. Now, it is a matter for my seniors," I intone.

"If females are being taken, then it is a matter for all Kijg." He looks around at his comrades.

"Females are not for the Drahon," the one I had by the throat says hoarsely. "The Council is wrong."

"Nari, you will come with me." Uncle Ingt takes her hands in his, his forehead butting against hers. "We are heading for a settlement to the south. I will send word to your parents that you are safe, and we will discuss with the southern kin how to deal with the Council."

"I need to get back to Kos," I announce. "I need to inform the seniors of this development."

"Then you need to head North, Gryn," Uncle Ingt replies. "It is a seven turn journey by foot, but for you, maybe two by air."

I bristle, my feathers shaking. Has he worked out I cannot fly?

"Lauren?" Nari walks over to my mate and takes her hand. "What do you want to do?"

Lauren looks at her, then her gaze slowly moves to me.

She is my mate. I know it with all my heart.

And if she chooses Nari over me, it will crack in two. Forever.

Lauren

Did Jay just call me his mate in front of all the Kijg? In front of Nari? When I specifically told him we didn't need to pretend anymore?

They keep on talking, but my brain races. It's racing with everything that's happened. My time spent in the bath where we got close, the escape, the Drahon, and now the very fact Jay won't let the mate thing drop.

What does he want?

And more to the point, what do I want?

I don't want to be used. I know that for certain. Been there, done that, got the T-shirt.

Anyway, I can't really be his mate. We've only known each other for a few days, and it's not that simple. For a start, we're different species.

But the electricity when I touched his lips...what did it mean?

"Lauren, what do you want to do?" Nari says, taking my hands in hers. "Do you want to come with me? The Kijg will give you a home, I'm sure of it."

She looks over her shoulder at the lizard man she called

'Uncle.' His black eyes don't give anything away, but his tongue doesn't taste the air. His skin is a resting blue.

I look slowly towards Jay. He stands tall, arms by his sides, his left wing still drooping. I shift my gaze up to his face, terrified to do so, but at the same time, inexorably drawn to work out if he really wants me. Or if this is the end and I have to let my gorgeous alien angel go.

Jay's dark eyes are pools of night. He stares at me as if he's trying to burn my face into his mind, so he can't forget me. For everything that's gone before, I know I can't leave him.

I should.

Why trust any male? Why trust him?

Because he doesn't move, doesn't speak. He just waits.

Waits for me to make a decision.

"Thank you so much, Nari. You've been a wonderful friend, and I don't know how I would have survived without you. Jay and I owe you so much for helping us escape, but I'm going to go with him. There are other humans with the Gryn, and maybe I can work out what's happened to us all." I squeeze her hands as tears jump into my eyes.

"You have been the best friend, Lauren. It was my honor to help you," Nari says, her voice just a whisper.

I didn't think that Nari could cry, but droplets form in her eyes. I wrap my arms around her thin little body and hug her hard. I am going to miss her so very much.

"There is a trading post to the Northwest. One day's flight for you, Gryn," Nari's Uncle says to Jay. "We can let you have provisions enough for you and your mate until you get there."

Immediately, the other Kijg start to dig into the bags they have slung over the enormous cow-like animals shuffling behind them.

When I look closer, I see that they have three eyes, each one blinking independently. I recoil.

Two large black pouches are located and handed to Jay,

then a further green one. He looks inside and nods with approval.

"Your assistance is appreciated, Kijg," he says. "I will inform my seniors of your help."

"Not all Kijg appreciate what the Gryn did for Ustokos under Proto's rule. It is causing a schism within our species, no doubt. Please don't judge us all by what our Council does," Ingt says. "We will spread the word about Nari and how you helped her."

Jay doesn't reply, and the Kijg pack up their beasts. I give Nari one last hug.

"When the Gryn mate, they mate hard," she whispers in my ear. "You have a long journey ahead of you. Trust him, and he will be true."

"I think he's mixing up reality and pretense," I whisper back. "He doesn't really want me."

"Oh, does he not?" Nari looks over her shoulder at Jay. "I guess that's why he nearly tore the throat out of a male who looked in your direction." She gives me a knowing look as he shuffles, staring down at his feet and avoiding our gazes. "Take care, my friend, but do not guard your heart so hard. You deserve happiness."

She releases me, and her uncle helps her onto the back of one of the cow things. I stand next to Jay as the entire cohort moves off, tears running down my face. He doesn't move.

"What now?" I ask eventually, once they are out of sight.

"We head North," Jay says. "We'll need to find some shelter for tonight. For all Ingt said about flight, my *eregri*, I'm afraid that will not be possible. Not today."

His wing droops farther, and I see for the first time the feathers are matted with blood.

"Fuck! Jay! Why didn't you say anything?" I grab at his wing and inspect the damage.

He jerks it away from me with a snarl. "I can protect you

even if I can't fly. It might take us a little longer to reach the trading post, but once we are there, we can join a Mochi caravan to take us back to Gryn territory."

"Can't you contact your friends to come and get us?" I ask him.

These are aliens. I'm on an alien planet, and I got here because there are spaceships. They must have something similar to a mobile phone.

Jay sighs deeply. "Ustokos was ruled for generations by a sentient AI called Proto which controlled all the tech. We haven't had access to it for a very long time. We may have beaten Proto in the last few cycles, but rebuilding a planet takes far longer. I have no way of contacting my commander or my unit." He stares off into the distance. "Until I can fly again, we are walking."

"I'm sorry, Jay. I had no idea." This time, I take his hand, and he looks down at where we join. "When we were with the Drahon, and all the technology they had, I just assumed you would have it too."

"Ustokos is a ruin of a planet. That's why the Drahon are here. They are attempting to fill the vacuum left by Proto, and I can't let that happen." He grinds out the words. "And I won't let them have you."

Jay

Every atom of my being was poised to grab my *eregri* and fly away with her if she had said she wanted to go with the Kijg.

And the relief following her decision to stay has all but drained me. Is this what it's like being a mated male? Exhausting isn't even the word for it.

If she thinks my injury makes me weak, well, she's wrong.

"Come, female." I stride forward as she jerks her hand from mine.

"Jay!"

Looking back, I see she has her hands on her hips and is glaring at me.

"I thought we were past 'female,'" she says, not moving from her spot. "And I want to check out your wing before we go anywhere."

My wing aches, a dull throbbing that can't be right. I don't regret getting us away from the Drahon, but I do regret that I can't just pick her up and make it back to the eyrie in a day or so.

"Fine." I bluster at her. "Make it quick. We need to find somewhere to camp tonight."

"Grumpy-wings," she mutters and grabs one of the water bladders.

"What did you call me?" I ask, incredulous.

"You heard. Now sit. I can't reach those grumpy wings if you're standing." She stares up at me, fire in her stormy, gray eyes.

"You don't have to look after me. Not now," I grump at her, thumping down on the dusty ground.

Lauren ignores me, inspecting the water bladder carefully until she pulls the small plug that allows the water to flow.

"Wing. Out," she orders.

I glare at her but extend the appendage like an obstructive youngling. It hurts like a bastid, and I suck in a breath.

Lauren pours some of the water into her hand and gently dribbles it over the area of damage.

"Flying has opened up the wound again. I wish we had the healing machine thing." She sighs, peering closer. "Maybe we should have asked the Kijg."

"Can't let them know I'm injured. An injured warrior is a dead warrior," I tell her.

"Of all the stupid things to say..." She puts her hands on her hips again, but then her face softens. "It's just you and me now, Jay. I want you to tell me if it gets any worse. Hopefully, we can find your friends soon. They'll know what to do, won't they?"

"We have a medic, if that's what you mean." I get to my feet again. "We do need to move. If any of the Drahon escaped the blast we heard, there's a risk they'll come after us."

"I bloody hope they didn't survive, especially Yuliat," Lauren spits out.

Brave mate.

"They may be like feather mites—just when you think

you've gotten rid of them, the bastids return with a vengeance, and we can't stay around to see if that will happen."

"Fine, but we're walking." She looks me up and down. "Just in case you were thinking of going all alpha alien male on me."

I shake out my feathers and immediately wish I hadn't. Lauren purses her lips at me. Not wanting to risk any more scolding, I take her hand in mine.

She doesn't resist, and her delicious perfume, the like of which I've never scented before, fills the air around me. If that was all it took to get me off the ground, we'd be back to the eyrie in no time.

But instead, we continue to wind our way through the dusty land on foot. Like all Gryn, I know which way is North innately, although that doesn't stop Lauren from asking me if I know where we're going.

"Are you sure this is the way?" she asks me for the thousandth time.

"If I didn't know, do you think we'd still be moving?" I grind at her.

Mating is much, much harder than I expected. And that's before the actual act. One I'm longing to participate in, finally.

"I'm sure we've been past that pile of sand before." Lauren points to a low dune.

"It's a pile of dust. They all look the same," I reply.

"But how do you *know* we're going in the right direction?" She stomps her little foot, and if I wasn't annoyed, I think I might have wanted to mate her there and then.

"I already told you." I turn away from her, exasperated and aroused in equal measure. "I just know."

Silence from behind me elicits a smile on my face. My mate has finally accepted my superiority in the knowledge of my own planet.

"We should be at the edge of the waste seas in the next hour, and then we can find some shelter," I add.

More silence.

"If there are any polokon around, I may be able to roast one for our evening meal." I reference the small, but tasty, furred creatures which provide many of the furs we use and which I often caught for a snack on an evening patrol with my fellow warriors, back before Proto fell.

Her refusal to respond is exasperating. Females are exasperating! I spin on the spot to find...

Nothing.

My *eregri* has vanished!

"Lauren?" I take a step towards where she was standing only seconds ago.

The place is desolate, a breeze whipping up eddies of the fine dust, but no mate. No Lauren.

"*Eregri*?" I begin to feel a sense of panic rising inside me.

The Drahon cannot have found us, nor stolen her from me without my noticing. My wing might be out of action, but the rest of me is functioning fine.

I take another step to where I last saw her.

And my entire world caves in on me. A swirling, twirling mass of dust, debris, and darkness, followed by light spins around and around.

Something hard pounds against my head, leaving it ringing and one eye refusing to function. A beautiful face peers at me. And the darkness claims me once again.

Lauren

Jay's huge body lands next to me in a heap. He groans once and lies still. Wherever we are, it's dark and hot.

"Jay?" I whisper, attempting to keep the urgency out of my voice. "Jay!" I gently shake him.

He is immovable next to me. I'm not even sure he's breathing, and a level of panic rises from my gut. I don't want to lose him.

Somewhere in the dark, there is a 'tink-tick' sound, like a fluorescent strip light firing up, and in the distance, there is light, and another, and another, racing towards me down a long, wide hexagonal corridor, until the entire place is illuminated, and I see that Jay and I have landed on a pile of sand.

But I also see that Jay has a head wound. It's pissing out bright red blood. He seems pale in this artificial light, and he is definitely unconscious.

"Jay—elite warrior of the Legion of the Gryn!" an artificial voice rings out, the lights dimming as it crackles from hidden speakers.

How does it know him? I'm pretty sure he didn't have a clue where we were, and if he did, he would have mentioned this place, given that technology is apparently so rare on his planet.

"*Jay—elite warrior of the Legion of the Gryn,*" the voice repeats. "*And human female.*"

I roll my eyes. Not the computer too with the whole 'female' thing. Jay shifts slightly, a small moan escaping his lips. His eyelids flicker, but he doesn't wake. If anything, the cut on his head runs with more blood, and a lump appears. I have to stem the bleeding, but we don't have anything.

Except the slave shift I'm wearing. I look down at the only piece of clothing I own and then at my downed alien warrior. He's already saved me more than once. I think I can sacrifice what I'm wearing for him. Pulling the shift over my head, I bundle it up and press it gently over his wound. The artificial voice calls out his name again.

"He can't hear you. He's hurt!" I shout back, not expecting an answer. Even if the computer recognizes him, it's a computer. It will have a stock response or no response.

"*Scanning,*" the voice replies.

"Helpful," I mutter to myself, checking on the wound. My shift soaks up the blood, but it's not slowing down.

He's a big male, but no one, alien or human, can lose too much blood. "Stay with me, Jay," I whisper.

I can't lose him. He might be stubborn, grumpy, and exasperating but that electricity of his touch...

I need to find out what it means.

"*Medical facilities can be located by following the red lights,*" the voice intones.

Immediately, a set of lights appear in the black floor of the corridor. They run a short distance and stop outside a doorway I swear wasn't there before. Not that it matters. It may as well be a mile away as Jay is a dead weight I can't possibly manage to carry.

He stirs.

"No medic. Only tranq," he half moans, half slurs.

"Can you stand, Jay? This thing says it can help, and your head is bad."

He grumbles to himself, eyes only partially open. I slide my arm around his shoulders and attempt to lift him. With an effort seemingly coming from his very soul, he gets to his feet with my help, and he leans heavily on me as we make it the short distance to the doorway. It slides open to let us in.

"No," Jay murmurs, sagging heavily against me as we find the only item in the room is a large chair. It looks like something out of a dentist's office, only without the usual scary light and spit attachment.

"What do we do?" I ask out loud and manage not to add 'Alexa' on the end.

"Place the warrior in the healing pod, and it will start automatically."

Jay complains quietly again, but all of his strength seems to have gone as I heave him into the chair, swinging his legs up as it whispers to life, shifting under him, stretching out to make a bed, and, out of the ceiling, a clear half-cylinder drops down, encasing him. His eyes open, staring directly at me. He puts a clawed hand on the glass.

I put my hand against it.

"I'll be right here for you."

His eyes close again, and my heart leaps into my throat.

"What's wrong?" I cry.

"He is undergoing treatment. Stand by."

I slam my hands against the clear covering. I want Jay to wake up, to give me that gorgeous smile he hardly ever uses, and for his dark eyes to twinkle at me. I want this alien alive and well more than anything I've ever wanted in my life.

Right now, nothing else matters but him.

Because Jay has become the center of my new world by

crashing into it like a kitten careering through the house. All enthusiastic, spiky predator.

How did this happen? When did my heart start to beat for *him*?

Finally, the machine hisses, and the cover lifts away, leaving a prone Jay in the chair. I grab his hand, holding it up to my bare chest. It's warm. He's warm. The scrapes and scratches on his torso are gone. The bloody wound on his head, healed.

"*The warrior requires recuperation. We have prepared a nest for him and his mate.*"

The chair judders, and I grab hold of Jay as we start to descend through the floor, looking around wildly. The whole contraption moves silently and smoothly as we drop into a dark hole, which lights from within as I look down.

The floor gets closer, and it's some relief when we touch down with a slight bump. I feel fingers curl around my hand, and immediately, my attention is back on my warrior.

Jay's eyes are open, deep, dark, and warm. He gives me the most disarmingly gorgeous, sleepy smile.

"Lauren." His rich, velvety voice twists around my name in a way which goes straight to my core.

Without any thought, I lean over him, pressing my lips to his and reveling in the spark leaping between us. His lips are soft, and he offers no resistance as I slip my tongue between them to explore. A hand delves into my hair, and he kisses me back, strong and powerful.

With a need that matches my own.

Jay

It's not possible for anything to be as perfect as waking and seeing your mate. I have never seen anything as beautiful as Lauren when I open my eyes.

Except for perhaps when she put her lips on mine, and I see the stars so close I might be able to touch them. Her tongue in my mouth, exploring my fangs, tasting me. Me tasting her, hungering for her. Needing her.

And I feel better than I have in a long time. Full of energy, fit, strong, and with an urge to mate that's causing my pants to constrict because my cocks are surging.

Lauren releases her mouth from mine, and I gasp for air at the loss of her touch and taste.

"What was *that*?" I ask, before I'm pulling her back to me for another one.

This one is even longer, and it makes me harder. I have to palm my cocks through my pants to get a little relief.

"It's a kiss," Lauren says, her lips trailing over mine, then down and over my jawline.

"A *kiss*." I wonder around the word.

"You've never kissed?" she asks, her crystal eyes dancing.

"I've seen my seniors touch lips with their mates, but not like this," I reply. "Your kiss is very different."

"Don't you like it?" Lauren makes to move away from me.

"On the contrary, I like it a lot." In a fluid movement, I'm sitting up and have her in my arms.

Her skin is soft against mine. She is almost completely unclothed, only wearing the barest scrap covering her pussy.

She squeaks with an initial alarm but lies still as I drop my head to hers and continue with the *kiss*. It's only when we resurface for a third time I actually take in my surroundings.

I'm sitting on a medi-pod. Most of our surroundings are in darkness, but it looks like an underground Gryn lair. More specifically, the nesting areas of an underground Gryn lair.

"Where are we, and why are you naked?"

"I don't know where we are," Lauren says, uncertainly and fear clouding her voice. "We fell in. You got hurt, and I used my dress to stem the blood. There was a computer voice that knew you and helped me get you to this thing." She pats the pod. "Then it healed you. Like magic."

She lifts her hand and brushes it over my forehead. A residual prickle suggests there was something wrong in the not too distant past.

"Magic?" I query the unfamiliar term, yet another one from my *eregri* today.

"It means something that defies explanation. Don't you have magic on Ustokos?" She smiles up at me as her hand cups my cheek.

"We have fate." I capture her mouth again for a long time, luxuriating in being in the moment with her.

Lauren's hands move over my chest, fingers skirting the waistband of my pants.

"Fate must want this then," she breathes.

I trace my finger over her skin, cupping her heavy breast and swiping my thumb over the hard nipple. Her breath hitches at my touch, her back arching, pushing herself into my hand.

"Do you want this?"

"I want you, Jay." She presses on my aching shafts through my pants, and I can't help but let out a groan of pleasure as they jerk against her touch.

"If this place is what I think it is..." I hop off the pod, Lauren still cradled in my arms, and lights come on, illuminating the large, open area.

Ahead of me are three deep alcoves, each one different from the other. I inspect each one, ignoring Lauren's protests until I find that the third has the right scent. The decoration might not be entirely to my taste, not nearly enough furs or hanging fabric, but it will do.

"What is it?" She licks over my neck, and my hips snap involuntarily.

I need to be sheathed in her. My desperation to make her mine has reached a peak.

If I don't mate, I'm pretty certain my cocks will explode.

"It is a nest," I breathe into her hair. "I would normally make my own, but these underground lairs have nests ready-made."

I step inside, and the door closes behind me, like in the other ancient lairs I've seen.

"What's happening?" She stares over my shoulder, and I gently lower her onto the soft, fluffy coverings.

"It's making the place private for us."

"You sound like this is something you've done before." Her voice trembles.

"I made my nest for you, back at the Drahon compound." I cage her in my wings. "But you didn't like it."

"That was for me?"

"A Gryn warrior must make the best nest for his female. He is compelled to do so by instinct for his mate, his *eregri*." I nuzzle at her breast, lapping my way over her salty skin until I reach the little peak, ruby red, and suck it into my mouth.

By Nisis! It's incredible. The feel of her, the taste of her. My cocks strain so hard at the maraha hide of my pants, the pain is immense.

"So, you really have always wanted me? All this time?" Lauren delves her hand down inside my clothing and grabs at my cocks, stroking up my lengths.

And I come, immediately, with a groan and instant regret.

Lauren

My head is whirling with all the new information and the incredible sensation of Jay's mouth on my nipple. He suckles at it like a man starved.

Like an alien starved.

Are we really doing this?
Did he really make a nest for me?
None of this has been pretend to him.

It's the last thought which sends my hands off on a voyage. Because I want Jay, all of him. Every single muscle, his handsome face, his huge feathery wings rising over us. When I thought I'd lost him, the singular blackness of being was something I never wanted to experience ever again.

I've never felt like that, not even about my ex.

Instead, all I want is him. My alien angel who makes my body sing like never before. Who feasts on me as if I'm his last meal.

Who is FUCKING enormous in the cock department.

And who has just shot his load all over my hands, prematurely.

"My *eregri*," he moans softly. "I didn't mean to come so

soon. I want to be inside you so much." He sounds both desperate and distressed.

"It's okay. We have all the time you need, don't we?" I lift his head up so I can see in his eyes.

There's something he's not telling me, and for an instant, my heart freezes. Can I have gotten things wrong?

Jay nods, biting on his bottom lip. "My sweet mate, I only want to pleasure you, worship you, fill you with my seed." Dark eyes plead. "We can try again, can't we?"

Suddenly, light dawns. I know exactly what's wrong. The answer is staring me in the face, and it's in the desperate eyes of Jay.

"Jay, my sweet." I press a kiss on his forehead. "Have you had sex—I mean mated—before?"

This time, the head shakes, slowly.

"No Gryn females means no mating, unless you wanted to go with a Mochi, but I didn't like the Mochi," he garbles out.

I shuffle under him until I can kiss his lips again. My huge, alpha predator is a virgin. A male who desires his female but is unable to control himself when just on the cusp.

I cannot even put into words how incredibly sexy this revelation is.

"I don't care, my darling. I only care that you feel good, that we both enjoy mating." I start to peel off his pants, but he stays my hands.

Instead, he explores down my body, claws catching in my less than sexy massive knickers provided by the Drahon. A ripping sound and they are gone. I feel the air on my pussy, cool against my soaking skin. Jay laps at my breast as a clawed hand explores my mound and just the tip of one finger presses against my clit.

"Jay." I catch his hand in mine as his tongue sweeps over my collar bone. "Let's just take things slowly, shall we?"

The last thing I want is for my big alien to explode

without warning because I know I want to ride what I felt in my hands until he comes again, inside me.

He is genuinely packing, and I need to know more, feel more, enjoy more. And he's got *plenty* to enjoy.

"I want to know all of you, taste all of you. Learn what you want, what you like," he murmurs as he delves a finger inside me, making me groan with pleasure. "You should be pleasured, worshipped, my mate." Jay slips in another finger, curling them and hitting my g-spot with uncanny accuracy as a clawed thumb presses down on my clit. My vision dims as I buck against him.

For a virgin, he's found parts of me no human man has ever even looked for.

I push at his waistband, and this time, he lets me as I roll him onto his back in order to get a proper look at the beast. Peeling away the leatherlike material, what springs out at me is even bigger than I ever expected.

And I mean equine large, but that's not the only surprise my sweet alien has for me.

"Holy shit, Jay! You've got two cocks!"

I am mesmerized by what I've exposed. Already hard, the two shafts jut up from a base of dark curls. The first one is larger, and that's saying something because these cocks are *massive*. A ridge runs the entire length, up to the bulbous head, and all along are small nodes. The second cock is slimmer, studded with nodes running in straight, even lines over the top half, underneath ridges like the skin on the belly of a crocodile. It weeps with clear pre-cum.

I reach for them, and his hips jerk at me as I take hold. A long moan escapes his lips.

"All Gryn have two cocks. Don't human men?" His eyelids flutter, and he thrusts himself into my hands involuntarily as I run my fingers over his members.

"They do not." I'm enjoying the feel of his cocks in my hands, and I drop my lips to the tip of the main one.

Running my tongue around the head elicits a deep groan and a clawed hand in my hair.

"Do you like that?" I ask but don't give him time to reply as I suck him into my mouth as far as I can.

"Lauren! I will spill my seed again!" His words are hoarse as I work both shafts, knowing that as long as he thinks about coming, and my mouth, and my hands, he can hold.

His hips jump at me, wings flop uselessly on the bed of fluffy, furry material. Jay writhes and groans beneath me until a pair of hands grasp my shoulders, and I'm lifted away from him with a pop.

"My turn," he growls, his dark eyes bright with a new intensity.

One of a male who knows exactly what he wants.

Jay trails his lips over my skin, making me shiver. He's exploring me with his mouth and fingers, which trip over my nipples and down, down over my abdomen to my mound. He rises over me, wings held high as he pushes my legs apart and plants himself between them. Clawed hands spread my thighs as he gazes down in wonder.

"So beautiful," he says, reverentially.

Then he drops his head over my pussy, nose nuzzling between my folds, tongue exploring my hidden depths.

"I want to make you feel good," he murmurs against my soaking flesh. "I want to taste what smells so delicious."

A tongue delves deep into me. "Ambrosia of the Goddess!" he exclaims, and his tongue is joined by a thick digit, slipping inside me easily, I'm so wet.

My hands are in his feathers, grasping at his enormous wings, and he grumbles his desire into my pussy, sending goosebumps running all over my skin. His mouth hitches, and he discovers my clit.

Stars are everywhere, behind my eyes, in front of them, as if the entire universe has come to visit me when he sucks the bundle of nerves between his fangs.

"Oh, Jay!" I'm convulsing, hips jumping, pushing myself wantonly into his mouth, flooding him with my juices.

"Sweet mate." He licks everything, lifting himself high above me, wings outstretched as he cleans his fingers of my wetness. "I have to sheathe myself in your hot cunt. I must mate you. I have to claim you, fill you."

His cocks nudge at me, main cock at the entrance to my pussy. "Do you want me, my *eregri*? Do you need me?"

"Yes! I want you. Fill me!" I hear myself yelling.

"I will be gentle," he murmurs, caging me in his arms as his main cock just breaches my entrance. "You are so small and tight." He groans, sweat rolling off him.

He is huge, and the stretch is incredible as he inches his way inside. I'm bracing myself for his second cock when I feel it pressing at my anus. Just as I gasp, it slips past the ring of muscle, lubricated by the slippery pre-cum, with a burning sensation quickly replaced by an incredible feeling of fullness.

"Oh, god." I breathe out slowly as Jay finally seats himself inside me. Dark eyes meet mine, and a clawed hand brushes my hair from my forehead.

"Perfect mate," he whispers. "This is everything I thought mating would be."

He withdraws almost his entire lengths and slams back inside me as I cry out in delight and pleasure. Each channel, the dark and the light, pulses over his enormous members as he circles his hips, thrusting and pounding while his lips meet mine. He adds his tongue to the invasion of my body, one I welcome willingly. Each movement sparks my desire, fanning the flames higher until my vision dims and my body gives up with the most intense orgasm I've ever felt, every single nerve ending concentrated on milking his cocks.

"My *eregri!*" Jay roars as he comes, hot seed firing out of him, coating every inch of my channels.

His irregular thrusts mean he's filling me over and over with his first proper climax that never seems to end, rolling with mine, our bodies desperate for each other, desperate to absorb every part of each other.

The nest is filled with the sound of our panting. My muscles tick at me, twitching as I come down from a high I didn't even think was possible.

And Jay showed me it was absolutely obtainable. My alpha alien. My virgin male.

"My love." Jay presses a kiss to my lips. "My *eregri*, my boundless flight. Thank you for being my mate."

He curls his arms around me, wings blanketing us both, and draws me to him in a delicious, warm embrace.

I'm not sure I've ever felt more loved than in this moment.

This surely can't be real, can it?

Jay

Mating was everything I thought it wouldn't be. Sensual, surprising, raw, and honest.

But the best thing? It was with Lauren. The female currently sheltering in my embrace, in a nest of my choosing, even if it's not of my making.

And I will be making a nest as soon as we return to the eyrie. One that is absolutely perfect for her. Maybe she might even allow me to fill her belly as well as her slick hot pussy.

A shudder of pleasure rolls over my body, and I already feel my cocks growing hard again, yet I'm still inside her.

"Ready to go again, tiger?" Lauren cups my face in her hands, gray eyes dancing up at me. She shifts and wriggles a little.

It all serves to make me even harder for her.

"I don't know what a 'tiger' is, but I'd mate with you forever, my *eregri*." I push my head into her hand, and she runs fingers through my hair, into my feathers, and the thrill bolting down my spine has me lifting her up so I can sit her on my cocks, cradle her in my arms, and explore her delicious breasts.

"You really are ready!" she chokes out as I begin to plunder her hot, tight channels once again.

"I need you. I need to mate you, make you mine," I groan against her sweet, salty skin. "But if you want me to stop, I'll stop."

"Oh god, no!" Lauren shifts, allowing me to go deeper inside her. "Don't stop!"

So, I don't stop until we lie panting in the fur, and she is full of my seed once again.

I dip my hand between her legs, and it comes up soaked with our combined essence. With a single digit, I spread some over her belly, up and over her breasts, twirling around her dusky nipples, covering her completely with my scent and my seed.

"You are mine. All of you, from your beautiful breasts, to this perfect belly that will swell with my youngling." I lap over her skin, tasting both of us on her before moving back to her mouth.

"I don't think I have much choice whether or not we have a child, not after what we just did." Lauren laughs.

"I have not filled you with my secondary cock, sweet mate. I can only fill your womb if you take my seed from both cocks. Until you are ready, I will happily take you in both delicious holes."

"A sort of natural birth control?" She runs a finger down my jawline, followed by her lips.

"Providing I can control myself around such a delicious mate." I nip at her breast. "Because I long to sheathe my cocks in your tight pussy and release all my seed."

Lauren moans softly, and I'm growing hard again for her.

"I want you too, Jay," she whispers in my ear. "But is there any chance we can have something to eat before round three?"

"Are you hungry?"

She looks at me, a mixture of embarrassment and need flitting over her face. I can't believe that I failed her at this first hurdle. She should never hunger, never want for a soft bed or the protection of a strong male. I'm not even entirely sure where I am, I was that desperate to mate her.

To claim her.

And now she is mine.

"You do know you're growling, don't you?" Lauren stares at me, her mouth quirked up at the corners.

"Because I have failed you, my *eregri*. You need food, and I don't even know where we are."

"Neither do I, but wherever and whatever it is, it helped you, so it can't be all bad," she says, sleepily.

"Come." I gather her up in my arms, and she protests. "We'll be back, I promise." I nibble on her ear, and she goes limp against me, a sigh of desire inflaming me once again. "First, we bathe and eat."

Because mating has made me ravenous too.

The wall slides open, and I'm confronted with exactly what I wanted as if the base knows my every thought. A bathing pool steams with hot water. I wade in quickly and lower my *eregri* into the liquid. She hisses slightly as she disappears under the surface.

You should have told me you were sore.

"What did you say?" Lauren looks up at me. "You said something, but your lips didn't move."

I'm lost for words. This cannot be happening so fast, surely?

"The thoughtbond," I gasp out.

"The what?" Lauren stares at me, swishing her hands in the water. Her emotions are a riot of color in my mind.

"The thoughtbond. It's the mind-link between mates. I believed only senior Gryn had it."

"A psychic link? I can hear your thoughts?" Lauren doesn't sound convinced.

"And I can hear yours."

"I know exactly what you're thinking." Lauren stares directly at my crotch. My cocks are hard for her again. The thought of her all slippery in the water has set my pulse pounding. "Without needing you in my head in some sort of weird psychic way."

I dive into the water, surfacing with hardly a splash. I pull her into me.

I want all of you, from your beautiful mind to your perfect toes.

She stills in my arms as I let her know just how the thoughtbond can be used.

I'm going to pleasure you until you come apart, until you ride me to completion, until you can't even speak your name, let alone mine.

"Jay!" she breathes as I surround her with my wings. "I don't...we..." Her words struggle out. "You're in my head."

"And I want to be inside you, but there are more important things." I butt my forehead against hers, then grab the strange white bars which sit on the side of the pool. They produce a foam I've seen other warriors use to cleanse.

Not something I care for myself, but I know my mate needs such soft, fragrant cleansing.

"Let me tend to you, then feed you. It is my honor. Only then will I ensure you are properly claimed, mated, and filled."

Lauren

I have a psychic link with Jay.

Let me just process that concept for a moment...

Except he's not going to let me. Instead, he's going to wash me *very* thoroughly, paying particular attention to the areas he plundered only minutes earlier, before he reverentially lifts me out of the water and puts me on my, admittedly wobbly, feet.

"How do we get dry?" I ask. The pool is in a circular room with walls that seem to be made out of polished concrete. Other than the water, there doesn't seem to be anything else in the way of towels or cupboards. "And what's the chance of clothing? Mine got ruined by your blood."

Jay gazes at me, heatedly, his tongue slipping out and wetting his lips hungrily. My body responds with a flood of moisture which I can't control. Damn him!

"I'd prefer to stay naked."

"So would I, but then hot food is out of the question." I cock my head to one side, planting a hand on my hip.

Because with Jay, I've developed some newfound confidence about my body I previously didn't have. Sure, like any other normal woman, I could do with losing a few pounds (maybe more than a few). I've got stretch marks in the usual places, along with various lumps and bumps.

But the way he looks at me, like I'm some sort of queen. I like that. It makes me feel strong. Strong enough to brazen my way through being this nude for this long.

Jay grins at me, then drops his mouth on mine for a long kiss. Something else he's mastered very quickly, along with the ability to control his hair trigger.

"Whatever you want, my mate," he murmurs as he releases me, and yet again, my chest is heaving at the intensity of his gaze.

Or is that what's in his head and mine? It's hard to tell, and I'm going to need time to deal with it.

"This way." Jay takes my hand and walks toward a blank wall. It's only when I think he's going to hit it that I see it's an optical illusion, and in fact, it stands on its own, just in front of a doorway that leads into a white room.

As we pass through, strong fans suck at both of us, and I feel my skin and hair drying. Jay shakes out his feathers several times, shuddering and shivering before stepping out of the doorway.

"I don't like that part." He pouts. "Prefer my wings to dry naturally."

I want to hug him. Cradle the adorable male in my arms for the rest of time. An alien predator who doesn't like a blow dry.

This is insane. I can't really be falling for him. He's gorgeous, huge, and I've just popped his cherry. Why the hell would he want to stay with me?

Jay looks over his shoulder, through his wings at me. Each feather is fluffed up; he grins and my heart melts.

Stupid heart.

"Clothing," he says, simply, and puts his hand on another wall that slides away to reveal rows of strange, shapeless items.

I delve inside and pull one out. It's a catsuit, matte black and likely to be very form fitting.

"Is this it?" I run the fabric through my hands. It's soft and silky. It would be nice if it wasn't, well, something out of a seventies pop video. "Nothing for females?"

"We don't have any females," Jay says, pulling on one of the suits.

I was right about it leaving little to the imagination, although I miss his acres of bare abdomen almost immediately.

"You said you didn't have any technology either." I wave my hands at our surroundings.

"This was built by the ancient Gryn. We're finding them everywhere now Proto has gone," Jay says, adjusting the crotch area in a movement which is clearly universal among males.

"Built by the Gryn when they had females," I prompt him. "Maybe?"

Because, presumably they had females at one point, given the 'natural' form of birth control the males of the species have. Although it makes me realize how little I know about the species of alien I've chosen to...enjoy.

This time, Jay's smile is somewhat sheepish. In a single pace, he has his arms wrapped around me, and he's dropped his head into my damp hair.

"Forgive me, my *eregri*. I have not spent much time around females of any species, and it didn't occur to me our lairs might have once been built with females in mind. We have been without females for so long. I don't even remember my mother."

Being in his arms, his warm wings enclosing me, is probably the nicest thing ever. My heart flutters for him, for the sadness which flows at his lack of memory of the one female he should remember. As much as losing my mum was terrible, at least I can remember how good things were when she was well.

My alien releases me and places a clawed finger on his chin as he studies the room. Then he crosses to the opposite wall and presses his hand against it. Another door opens, and this time, it looks a bit more promising.

Before I can reach the wardrobe, Jay has pulled out a couple of garments and is staring at them.

Yep, his suit leaves absolutely *nothing* to the imagination.

"Do females really wear things like this?" He holds out the silky black dress.

It's backless, presumably because the female Gryn also had wings, but it's also floor length.

"I thought there were females back at your eyrie? Human females. What do they wear?"

"Not this." Jay goggles at the dress a little longer, running a claw over it with a certain reverence.

Which is like a red rag to a bull, or should I say, silky ballgown to a woman who always wanted to be a princess. I sashay up to him, pull it teasingly out of his hand, and shimmy into it, fully expecting that the material will reach my thighs and stop.

But it doesn't. It clings deliciously to me, slithering over my skin beautifully. Only when I hook the straps over my shoulders and look back at Jay do I see his jaw hanging loosely. I spin on the spot, allowing the fabric to ripple and flow, fluttering almost like wings.

Jay palms his crotch, eyes not leaving me for a second.

"What was it you said about food?" I ask him, innocently.

He hesitates, clearly struggling to process his emotions, and yet again, my heart pulls in my chest. I shouldn't tease him, but I can't help it. He is just so gorgeous when he's trying to deal with his newfound lust.

And a *pair* of cocks with a mind of their own.

"Yes, my *eregri*." He stalks towards me, wings held high and, in a movement which is impressively quick for a seven-foot powerhouse of a male, he's grabbed me by my waist and lifted me off my feet into his arms, as I squeak pathetically in alarm. "My job is to feed you."

With that odd suggestion, we're striding out of the changing room and down another corridor.

"Food!" Jay bellows out.

"*The dining hall is on your left, Jay,*" the computer voice says.

Jay huffs, his dark eyes hardening and his grip on me tightening.

"What's wrong?" I ask.

Jay

The voice, it goes right through me. I know it's friendly, but that doesn't stop all of my instincts firing up.

"It's nothing," I say. "It just reminds me of Proto. I should be used to it by now."

A doorway appears on my left as if out of the wall. Whatever lair this is, it's far more sophisticated than any I encountered before with my unit.

"Proto? The previous ruler of this planet?" Lauren queries.

I inhale her scent deeply. It's calming and arousing in equal measure. Both of these things war within me, but my desire to please my mate is uppermost.

"The sentient AI. It destroyed Ustokos and sought to destroy all organic life, or so we thought." I step up to the doorway, and the doors slide into the walls, revealing a room not dissimilar to the underground lairs I have seen and used. "Until we found it had partnered with the Drahon to sell Gryn to the rest of the galaxy."

I carry Lauren over to a table and put her gently on her feet. I do not want to let her go, having to force myself to release her if I'm to get food. She chews on her bottom lip in the most gorgeous way.

"Is there anything else you want to tell me about how horrible this galaxy is?" she asks.

From somewhere, I get a prickle of fear.

My mate will never be afraid.

"But we're safe here, and you're with me," I say, proudly. "Once we get back to the eyrie, you'll see what a force the Gryn are and that the Drahon are no match for us."

I approach the wall of food heaters and look around for the ration packs, finding them neatly stacked in alcoves. The writing on the wall is ancient Gryn, but it looks like each one relates to a flavor of food. I grab two, peel off the lids with some difficulty, given my claws, then place each one in a heater with a flourish.

"Is that going to be okay to eat? If this place is as ancient as you say it is, won't it be...oh!" Lauren lifts her head and sniffs at the smell of hot food.

"I wouldn't give you anything if I didn't think it was edible, my mate." The heater chimes, and I manage not to jump at the sound, just flare my wings a little and give her a hesitant smile. "Tech. I'm not going to get used to the fact it doesn't want to kill me for a while."

"The microwave used to want to kill you?" she asks, watching as I remove the food trays and place one carefully in front of her. Then I return to the preparation area and use the dispenser on the wall to obtain two cups of cala.

All of which is as fresh as if it had been prepared in the eyrie's kitchens. The ancient Gryn certainly knew how to treat themselves.

I'm not entirely sure what to do next. Lauren looks up at me and then pats the seat next to her with a smile. "Let's eat. If I'm hungry, I bet you are."

She's not wrong. I practically inhale the first tray of food, and I'm up for more just as quickly. At the third tray, I remember why eating was important to me and meet Lauren's gray eyes. They crinkle deliciously at the corners as she dips her head, hiding yet another smile.

"I could look at your smile all day," I blurt out.

"Subtlety isn't a thing for the Gryn, is it?" Lauren picks up a piece of meat using her fingers, blows on it, and then pops it into her mouth in a way which has an alarming effect on my cocks.

"What do you mean?" I shake out my feathers. "I can do subtle."

"A being your size and fluffiness? I doubt it." She laughs, inspecting a round, yellow object which I believe is some sort of berry. As I'm not a fan, I have piled mine to one corner of my tray. As she chews, she lets out a low groan which, all at once, sends my desire to mate into overdrive and has me terrified for her safety.

"What is it?" I ask urgently.

"This is delicious!" She opens her eyes and continues to chew. "Why aren't you eating yours?" She points to my empty trays of food—empty save for the yellow things.

I shake my head. "Prefer meat."

"I bet you do." Lauren picks up one of the orbs and holds it up to my lips.

This is wrong. I should be feeding her, not the other way around and especially wrong as I don't want to eat the berry. Her eyes dance, part challenge, part something else.

I open my mouth and gobble the fruit, along with her fingers, which taste both sweet and meaty as I lick them clean. Lauren's eyes widen, and the scent of her arousal perfumes the air. Another flavor bursts over my tongue, the berry. It's sweet, sour, and I'm not sure I like it.

Lauren bursts out laughing, a raucous sound, full of life. If

I never heard anything else in my life, I'd die a happy Gryn. I swallow the remains of the berry. "What?"

"Your face!"

"What about it?"

"You didn't like it at all, did you?" She winds her arms around my waist and presses a kiss on my collarbone, hands slipping into my feathers and stroking them as she leans into me.

"Not really." I'm already wondering if there's anything else I might not like if she cuddles me this way every time.

"Fruit and vegetables are good for you." She settles farther into me. "Tell me about the Gryn, about your eyrie." Lauren lifts her head from my chest, fixing me with her steely gaze. "Let me know exactly what I've gotten myself into."

I continue consuming my food for a short while. I should tell her about what happened to my unit. I should confide in my mate how worried I am, how I don't know if they live, what will happen if I return and they are not there.

"We are not numerous, but we are the protectors of Ustokos," I begin.

"All of you?"

"When Proto ruled, some of the Gryn were captive. The rest of us, the free, we offered services to the other organics. Protection, medical supplies, weaponry, in return for supplies," I explain.

"That explains why Nari's uncle said not all the Kijg were appreciative of the Gryn," Lauren says, her fingers stealing towards another leftover berry.

"The Kijg in particular disliked being in our debt. The Mochi were pleased to be able to get on with their lives without having to concern themselves with such matters." Just as I finish speaking, quick as a flash, she pops the berry into my mouth, and I have no option but to eat it with a wince.

"Now Proto has gone, what do you do?" Lauren asks, smirking happily as I chew and swallow.

"This is a planet which requires rebuilding and protecting. Our seniors are set on finding as much tech as they can. We have a planetary defense system..." I hesitate briefly, and Lauren studies me. "My unit and I were tasked with getting it online. That's when the Drahon took me."

"No wonder you want to get back," she says, one finger stroking over my cheek, making me want to capture it with my mouth. So I do, sucking on it until I release it with a gentle pop.

Lauren breathes out, shuddering as she does so.

"I'm happy right here. With you," I say.

Lauren

A strange emotion rolls through me as Jay releases my finger, part unbridled desire, part sadness, although the sadness dissolves immediately. Is this part of the 'thoughtbond' he mentioned?

I'm not sure. All I know is I'm back in a pair of muscular arms and being marched through the underground corridor by an alien angel who growls deep in his chest.

"Where are we going?" I wriggle in his arms.

"Don't move, little mate. I'm taking you to our nest."

"I can walk." I wriggle again.

"If you don't stop that, I will mate you right here and now," Jay snarls, one lip hitched to show his sharp fang and his lust.

I shift in his arms, reaching up to kiss him. I'm spun around with dizzying speed until I come to rest, back against the corridor wall, legs dangling as Jay presses himself between my thighs. I've no option but to wrap my legs around his torso, feeling every long inch of his cocks grinding against my core.

"You were warned." His voice is feral, as are his eyes, dark with need. "When I need to claim you, I need to claim you. It should be in my nest, but anywhere will do."

"Anywhere?" I rasp.

It appears a virgin alien can be as kinky as fuck with the right incentive.

"Anywhere." He growls over the skin of my neck, teeth nipping as my pussy floods with moisture.

Jay's hand snakes under the fabric of my dress and finds my soaking folds. "And it looks like you'd let me take you anywhere too, dirty little mate."

"I don't think you'd really mate me here, would you?" I whisper in his ear. "Not when we have a nice nest waiting."

"Oh, you don't think I'd fill my mate where she stands?" Jay's gaze gets even darker. "That I'd fill her until she can't take any more, until she swells with my seed, right here."

A zipping sound, and something huge breaches my entrance, more than just one something.

"Fuck, Jay! You are *big*." I gasp as he thrusts hard at me, and I'm suddenly fuller than I've ever been in my life.

He lets out a long groan of pleasure, circling his hips to seat me on him. Every single node and ridge scrapes over my sensitive channel, and I already feel the flutter of my climax.

"I'm going to breed you, my Lauren, you know that don't you?" Jay murmurs, withdrawing almost all the way out and slamming back into me again, shaking my body. "You will take my seed and make a youngling."

"Is that what you want?" I'm struggling to breathe, to take in the invasion of my body, my huge, winged alien who wants to possess all of me, who wants to get me pregnant.

"More than anything. I want to mate you over and over when you are full of my child, and I can feel your swelling." His words are getting hoarser, and he continues to plunge into me, his thrusts getting more and more irregular.

He's close and so am I.

He's a male who wants me, body and soul, who shares a mind link with me. *Who wants me pregnant with his child!* So why am I still scared to give him my heart? Why can't I just let go and be with this fluffy, feral predator?

Jay sinks his teeth into my skin, not enough to break it but enough to tip me over the edge of my orgasm.

"Jay, Jay, Jay!" I chant through the pleasure and the pain. "I don't know." I moan as I convulse in his arms, soaking his cocks with everything I have as my entire body gives itself to him, his cocks and gorgeous eyes.

"If you're not ready, then you don't get all my seed." Jay laps over the place where he bit me, sending even more sparks through my body but then withdraws from me completely, and I moan at his loss.

Instead, I'm being spun until I face the wall. Jay kicks my legs apart, and suddenly, I'm invaded again, only this time with only one cock. The other runs through my folds and hits my clit.

I thought multiple orgasms were a myth.

I was wrong.

The ridges on his second cock are absolutely made for massaging my clit, and stars spiral from the heavens for the second time, or is it the third? I have no idea, not anymore. All I know is Jay's weight behind me, pounding me as he grips my waist, growling low in my ear.

"If a mate doesn't want her belly full, then a mate has to be punished until she can't come any more." Jay roars, pinning me to the wall. He thrusts up once, twice, and I feel the hot fountain of cum from his secondary cock as his main cock fires everything he has inside me. He groans his pleasure into my neck, his wings enclosing us in a feathered cocoon.

"I cannot get enough of you," Jay murmurs into my ear. "My little mate, so delicious, so edible, so ripe." He inhales deeply, his cock slipping free, and it's followed by yet another rush of our combined juices.

Jay turns me to face him. "I only ever want what you want, Lauren. But you have to know I want you, in my nest, over and over again. I want you always by my side and in my heart."

His lips find mine so very easily, and the kiss he extracts is tender beyond belief.

"Jay," I say as soon as he releases me. "I don't know what all of this is but..." I drop my chin to my chest, fingers entwining with his feathers as I wonder exactly how to tell an alien who only believes in fate about ex partners who cheat.

Who lie, who destroy every iota of trust you might have in another man. Who make you believe that love will always be out of your reach.

Until Jay.

"Lauren."

His face is right next to mine, liquid dark eyes taking in every aspect of me. An equally dark emotion swirls between us.

"Who hurt you?" he demands. "Who made you believe you were not worthy of a Gryn warrior?"

"It's not important," I say as I'm swept up again, and Jay strides through the corridors until he reaches the nesting room.

"It is important to me." He places me like a feather on the bed and begins to lift my dress over my head, but I stop him. "Because I don't want anything to get in the way of us."

He means it. He genuinely means it. I should just let it go, put my trust in this alien angel who has only ever worshipped me. But my mouth takes over, as usual.

"There was a man on Earth. He told me I was his everything, and then he cheated on me with another female."

Jay is silent. His hands ball into fists, and a muscle ticks in his jaw.

I've blown it with him. This kind, caring and, as I've discovered, very, *very* dirty male. He knows I'm damaged goods.

Why would he ever want to be with me?

"Males on Earth do such things? Toy with a female in such a way?" He growls. "Do they not know how precious females are?"

In a blink, I'm surrounded by feathers, a heavy warm body on top of me, a handsome face kissing my lips to oblivion.

"His loss is my gain. You are the most precious thing on Ustokos, my Lauren. And you are mine. Always. Anyone who tries to get in my way, they will feel my fury."

Jay

All I want is for Lauren to understand just how special she is to me. I've mated her *and* made my nest for her. But she's still not sure I want her and only her. I can feel her trepidation as a weight swinging from the bottom of my heart.

I kiss her, hoping it will change how she feels. A human kiss for a human, proving to her I can be better than any human.

"I am yours, Jay." She stares up at me when I release her. "No one else's."

"Good, because once we're back at the eyrie, I'm going to take a ship to Earth to teach human males about females." I'm vibrating with anger that any species would treat a female the way my *eregri* has been treated.

"You don't need to do that, Jay." Lauren dips her head, and when she looks back, her eyes are full of tears.

"Do not cry for him." I use my thumb to catch the water. "Never cry for him."

"Oh, god, no, Jay!" She chokes out something that is half sob, half laugh. "I'm not crying for him! I'm crying because you're the sweetest, kindest male in the entire universe! You are utter perfection, and I don't deserve you."

"*Eregri.*" I breathe the word as it is meant to be said, like a prayer to the Goddess. "You deserve to be happy, and I will make it so."

Lauren runs her little pink, clawless hand through my feathers as I settle in beside her. She toys with the smaller ones on the ridge of my wing, and I do my best not to allow her to see my growing arousal. I'd mate her all the time if I could. After a while, she sleeps, her eyes closed and face at rest.

I stare up at the ceiling and turn my worries over in my mind. Lauren has me as her mate, but she thinks I might reject her in the same way as the unworthy human male did. Maybe my nest *isn't* good enough. It's not like it's one I've made. And a pre-made nest can't possibly be the same as one created by me. If I want my *eregri* to be the happiest female on Ustokos, and I do, then I'm going to have to up my nest making game.

When I'm sure she sleeps soundly, I very carefully unpeel myself from her and go see what can be done.

"OH, JAY!" LAUREN CONVULSES OVER MY COCKS AS I have her pinned on her front against the wall of our temporary nest.

"Let me paint you with my seed, sweet mate," I growl in her ear.

She's boneless as I withdraw and drop her onto the furs, ready to be mated some more. I pump at my cocks, readying myself for the eruption of seed which I can spread over her creamy skin, making sure our scents mingle, and I can ensure she is marked as mine.

Later, I will show her exactly what she means to me, but

only when I've finished what I started when I kissed over her entire body this morning.

She rises on her knees until she's level with my cocks and takes hold of them, pumping them in time with my hands, and then her pink tongue swipes over the end of my main cock. I grunt with the effort of not coming immediately.

"Let me pleasure you, darling," she says, and before I can reply, her mouth encircles my cock, and she's licking and sucking it deep into her mouth.

I can't believe how incredible the sensation is, especially when she separates out my secondary cock and strokes it, too. My hands are everywhere, in her hair, on her shoulders. Wings flail behind me as I'm lost in the sensation of her tongue lapping over every inch of my cocks.

Then she takes both into her soft, wet mouth, and I know I cannot hold.

"I will spill my seed." I moan, "My *eregri*. I will..."

When my climax hits, I'm not sure my legs are going to take my weight. Each cock fires out so much seed, it can't be possible. Yet Lauren laps it up, swallowing my essence, letting some fall on her delicious globes where I can trace patterns over her skin.

"That should have been inside your cunt, sweet mate." My knees give way, and I drop onto the floor, pulling her into me so I can spread my cum across her breasts, like I intended.

"You really mean it, don't you?" Lauren swipes over my mouth with hers, and I can taste myself on her, as well as tasting her sweetness from where I pleasured her earlier. "You want to make a baby with me?"

"It is my instinct. Mating and younglings is what every strong warrior should do," I tell her. "I need to fill your womb as surely as I must fly."

Lauren stills in my arms.

"How are we going to get back to your eyrie?" she asks suddenly. "Your wing is healed, so are we going to fly?"

It is a matter I've given some thought to. I've even gone so far as to ask the lair's AI about contacting the other Gryn. But going back means I have to face what happened. That thought sits like ice in my stomach. And something gray sits in the back of my mind. It is my mate. Something troubles her.

"We can fly, once we're ready. But I won't be ready until I know you understand what being a mated male means to me."

"It means you knock me up. Me or any other hapless female you happen to encounter," Lauren says, clearly trying not to sound upset, but the thoughtbond tells me different. "Breeding humans is all you bloody aliens want to do."

Her hatred for the Drahon is strong. And it only makes me love her more.

"Come." I take her hand. She reluctantly gets to her feet.

I swipe a soft artificial fur from the floor for her, wrapping it around her lush body before pulling on my pants, then I lead her out of our temporary nest.

"Jay, what's going on?" she asks, dragging her feet.

We reach the door, and I press my hand to the pad to open it. Lauren stands next to me, her hair tousled in a delicious post mating manner, my scent strong on her. The nest door opens to reveal my creation.

"What have you been doing?" She stares at the nest I've spent hours preparing from scratch.

I think it's my best work. The underground lair's AI was relatively helpful in providing me with directions to the items I thought I might need. The result is a nest that is resplendent in dark fur-like materials with easy access to the healing pool.

I have found plenty to decorate the rest, colorful fabrics, shiny discs, shinier pieces of see-through material which sparkles beautifully, like her eyes. It has to impress her. It has to show her just how much she means to me.

It has to tell her I'm a powerful male who can make a good nest and provide for a youngling. Or younglings. Hopefully many younglings.

"I have finished our nest, a proper one, not one made by the ancients." I wrinkle my nose. "This is all my work. I made it for you."

"Oh, Jay." Lauren doesn't look at me. "You did all this for me?" She holds her fingers to her lips, and I see her tears on her cheeks. "Why?"

I'm on my feet, enclosing her in my arms. "I did it because my last one wasn't good enough for you. I wanted to prove to you that you are my *eregri*."

"It's me that should be apologizing, Jay." She smiles through the tears, melting into my arms. "All of this is so new, I thought I could go with it, and it would be okay, but it's not. It's overwhelming. I want it all to be real, for you to be real, for what I feel for you to be real." Her eyes trail over my nest once again. "It is real, isn't it?" she whispers into my chest. "You are the male who will protect me. An honorable warrior, just like Nari said."

I clutch her to me, realizing too late my mistake.

I built my nest; I proved myself to her.

Only I haven't told her what I did, and when we return the eyrie, she will discover just what a terrible male I am.

Lauren

I don't know what to think anymore. Jay has obviously spent ages planning out this room and decorating it in such a particular manner. It's at once gaudy, brash, and beautiful.

And he did it for me.

Because mating is more than simple copulation for him, and he wanted to prove it. Which he's done in an incredible, delightful alien way. He's even made sure there's a spa pool.

I snuggle into his feathers, breathing in all their spicy warmth, taking comfort from this incredible male who will seemingly do anything to show me how much I mean to him.

But, stupid Lauren, I've failed to see past my self-imposed blocks, right up until now, when I'm seeing, for the first time, a male who adores me.

Me.

"I'm sorry, Jay. I didn't mean what I said about other females. I guess I thought I understood males, but I don't know Gryn males. What I said was wrong, and this is the most beautiful thing anyone has ever done for me."

I run my hands through his feathers, and he hums with

pleasure. It's a feeling I can almost taste, like candy floss and strawberry jam, a swirl of cream and pink.

"I'm pleased you like it, my Lauren."

"Maybe we need to be more open with each other," I say to the male who is so open he might as well be a book in the wind.

"A male hurt you, and he won't do that ever again, not while you are here on Ustokos with me," Jay says fiercely, his strong arms squeezing me.

"I don't think I'm leaving Ustokos."

Jay looks down at me, dark eyes which are pits of desire. "I hope not."

"I'm not leaving Ustokos." The reality hits me, hard, like a punch in the gut. I'm not leaving Ustokos because I'm never leaving Jay.

"Good, because our mating, it is fate, my *eregri*. Fate is never wrong." He croons into my hair, his belief very strong, even if something else hovers in his mind like a dark cloud. "I've been exploring this underground lair if you would like to see some more of ancient Gryn tech?" He adds, "Get to know your new planet?"

"I'd love to." I smile up at him. "Sounds like a date."

"A date?" he queries, leading me out of our nest, which I give a longing look, and into the bathing area. "What is a date?"

I contemplate the answer. "It's where a male and female spend time together but not mating." It is the best I can do.

"I want to spend time with you either way, although I like mating." Jay grins at me over his shoulder as I drop the blanket to the floor and walk into the pool. "I like mating a lot."

"I've noticed." I sink down in the warm water as my predator joins me. Something tells me this will be quite a long bath.

"This is a control room, I think." Jay shows me into another room.

So far, I've seen a storeroom full of boxes, a training room, which was empty save for mats and the very slight whiff of testosterone, and an armory, which was full of laser guns.

Jay was quite fond of that room.

This is different. My knowledge of computers doesn't extend much beyond my laptop and smartphone, but this is definitely technology far beyond that of Earth, in that I haven't a clue what I'm looking at.

It's full of waist-high consoles (providing you are Gryn sized—they come halfway up my chest), all blank, as if they are touch screens waiting to be activated. One wall is also black, and it makes me think it might be some sort of viewing screen.

"So you say this place was built by your ancestors?" I ask, running my hands over a blank console.

"All the other ones we've found were. Our quartermaster and his mate said these places scan for Gryn DNA, which allows us entry. Other species on Ustokos which might have come across them wouldn't have been able to get in."

"How do you find them? The bases, I mean." I poke at a console, but nothing happens.

"Mostly by accident. We're still figuring tech out." Jay shrugs.

"And you like the blowing stuff up part?"

His stunning grin tells me all I need to know and, despite not being a 'blowing things up' kind of girl, his enthusiasm makes my lady parts tingle.

"I like the investigation of ancient things part," I say. "On Earth, the study of ancient things was my job." I jab at the console again.

"We could do with help in deciphering what happened to

the Gryn, not just the tech," Jay says, putting his hand on a console and watching as it lights up. "There's so much we don't know, and yet, with the Drahon on Ustokos, we need to know to ensure we can fight them."

"I'm all about fighting the Drahon," I agree, walking over to where his console has lit up.

The characters are not unfamiliar, but I'm not sure where I've seen them. If I had access to my books, I'd be looking it up. Except this is an alien planet. Nothing should be familiar. However, before I can explore that thought, another one occurs to me.

"If your friends also have one of these — lairs — then can you not communicate with them?" I look up at my big alien excitedly.

"Communicate? How?"

"Like send a message."

"Does Jay wish to send a message?" the strange artificial voice suddenly chimes in, making me jump.

"It does that."

"Well, hello, Siri," I mutter to myself, ignoring Jay's confused frown. "Yes, er, computer. Jay does wish to send a message to the other lairs."

The black wall I suspected suddenly lights up and an image of me and Jay is reflected in it. Jay flares his wings in alarm, huffing out a breath, then his innate curiosity takes over, and he stalks towards his image, holding up first one hand, then the other. He extends a wing and watches TV Jay mirror him.

"Fascinating," he admits. "I wonder what it is."

These aliens really have not had any access to tech, that much is abundantly clear.

"It's a camera of some sort, Jay. If I had to guess, you can link up with the other lairs and either send a message or talk directly to them over a video link."

His confused face says it all, a handsome face that suddenly darkens. "I'm not sure we should," he rumbles. "In fact, we don't know anything about this tech. We shouldn't touch it. I forbid you to touch it!" He turns on his heel and stomps out of the room, feathers flying.

I stand, rooted to the spot. He can't be afraid of the tech, given he's gone to such pains to tell me how much he's enjoying learning about it. Weapons in particular are his thing, and he's almost as enthusiastic about them as he is about mating. Almost.

So to dismiss the opportunity to show me how wonderful Gryn tech was. To speak to his 'unit' or his 'seniors,' both of whom he holds in high regard. There's something not right. And I like to think I'm getting to know Jay just a little better with every passing moment. Notwithstanding the strange psychic stuff which I'm trying to ignore.

Regaining the use of my legs, I hurry out of the control room and follow the sounds of destruction. Whatever has upset my sweet warrior, I think he might be taking it out on a part of this lair.

Jay

I steady every part of me as I line up the laser sights with the target. Breathing out slowly, evenly, gently before I take the shot down the range. The bolt hits the center with a satisfyingly loud zap, and I line myself up for the next shot.

Only this time, someone blows in my ear, and the bolt goes wild, ricocheting off the wall until it fizzles away.

"Hey," Lauren says, her scent invading my senses in such a way I know I can't shoot straight even if I want to. "I'm here."

"I'm shooting," I grump at her. "Need the practice."

She watches me loose the next three bolts and miss the target every time.

"Yep, you need the practice," she says.

"You're putting me off," I half-snarl.

"Good." She snatches the laser rifle out of my hand before I have time to process it. "Then you have time to talk to me."

"Give that back!" I reach for it, but she dances out of the way and down the range. "It's dangerous for females."

That was the wrong thing to say. Lauren bursts out laughing, turns, faces away from me, and lets rip with five bolts which all hit the centre.

"Definitely dangerous for girls," she says over her shoulder. "Now, are you going to talk to me?"

I rattle my feathers in frustration. I don't want to admit I have no idea what I would be going back to, if we do manage to contact the eyrie, or that the loss of my unit was all my fault. I don't want her to think I am a poor warrior, without honor.

I just want to stay here, in this lair, in our nest, and mate, and feed, and spend time together on a 'date,' like we were doing before she suggested contacting the other lairs.

Lauren walks up to me. The short red outfit she has on today leaves nothing to the imagination, and yet everything is covered. The silky fabric clings to her every delicious curve, like something which needs unwrapping.

"Why don't we go eat?" She hands me back my rifle. "You like that."

"I killed them all," I blurt out and stumble away from her, turning and running like the coward I am because I don't want to see the look on her face when she realizes I'm not the mate she thought I was.

"Jay!" Her voice echoes after me. "Wait, please wait!" I slow my pace because the pull of the thoughtbond, her thoughtbond, is too great.

I drop my head to my chest, staring at my boots, knowing I have no option. She knows, and she will hate me for it.

"What the fuck is going on, Jay?" An angry looking Lauren confronts me. "You don't say shit like that and run away. Not ever. That is absolutely not a thing on any planet, and the last thing I want to happen to me. I've had enough secrets and lies to last a lifetime." She bristles with annoyance. "Tell me what happened."

I lean against the wall, closing my eyes and tipping my head back. A small, warm hand slips into mine.

"Literally, there is nothing you could say that will change the way I feel about you, Jay," Lauren says, winding an arm around my waist.

I add my arm to her waist and draw her into me, inhaling her scent and knowing I have no options left.

"I told you I was on a mission when I was captured by the Drahon," I say as Lauren nods. "It's partially true. We were in the Drahon ship, searching for my commander and some humans. I was distracted because I could scent something I wanted." I inhale again. "It might have been you." I trace a claw over her cheek and tilt her chin up to me. "But I shouldn't have been distracted. Next thing I know, I'm separated from my unit, trapped in an escape pod, which blasted away, leaving the rest of the ship to self-destruct, with everyone on board."

"How is any of that your fault?" Lauren's eyes flash. "Should you have stayed there to get blown up with them? I don't understand."

"I left them, Lauren. I am a male without honor."

"But really, you don't know if they were in there at all, do you? Not until you contact your friends and find out," she says, full of fire. "And it was hardly your fault that the Drahon captured you. If you were looking for me, then you were doing your job, weren't you? Looking for humans?" she adds in a softer tone.

"I suppose."

"And you found me, too. Would you want to change that?" Her voice cracks slightly.

"By the Goddess, no!" I have her face cupped in my hands, my lips on hers to show just how much her human kiss means to me. "I'd rather tear my wings off than lose you again, sweet mate. All of Ustokos can burn if I don't have you by my side. I love you with everything I have."

Tears hover in her eyes. "Jay, you shouldn't be scared

about finding out what happened to your friends. You did what you thought was right, and that's what matters." She pushes her cheek into my hand, holding it against her soft skin.

My mind blooms with her emotion for me all at once, and it's like being buffeted by the strongest winds on Ustokos. She is only concerned with my happiness, not consumed with shame or doubt. She believes in me completely.

"But what if..."

"I understand betrayal and failure, more than you can ever know, Jay. What you did, what you have done is none of those things. You escaped the Drahon. You blew up their base. You rescued me and Nari. If that's not an honorable warrior, I don't know what is. Your seniors should be proud of you."

She pulls back from me. "So let's go and contact them, shall we? Because there's an alternative you haven't thought of while you were blaming yourself."

"What's that?" I frown at her, still unsure of the correct course of action.

"What if they think you're dead, and they're all missing you?"

Lauren

Jay still seems reluctant as I tow him back towards the control room. I guess he really didn't consider the possibility he was being missed.

But if you tell yourself something for long enough, you start to believe your own lies. I should know. It took an alien abduction and a huge, winged predator to convince me I wasn't the one in the wrong.

And when you care about someone, when you love them, you will do anything for them, including making them face their fears.

Or building them a nest.

Jay has made me whole again, and it's about time I returned the favor. We reach the control room, and the screen remains on.

"What do you think we do?" I ask. It is his technology, after all.

"Lair, connect me to another Gryn lair," Jay calls out, staring at the ceiling.

"I'm not sure that makes sense." I stare at the pair of us on screen, marveling at Jay's feathers and impressive set of abs which look even better on the telly, given he's returned to his usual bare chest and leather pants combo. Because apparently the suits were 'too tight.'

"Connecting to lair four," the disembodied voice says.

Much more helpful than Alexa.

"What's at lair four?" I take hold of Jay's hand again, trying to keep his mind calm.

"I don't know. I didn't even know they had numbers," Jay says, his voice low as he studies the screen.

"What the vrex is going on?"

Our faces are suddenly replaced with a *very* up close and personal view of a nose.

"Why is it making that vrexing noise?" someone else asks.

"Is it going to explode?" a third voice adds with some glee.

Looks like the desire for destruction is universal among the Gryn.

"Ayar?" Jay steps closer to the screen, and I pull him back.

"You need to stay where you are so they can see you. If you get close, that's all they will see." I point at the screen which is currently showing half of a face, and most of that is a dark eye.

"Jay? Is that Jay?" the first voice comes again.

"Stand away from the console," Jay calls out, smiling knowingly and a little smugly at me. "It is me. Is that Ayar and Mylo?"

"Jay!" Finally, the Gryn in front of the camera steps back, and I see three of them.

All are naked from the waist up, just like Jay. All sport huge wings. All are impossibly good looking, although one of them is somewhat disheveled and scarred.

"Guv?"

The slightly taller of the three steps forward.

"Jay, we thought the Drahon had taken you off world. How are you talking to us? Did you escape?" he asks, his voice calm and controlled.

"They didn't take me off Ustokos, Guv. They had a base in Kijg territory. I — we — found another underground lair under the waste seas. That's how I'm contacting you now." A clawed hand draws me into him. "This is my mate, Lauren. She was also a slave of the Drahon," he adds proudly.

"Hi!" I wave at the camera, and to my delight, all three hesitantly wave back.

"Lauren, this is my Guv, Strykr, commander of the Legion of the Gryn." The big warrior nods. "And also Mylo and Ayar."

I'm not entirely sure which is which, but the pair grin like Cheshire cats at the screen.

"Did everyone else make it?" Jay asks, stiffening with his question.

"Make it?" Stryker asks.

"Out of the Drahon ship when it self-destructed?"

I squeeze his hand again as he stares hard at the screen.

"Not only did everyone make it," Strykr laughs, *"we gained three human females and a Gryn warrior. And now we have you back too!"* He's clearly delighted.

As is Jay. His feathers pricked, he runs his hands over my shoulders and presses a kiss to the top of my head.

"The best news," I whisper up at him.

"I'm interested in the Drahon base down there," Stryker says, rubbing his chin with a viciously clawed hand. *"I think we'll come to you. This new lair sounds interesting. Stay put, and I'll get Syn to work out how this vrexing thing operates."* He peers again at the camera. *"Go get Syn,"* he says over his shoulder to one of the others, and they disappear.

"Yes, Guv!" Jay's happiness rebounds through me. "Only one thing. I might have, accidentally, blown up the Drahon base."

Stryker performs possibly the best face palm I've ever seen. It's all I can do not to laugh out loud.

"He had no choice," I chime in before Jay can speak. "It was us or them."

"*It always is with this unit,*" Strykr replies. "*I'll need to speak with Ryak and the other seniors, but we should be with you in two turns max. Will you be able to stay in your lair until then?*"

Jay looks down at me, his gaze heated. "I think we'll manage, Guv. For a few days," Jay replies. "Comm off," he adds, and the screen goes dark.

Then I'm swung off my feet, and the control room disappears in a flurry of feathers.

"When did you learn how to do that?" I gasp as his pace increases, and I know exactly where he's taking me.

"I know how to turn things off. And on," Jay growls. "And right now, all I want to do is turn my mate on, devour her, and ensure she is pleasured so hard she doesn't remember where she is for the next two turns."

"Is that a promise?" I pant as my mind fills with everything Jay plans.

"I don't have to promise, little mate. I only have to show you."

We reach the nesting area, and he practically breaks the door down. As I'm tossed onto the furs, there's a ripping sound, and my cute red playsuit is torn away.

Jay holds the remnants of the fabric in his mouth, sharp teeth white against the scarlet. Onyx black claws grasp my thighs as he spreads me wide; his huge wings open like an avenging angel. He drops between my legs, pinning me in place with one hand on my stomach.

With one single swipe of his tongue, I'm spinning as all my nerve endings fire at once. Jay keeps his eyes firmly on me as he works, unerringly finding my clit and fastening his lips on it. I groan, grabbing at him and making contact with a feathery wing.

"Eyes on me, mate," he orders before continuing to feast. "Eyes on me at all times." He laps over my wetness.

The suction is incredible, and without any warning, my body gives in to him, an orgasm slamming through me as I buck under his touch.

"Completely delicious," Jay murmurs over my pussy as he licks me clean. "Ambrosia from the goddess herself."

He rises over me, unfastening his pants and releasing two huge throbbing cocks which I know need some attention. I reach for them, but he bats my hands away with a growl.

"Not for you, mate. I have far better ideas on where I'm going to put these, and it's not in your clever hands or mouth. Not yet." He pumps at his enormous members, pearly pre-cum spilling from the tip of each one.

"Where?" I ask, my voice hoarse as he watches my every move.

"Where, indeed?" he rasps, and he lifts his hand to his mouth. Placing his index finger between his lips, he bites down, spitting out the claw.

He sucks the same finger into his mouth, then he slides it inside me, curling it up until he hits my g-spot, and my vision goes again.

"Should I put them in here and breed you?" he rumbles, raising his eyebrows and his dark eyes glittering as he probes deeper. "Fill your womb with my seed? Make your belly grow big and round with my youngling?"

I exhale all the breath in my lungs. Right at this moment, I want his cocks deep inside me, fucking me hard, and I don't care if I do get pregnant because the baby would be his. I would be his.

We would be his.

And I want nothing more than to be the mate of this fluffy, sex mad alien angel who only lost his v-card recently and is shaping up to be insatiable.

And adoring.

And would probably make the best dad ever.

"Or how about I put them both here?" Jay slips his finger free and circles my tight pucker, pushing his way inside oh-so-gently. "So tight!" He groans as he slides his digit deeper and presses the head of his main cock up against my entrance. "I love how tight you feel with me inside both holes," he rasps, barely holding it together. "By the goddess, I want to breed you, sweet Lauren."

Sweat rolls off him, and he is entirely still. Unable to move.

"Jay?" I whisper up at him.

"I cannot hold, my *eregri*. I must claim all of you, and you don't want it. I can't."

In the moment, this single moment, I understand what it is to be an *eregri*, a fated mate, bound to one by something otherworldly.

"I want you." My voice is strong, desiring, needing. "I want all of you, Jay, every single inch, everything you have. Give it to me, over and over." When I breathe in, lust shudders my body. "Breed me, my darling." My pussy floods with moisture, slick and hot.

"Vrex!" Jay's hips fire forward, and both cocks stretch me wider than I could ever imagine. "Oh, my mate, you are absolute perfection." His dark eyes pin me down. "Perfection I will gladly corrupt with all my cocks have." He circles and then withdraws, nearly all the way, before pounding back inside me.

One of his enormous cocks in my pussy was good, two are simply incredible, stretching me to my very limit. The ridge and nodes on the main cock hit my g-spot with every single thrust as Jay cages us with his wings, and his spicy scent intoxicates me. His eyes never leave my face, one hand on my hip and the other planted firmly next to my head. He moves in a sinuous, rhythmic fashion, ensuring that every part of me is being plundered by his huge members.

"All I've ever wanted is to breed you, from the moment I saw you. Today, you are ripe for me. I can scent it and I will fill your womb." He growls. "I will make you mine, forever."

His words tip me over the precipice, and I'm coming, convulsing, pulsing even though there's hardly any room.

"Lauren! You make me—" His sentence is cut off as he roars out his own climax, and I feel a further intense, painful stretch which disappears the instant his hot seed fires inside me, both cocks exploding at the same time.

My body responds in unison, milking him for every last precious drop. I can't move, can't think, can't even breathe with the orgasm rolling through me, intensity ramped up to maximum. It's as if all of me is on fire, and Jay is the only one who can put me out.

He drops his lips to mine, his skin damp as he kisses me.

"How long do we have until your friends get here?" I say, as I try to catch my breath.

"Not long enough." Jay gently pushes a lock of hair from my forehead. "Not if I'm to ensure you are thoroughly claimed before they arrive."

Jay

My beautiful mate is even more stunning underneath me, full of my cocks and my seed. Her crystal gray eyes take in everything because she is a brave and clever mate.

Who wants me, who wants to have my youngling. Who helped me see my folly wasn't that I might have killed my unit by my actions, but I shouldn't have shied away from finding out the truth.

And now I'm going to be reunited with them, and I have her.

I shift position over her and find I can't withdraw.

"What's wrong?" Lauren asks, her face calm.

"I'm — stuck," I say. "My secondary cock has swelled!" I add.

"Um." Lauren bites down on her lip. "Is that supposed to happen?"

"A Gryn male's secondary cock should swell when he claims his mate. It ensures she retains his seed," I say, proudly. "As mine has done."

I swing my hips, pressing back into my mate, and she gasps gorgeously.

"How long?"

"Long enough."

"Just when I thought I knew everything about you, Jay, you go and surprise me again." She smiles, cupping my cheek in her little pink hand. "Anything else you want to tell me?"

"Probably just everything. But mainly you are mine. Now and forever," I growl. "You are truly my boundless flight."

"A party?" Lauren queries me as she offers up another of those interminable yellow berries to my lips.

I have to admit in the last few days I've gotten used to them, but I still wince out of instinct as I take it from her fingers, making sure I lick my way over her skin and make her giggle at my touch.

"Party. It's what we do to let off steam."

Lauren tips her head to one side. "I'm trying to imagine a hundred Jays having a party. Does much stuff get exploded?" she asks with a laugh.

"Not exactly, but things can get...interesting. Like you said, with a hundred Gryn warriors, or mercs as the seniors call us, there can be a bit of a mess."

"Ah, so that's why you need the humans? To clear up after you?"

"Oh no!" I reply, horrified. "Whatever mess we make, we clear up or the Prime would have our hides!"

"Party animals which clean up after themselves? Are you Gryn the perfect males or what?" Lauren replies, spooning a mouthful of something she says reminds her of *isscream* from Earth.

We've been mating, talking, dating, and mating again for the past turn, and I've reached the point where I can't wait to show her the eyrie and the lair. At the same time, the thought of her being in the presence of other males boils my blood, and I want her all to myself.

And all of this is before any of my unit have set foot in this base. Life is going to get difficult for me all over again. Still, I've got at least another turn with my mate until that bunch of vrexers gets here.

"What is that noise?" Lauren asks, lifting her head and looking out of the canteen door. "Sounds like…"

"Vrex!" I stand immediately. "There's something in the base."

"Shit!" Lauren fires out. "Do you think it's the Drahon?"

"If it is, they picked the wrong ground to fight on." I grab her hand and, meal forgotten, I race the short distance to the armory to grab my rifle.

Lauren watches me as I sling it over my shoulder and buckle on a belt with a laser pistol and dagger.

"Any chance I could have something to defend myself?" she asks, arms folded.

Instantly, I have her in my arms. I nuzzle my face into her fragrant hair. She smells perfect, all maraha hide and warmth. She smells like home.

"You don't need a weapon, my *eregri*," I rasp out. "I am your weapon, your protector and your shield."

I'm in her thrall; she is so completely perfect. It's the sound of noises outside in the corridor which breaks our spell. I tuck her behind me and lift the rifle from my shoulder. Leaning slightly out of the doorway, I take a quick glance out. All I see is a hint of movement as something large disappears into the canteen.

"Did you see anything?" Lauren whispers, her hands in my feathers in a very distracting way.

"There's definitely something here. It's gone into the canteen," I reply in a low voice. "Stay close to me."

On the one hand, I want to put her somewhere safe, rather

than have her following me around, but at the same time, there's no way I could leave her behind. Safe is with me.

We edge out of the armory, and I flatten myself against the wall with Lauren in tow as we approach the canteen. Inside, there are scraping sounds of furniture being moved and rustling which is somewhat familiar.

"Wait here," I mouth in Lauren's ear before I press her back onto the wall and take several strides to the canteen door, rifle raised, I step into the doorway, ready to deal with the Drahon scum.

Instead, I'm presented with three Gryn warriors, one with bulging cheeks as he chews on the remains of my meal.

"Jay? Jay!" Ayar closes the distance between us in a single beat of his wings, and my rifle goes flying as he leaps onto me, enveloping me in a hug of Ayar proportions which is only matched by his musky scent.

"It's Jay!" He releases me for a second, turning to the others as if they don't have eyes in their heads. "I told you, he's alive!"

"We can see that, Ayar." Vypr lounges against a table.

Ayar breathes in deeply. "And he's *mated*! Our little Jay is *mated*!"

"Ayar!" I groan and attempt to disentangle myself from his grip. "It's not that big a deal."

"I think you'll find it is." Mylo ambles over, shoving Ayar to one side with a wing and eyeing my carefully before he wing bumps me amicably. "Always thought you'd be too terrified to mate," he adds as I shake my feathers at him.

"Are we going to meet this mate or what?" Vypr asks, and I spin to the doorway, to see Lauren backing in, followed by Strykr, Syn, and another Gryn I don't recognize.

"Is this your female, Jay?" Strykr rumbles.

Lauren bumps into me, and I enclose her, feeling her body

vibrating with fear. I'm growling low, unable to help myself with so many males in the room with my mate.

"Lauren. This is my unit," I murmur in her ear. "They are entirely harmless, most of the time, and will not hurt you in any way."

"Okay," she stammers out.

"Honored brothers, I give you my mate, Lauren." I bare my teeth at them all, wings held high.

Making sure they all know she's mine.

Lauren

Good god, ALL of these Gryn are huge.

Together, they fill the canteen which I thought was quite large. But it's absolutely not with seven massive, winged warriors crammed inside. Suddenly, it's gone quite claustrophobic.

It doesn't help that Jay's thoughtbond is going off the chart. He's aroused, happy, and growly jealous all at once. I do the only thing I can, the one thing I've learned in the last few days. I shut it down. It means he can't feel me either (and, believe me, during sex it is *astonishingly* good), but it means I can think clearly.

"Er, nice to meet you all," I offer as six pairs of dark eyes turn on me.

"I'm Strykr." A Gryn wearing a weapons belt across his chest steps forward and offers me his hand. Jay snarls, but Strykr stands his ground. "I'm your mate's *commander*. He's been missing for a while and might not remember his training," he says pointedly.

With some considerable reluctance, Jay relinquishes his

hold on me, but he doesn't move away. I take Strykr's hand, and he shakes it up and down with exaggerated slowness.

"Pleased to meet you," he says, as if repeating a mantra.

"There really are humans on this planet." I twist to look up at Jay, who glowers at Strykr. "British ones, like me?"

"My mate, Kat, is Bri-*tish*. Or so she tells me," Strykr replies with a shrug. "It's some sort of designation the humans give to other humans living in different areas of their planet," he tells the others.

"Got any more rations?" one of the broader warriors asks. He has the most enormous gun on his shoulder.

"Mylo!" the others groan.

"What? A Gryn gets hungry when he's looking for lost warriors." He grins at me. "I'm Mylo. The closest this one has to a friend." He bumps his wing against Jay's and receives a glower in return.

"Mylo is only my friend when he thinks I have rations for him," Jay replies. "The ration trays are over there." He points out the neatly ordered trays on the other side of the room, and Mylo heads over, making happy sounds, feathers fluffed.

It looks like these fearsome predators are anything but fearsome.

"Where's the control room?" a warrior holding something which resembles a tablet asks.

"This is Syn, our tech expert," Jay says. "It's three doors down."

The warrior doesn't even look up from his pad as he heads out of the door.

"Still friendly, I see," Jay grumbles.

"As always," a warrior behind me replies. "I'm Vypr, and this is Ayar." He slings his arm around the shoulder of a scarred male with longer hair than all the rest and disheveled wings.

"Hi. You were on the video call, weren't you?" I recognize Ayar.

"The picture on the wall?" He gives me a somewhat unhinged smile. "I saw you."

"Ayar doesn't do tech," Jay says, knowingly.

"No, I vrexing don't!" Ayar fires out, and as if to underline the point, one of the alien microwaves pings, and his feathers lift involuntarily, like a cat's fur sticking on end.

"Who are you?" Jay stares at the last warrior who is leaning against the doorframe, looking insolent and dangerous.

"This is Huntr. He was on the Drahon ship when they captured me," Strykr says. "He's part of the unit now."

"Only so I can destroy the vrexing Drahon," the warrior growls. "When that's done, I'm done." He pushes away from the wall and stalks out of the room.

"What's his problem?" I ask before I realize what I've said, mouth running away with itself like usual.

"Ignore him," Mylo replies, mouth bulging with food. "Everything was wrong with him, and now he has female trouble."

"You were definitely on Ustokos when you escaped the Drahon?" Strykr asks Jay, taking a seat next to Mylo who is happily stuffing his face. "We saw the escape pod leave the ship, but we believed it had left orbit before Syn could complete the activation of the defense system."

"The Drahon base was around half a turn's walk from here," Jay says, indicating I should sit too, while he remains standing.

"Walk?"

"It's a long story, but my wing was injured before we found this base. Lauren got me into a healing machine."

Mylo chokes and coughs, slamming a clawed fist into his chest. "You used one of those things? By the goddess!"

Strykr studies me carefully, as if he's weighing up what I am.

"We fell in. Jay hit his head. When the base computer recognized him, I decided to trust it rather than let him die." I bristle.

The senior warrior breaks into a smile.

"That's one brave and resourceful mate you have, Jay," he says with genuine warmth.

"I know," Jay replies, gazing at me with liquid dark eyes, and the pleasure flowing from him fills my heart.

We might not have had all the time on our own we wanted, but he has his unit back, and he has me. My alien angel is happy.

"We're going to need to see the Drahon base," Strykr says. "We need to find out why they are still here and didn't just leave the planet when they could."

"I'm not sure how much of the base is left," Jay says, shuffling his feathers and a naughty look stealing over his face.

"Like I said, it blew up a bit when we left." I grin. Somehow, Jay's desire to wind up Strykr is infecting me.

"A bit?" Strykr queries.

"We didn't exactly stop to find out how much," Jay adds.

I hold my breath, hoping I might see the epic facepalm in person, but Strykr just sighs.

"If there are any Drahon alive, we need to interrogate them. They won't have been able to get off world."

"Why do you want to have anything to do with them?" I blurt out. "They were going to sell Jay and had plans to get me pregnant and sell me too. Filthy creatures!"

"That's the exact reason we need to find out more about why they are here and how we can beat them," Strykr says. "Ustokos has to become out of bounds for those who wish to enslave the Gryn."

"It's not just the Gryn," Jay says. "There was a Kijg female who escaped with us. We helped her find her family, but from what they told us, the Kijg Council are selling their own to the Drahon, and it's not something they all agree with."

Strykr's face darkens.

"Then we do need to find out more about the Drahon. I appreciate you've found your mate, Jay, but we're going to need you to come with us."

"I will be coming too," I say quickly. "I want to see the Drahon pay as much as Jay does."

Jay turns to me, one hand tracing gently down my arm. "I can't put you in danger, sweet mate. I don't want to risk you falling into the hands of the Drahon."

"And what about you?" I push his hand away because his touch calms me, and I don't want to be calm because I don't want him to go. "The Drahon captured you once. What if they do it again?"

"It won't happen again." Jay ducks his head, and his lips are on mine before I can move away and, stupid me, I melt into his kiss. "Because I have you to come back to. I will never, ever leave you, Lauren."

Jay

I'm fired up to be back with my unit, but something tugs at my insides.

Not just something. It's Lauren. As much as I want to be part of what I thought I'd lost, I want her too. I also have an instinctive desire to protect her, and even if she wants to come with me to fight the Drahon, I can't let her.

I can't risk her.

Looking on to Lauren's eyes, I see she can't understand why I would go and leave her behind.

"I'm going to see if Syn has had a chance to look over the control room," the Guv says diplomatically. "If you've quite finished eating your bodyweight, Mylo, go and check Huntr isn't destroying anything he shouldn't be." He looks over at Ayar and Vypr.

Ayar paces like always; Vypr watches him move back and forth with a caring gaze.

"You two, find the armory and do an inventory," Strykr orders them.

All warriors troop off to their assigned tasks. "Guv?" I query, expecting my orders.

"I'll let you know when we're due to leave, Jay." He gets up from the table. "I don't want to separate you from your mate, but this is important," he adds, not moving his gaze from me. "She will be safe here, and we'll be back before you know it."

He heads out of the canteen, and we're left alone. For a long time, Lauren doesn't say anything. I feel as if we're back to where we started. I don't know what to say, and I've already made her a nest.

"I understand what you have to do, but I don't have to like it," Lauren says, finally.

She's closed the thoughtbond to me, and I'm frustrated. If she let me in, I might know what I should say to convince her I'm right.

"It is my duty, sweet mate. It won't take long, and like the Guv said, you'll be safe here. You've seen my unit. We're perfectly capable of defending this base and you."

Lauren's lips go into a thin line, still unsure.

"Yuliat was fucking slippery. If anyone escaped the compound, it'll be her. I want you to be so careful, Jay. If I lost you..." Her eyes fill with tears. "Fuck! I'm fucking crying again. Why do you do this to me?" she sobs out, anger rolling from her as the thoughtbond kicks into life.

I don't know what else to do, so I kiss her, tasting her salty tears, running my hands through her silky hair, making sure I imprint every single part of her on my mind. After a while, she kisses me back, her hands slipping into my feathers and her lush body molding against mine.

"Exactly how long do we have before you leave?" she asks me, breathlessly.

"Long enough." I toss her into my arms and race out of the canteen, needing to get her into my nest so I can properly pleasure her.

So she stays pleasured until I return.

Somewhere behind me, I hear a sound which can only be described as a cheer. Vrexing Gryn!

Our nest is deliciously dark, full of the scent of us and our mating. I snuffle my way over my mate as I claw at her clothing, getting her nice and naked for me.

The scent of her arousal draws me inexorably down to her juicy cunt.

"Already wet for me, mate?" I growl over her, lapping gently at her sensitive bundle of nerves as she grasps at my wings. "You know I'm going to devour you then mate you, ensuring you're so full of my seed, it will run out of you for turns on end."

"Fuck!" she groans in her strange language. "Jay, you're going to finish me!"

"I am." I fasten my lips around her sweetness and suck hard, my cocks bursting to be free of their confines as she bucks at my mouth. I hold her in place as I spear her with first one digit, then two until she's milking me for all she's worth, her orgasm flowing from her like a river.

My pleasure is infinite. I pleasured her, she lies beneath me, boneless, and I know exactly what I want to do to her.

Lifting her into my arms, I push her up against the nest wall, spreading her legs. I notch my cocks at her entrance.

"Are you ready to be mated, little one? Are you willing to be filled to the brim? You know I can't go easy on you. Your body calls to me, ripe and perfect."

"Jay, I want all of you, every single inch of you, my gorgeous alien angel," she rasps, looking over her shoulder at me, eyes half-lidded in the aftermath of her orgasm.

With one thrust, I'm buried inside my *eregri*, knowing it's the one place I want to be, for the rest of time. Her slick, tight channel grips both cocks, holding me until I withdraw and plunge back in. My lips on her neck, my teeth in her skin, the taste of her, the scent of her, it's all I ever wanted but never knew I could have.

She is my everything, and when I come, it's like there is no tomorrow, like I will never be inside her again.

Lauren

Jay makes my body sing again and again. He uses his lips, his claws, his cocks, and when he's done, I'm a puddle.

He wants to prove to me I'm his and only his. Which I want to believe, so very much. If only he wasn't about to just walk out of my life into the unknown.

About to leave me, even if he's not leaving me. I can't possibly compare him to the dratted ex, but the ice in the pit of my stomach, it's the same as when I thought something was wrong before. The ice that grew and grew until I found out what the problem was.

And then I was told it was all my fault.

I can't let this be my fault. I need Jay in my life. The alien who has stolen my heart.

Fuck! He really has, hasn't he?

I let him in, and he's taken it all. Which means I can't possibly fuck this up. I have to be the female he wants.

Jay lies next to me in the nest he built for us, dozing happily in a post mating haze. I'm enveloped in a blanket and bed of feathers. Their scent is incredible, like nothing I've ever experienced and one I'd recognize anywhere.

Another reason I don't want to let him go and I hate myself for it in exactly the same amount I love him. Damn it!

"My Lauren." Jay smiles a sleepy smile at me, reminiscent of the first day we met. When I should have seen what he was, underneath the fire, fight, and blood.

He's a male who thrives on being part of something. His unit, our union. These things make him whole.

"Don't go," I blurt out suddenly. "Please?"

"Mate, I must go." Jay runs his hand down the side of my face to cup my chin with his claws.

"You don't have to be a hero," I mutter.

"I have to ensure the Drahon have either perished or left the planet. If not, we have to capture them so they cannot enslave any more Gryn, Kijg, Mochi, or humans," Jay says, patiently. "It is what we do as Gryn warriors, and it is what I do as your mate."

I wrench my head away from his touch. Damn his logic! Damn him for being such a reasonable, gentle, vicious predator!

I know you think I'm leaving you, but I will always return.

His love flows down the thoughtbond, hot and sweet, a riot of colors. He places a single finger under my chin and turns me to face him, his dark eyes which I could get lost in, and which hold no secrets, not anymore.

A loud knock echos through the nest.

"Jay! Pants on, it's time to go!" a male voice shouts through the door.

"Vrex off, Mylo!" Jay calls back over his shoulder. He leans in and extracts a kiss from me. "I'm coming," he adds.

I WATCH THE SEVEN ENORMOUS WARRIORS AS THEY get ready. They move around with an impressive grace despite their huge wings, and given I've just watched Ayar thump Syn hard with a wing because of some perceived slight, these appendages are not just for flight. The blow rapidly descended into a full on fight, wings, claws and everything else, until they were pulled apart by the rest of the unit.

All seven are preparing to fly out to the site of the Drahon compound. Apparently, this base has a wealth of tech which hasn't been seen before, including more sophisticated weaponry, to the delight of Ayar and Vypr, a pair of Gryn warriors who seem very close.

More than close. After Ayar's angry incident with Syn, Vypr takes hold of his head and butts it with his, gently nuzzling at Ayar's ear, and the big warrior calms. He goes back to picking over the laser guns which excited him earlier.

Syn goes back to glowering, which seems to be his default setting. Jay takes Mylo through the finer points of his new, long laser rifle with a smile a mile wide.

He's so happy, it resonates through the bond, and I should be happy too. Happy for him because he has his family back. Happy because I'm with him.

I just can't stop the pit of dread in my stomach from deepening. I know Jay leaving is nothing like what happened with my ex. There's no betrayal here.

I wish my emotions would sort themselves out. I want to be happy, to have confidence in what I've found with Jay, to believe in, to trust he loves me.

Like I love him.

But it's the love part which is causing the pit. I thought I loved once, and it was torn away from me. Now I'm a million, million miles from Earth, and I feel like I'm risking my heart all over again.

Unable to watch anymore, I back out of the armory and head down the corridor to the canteen, where I help myself to a cup of what Jay calls 'cala' and which today tastes more like coffee than it has in the past. Taking a seat at a table, I warm my hands on the cup and attempt to sort through the wreck of my mind.

"Lauren?" a deep voice rumbles across the room. I look up to see Strykr standing in the doorway, arms folded over his muscular chest.

"Oh, hi." I get to my feet. This warrior is Jay's boss.

"Cala?" He nods at the cup.

"Yeah."

"My mate says it's a bit of an 'acquired taste' for humans." Strykr doesn't move into the room. He stays exactly where he is.

"I like it, but then I'm what humans would consider 'strange,' anyway." I say. "Why do they call you 'Guv'? It's a very specific Earth term."

Strykr's mouth quirks up at the corners. "You are a curious one, aren't you?" he says, still remaining in position. "It's a long story, but when our unit was formed, our first commander had a human mate, and she introduced us to the term. It's sort of stuck."

"Yep, sounds like humans for you." I take a sip of the cala.

"Don't judge Jay for wanting to go on this mission," Strykr says.

"I'm not judging. You ordered him to go. He's going." I look into my cup, anything to avoid looking at him because if I do, I might say something I regret.

"But you want him to stay, and I understand."

"Do you?" I get to my feet, the chair skittering away behind me. "Do you really? Were you there when the Drahon had him drugged to the eyeballs and tortured him? Were you here when he was about to die and all you could do was try to stem the blood with your clothing?"

Hot tears are streaming down my cheeks. I've never cried

this much in my life over anything, not even my horrible ex and what he did to me. I'm not sure I even cried at all.

But Jay...Jay. He's got to me in a way I didn't expect and didn't even think I wanted.

Now all I want is him.

"Sweet female," Strykr rumbles. "He is indeed a very lucky male to have a mate like you."

"Fuck! Fuck! Fuck!" I swipe away the water from my face. "I know, I know. If you love something, set it free. Story of my fucking life!"

I stare at the big warrior, who remains impassive and immobile.

"Jay is only ever going to be free when he nests with you, Lauren. I will not keep you apart."

"And I'm not going to stop him from doing something he wants to do." I stare at my shoes.

"Lucky male," Strykr says again and steps away from the door as a growl sounds from behind him. "I was only speaking with your mate, Jay. Telling her about Kat and the youngling." He holds up his hands and stands aside to allow an angry looking Jay to enter.

Jay's gaze rakes over me, but once he's sure I'm unharmed, he turns back to Strykr. "Unit's ready to go, Guv. Ayar still wants to kill Syn, so we should probably give him something else to think about."

Strykr claps his hand on Jay's shoulder. "Time to be in the air," he says with a grin which is answered by a raucous cheer from outside.

Jay

At least the Guv wasn't in the canteen with Lauren, or I might have had to do him some damage.

Given that he's my Guv and under normal circumstances, he'd probably kill me in a fight, since he's the lair's dirtiest pit fighter, the fact I'd challenge him without thinking means my mating fever is getting out of control.

Boots sound out as the rest of the team make their way back to the actual exit from the lair, not the hole Lauren and I fell through, and I'm across the canteen in two strides to capture her in my arms.

To inhale her.

"We'll be half a turn at most." I kiss her lips. "Providing Ayar doesn't blow anything up. Actually probably less if he does. Then Syn wants to do a reccy of the area, above the lair, and we'll head back to the eyrie after that." I'm babbling, but I want to prolong this moment. "I want you to stay in the ship at all times."

"The ship?"

"The Guv and the unit, they came in one of our ships.

Given that this base is, well, damaged, the Guv suggested you stay in the ship instead."

"A real life spaceship?" Lauren asks, her eyes shining. "Like out of Star Trek?"

"I don't know what that is, my mate, but if that's what you want..."

I'd give her anything to make her happy, and although her fear for me, her sadness at our parting, still swirls around her like a dark blue cloud, there is a pinprick of pleasure which has been generated by the thought of going on the ship.

"Do you absolutely, one hundred percent, promise me you will not do anything stupid, and you will come back in one piece?" Lauren has her hands on my shoulders, standing on the tips of her toes to look up into my face. "Because you know if you come back dead, I will kill you," she half sobs.

"I have my brother warriors with me. No Drahon, not even Yuliat, is a match for a Gryn patrol. We kept the organics on Ustokos safe for many, many cycles because we are who we are. You need not have any fear." I kiss the tip of her nose, rubbing her silky hair through my fingertips, wanting to always remember this moment. "I'm probably more at risk of getting caught in the crossfire between Ayar and Syn."

I take her hand in mine and lead her through to where the rest of the unit are waiting. Huntr stands to one side and appears to be attempting to rival Syn in the glaring stakes.

Given the unhinged nature of his glare, I'd say he's winning.

Mylo wing bumps me affectionately. "Ready to show your mate where she'll be staying?"

I grumble at him for mentioning Lauren, and he backs off immediately, pushing open the doors to a howling wind.

"What the vrex?!" I shout over the noise.

"Vrexing waste seas," Mylo hollers back. "Often get these

storms. Come on. Quicker we get to the ship, the quicker we can get into the air."

I wrap a wing around Lauren as we push into the wind. It's not too bad for flying, but the dust being whipped up is no fun at all, and she coughs despite my attempts to shield her.

The ship looms out of the strange half yellow light that the dust storm has created.

"This isn't the *Perlin*?" I yell at Mylo.

"No, this is one of the ones we got from the Drahon," he shouts back as we troop up the exterior ramp and are finally out of the wind.

"In fact, it's the one you were on," he adds.

"I thought it exploded." Lauren coughs out a mouthful of dust and wipes at her eyes. "Jay seemed to think it had been blown up," she clarifies, giving me a smile.

"It did, but it appears that the Drahon are not exactly great at many things, one of which is doing a good job. Lyon, Syn, and Huntr worked with Kyt to fix it up, and here it is, as good as new."

"Huntr knows about tech?" I ask, surprised the dour Gryn knows about anything other than glowering.

"Like Lyon, he was a Drahon slave, only let's say it didn't agree with him as much. He had the same memory downloads."

Lauren snorts out a laugh. "Given how badly the Drahon seem to do everything, especially control you lot, I'm surprised their business model still includes enslavement of Gryn warriors."

"What does she mean?" Mylo asks.

"I wasn't a good candidate for slavery either." I grin at him.

"Oh, I don't know." Lauren winds her hands into my feathers, and I have to hold back a groan of pleasure in front of my fellow warrior. "I'd say you made a pretty gorgeous slave."

I hold her to me, tight so her scent is everywhere over my entire body. No part of me wants to leave this clever, resourceful female who cares so intensely about everything. But every part of me wants to vanquish the Drahon from Ustokos so she remains safe forever.

Mylo speaks to break up our embrace. "You'll find the bridge is up this corridor and to your left." He holds out a small black box to Lauren. "Once we're gone, press this, and it will secure the ship."

"How will I know to let you back in?" she asks.

Mylo holds up another black box. "We'll let ourselves in." I immediately snatch it from him, and he gives me a hurt look, even as I grin at him.

"Vrex off," I growl. "I'll meet you outside."

Mylo opens his mouth to say something, sees the look on my face, and closes it again. He shakes out his feathers and leaves, walking back down the ramp into the wind.

"Are you going to be okay flying with the wind so strong?" Lauren's gray eyes study me. "You've not flown since the chair thing healed you."

"Wing's better than ever, my mate." I extend it, slightly twisting it one way, then the other. "Good as new, honestly." I push my confidence down the bond at her and feel her heart lighten.

She holds me, arms around my waist, head resting lightly on my chest.

"Please come back to me, Jay." She sighs.

"You know I'll come back." I stroke her hair. "I didn't want to admit it, my *eregri*, but you've stolen something from me."

"I'm not a thief, Jay," she cries out. " What could I have possibly taken from you?"

"My heart, Lauren. You've stolen my heart."

Lauren

I'm resigned to his leaving. I managed all those months in captivity with the Drahon without him, without a male, and without even thinking about love.

I can manage another day without him, surely.

Only what I told him before he left was true. I didn't mean to let the big, fluffy, feathery alien in, but he got in anyway, purely because he made me a nest.

And fucked me like there was no tomorrow.

And is the dirtiest virgin the universe has ever known.

As I hear the outer door of the spaceship closing, I wander down the corridor towards the bridge of the spaceship like Mylo told me. A set of double doors swishes open, and I'm confronted with something straight out of a movie, all flashing lights and, more importantly, a view to the outside.

Unfortunately, the view is swirling dust. Even if Jay and the others are out there, I can't see them. I find myself hoping the rest of Ustokos isn't a dusty wasteland.

In a move I never saw coming, I want to stay on this planet. With Jay.

It's a bonkers concept which is going to take some getting

used to, especially if his friends are an indication of what I'm going to meet when we get back to the more inhabited parts of Ustokos.

Dysfunctional as a description doesn't quite cover what I've witnessed so far from his friends. Mad, bad, and dangerous to know almost covers Ayar. As for the rest of them? It looks like they really needed Jay back.

Almost as much as I do.

Somewhere outside of the bridge, I hear a scraping sound. I'm out of the doors and running back to the exit with hope in my heart.

"Did you forget something?" I call out, grinning stupidly from ear to ear.

"Not at all," a voice I'd hoped never to hear again calls out. "But it looks like we found something we've been looking for." Yuliat steps through the doorway, her scaly green face even grimmer than the last time I saw her.

Probably due to the rather nasty burn down one side.

I'm not normally someone who would revel in another's misfortune, but given as Yuliat tried to feed me to the squid-lion in order to trigger my sweet Jay into breeding me, I'm going to make an exception in her case.

"Oh, hi, Yuliat." I give her a little wave, contemplating both my options and how the hell she managed to get into the ship. Behind her, two of her guards step into my vision, both toting very big laser guns, which narrows my odds. "You've got a little something…" I brush my hand over my face, mirroring hers.

"Zarking human!" she snarls. "If you hadn't mated with the Gryn, I'd be destroying you, right here, right now." She's lowered her voice to the level of 'nasty villain.'

Her black eyes flash and her blue tongue flickers. Yuliat never uses her tongue. Something is definitely wrong.

"I don't give a shit, Yuliat. I'm with the Gryn now, so why

don't you crawl back under your stone or something." I begin to back away from her, hoping there's somewhere in the ship I can hide or find a weapon.

"The fact you are carrying a Gryn hybrid is most definitely my business," Yuliat simpers. "You've been doing plenty of mating, and the Gryn is a virile male."

Okay, my mind officially goes into 'WTF' mode. Not only is she suggesting I'm pregnant already, but somehow, she knows what we've been doing.

"Did you not think I would want to monitor your vitals?" Unfortunately, Yuliat has seen my confusion, and she's one smug lizard lady. "I injected you with the tracking chip some time ago." She pulls out her tablet device and studies it. "You and the Gryn *have* been busy."

Her voice drips with venom.

"What do you want, Yuliat? It's not just Jay with me but an entire patrol of Gryn warriors, all armed. They're specifically looking for you as they have questions they want answered. If I were you, I would not be hanging around here."

"I was hoping to take back a fully grown, fully trained Gryn to Drahonia, but as we have lost our regular supplier of these items, you have suddenly become worth far more. A female, pregnant with a hybrid? Not only is your young going to fetch an impressive price, but as you have demonstrated your compatibility with another species, so are you." She bares her teeth which glitter sharply.

"The thing is, Yuliat." I speak slowly and take a step backwards. "Your plan relies on me coming with you, and to be entirely honest, I don't want to. So I'm not."

I spin on my heel and sprint back down the corridor.

I'm pregnant, apparently, and the Drahon want the baby, so they are not going to risk injury to either me or it. That should be enough to give me an advantage and a head start. All

I have to do is not let the Drahon catch me until Jay and the others get back.

Can't be that hard, can it?

As I skitter around the corner heading back towards the bridge, something hits me smack in the center of my back, and I'm sent flying through the air. The floor comes up to meet me in a way I know is going to hurt. A lot.

I land with my arms outstretched like an idiot, and the crunching sound from my wrist is immediately matched by the intense spike of pain which follows.

This is not going how I'd hoped it would. I'm alone on this bloody ship, Jay's nowhere to be seen, and as I look up from my prone position, clutching my left wrist to me, Yuliat swims into view.

She crouches down next to me.

"Pathetic," she hisses. "You think you're feisty, but I've been training Gryn for a very long time. You are no match for them."

"I don't need to be," I fire out at her. The pain in my wrist is agony.

"Oh," she puts her hand to her mouth and snorts, "you think your Gryn mate is coming for you? Think again. I've arranged a surprise for him and the rest of his untrainable warriors, which they are unlikely to survive."

She jabs a silver tube into my arm, and although I welcome the pain relief, I fight the effects of the sedative for as long as I can. Holding her gaze with mine, wishing she would expire on the spot.

Just before I pass out, an image of Jay floods my mind, as if the weird psychic link we have has fired back into life. He's so happy to be with his friends, to know I am his mate, and I'm waiting for him.

Only it's not going to end that way. Yuliat is going to take me, and if what she says is true, Jay is never going to know he's a father.

"Jay." His name is a mere whisper on my lips as everything spirals into the depths.

Jay

It doesn't take much height or distance to get out of the dust storm. My wing is feeling so strong, it's as if I could fly forever. Once we're clear of all the dust, Ayar flies ahead, shaking out his wings as he goes and looking as if he's having some sort of fit.

For a warrior who isn't very interested in bathing, he sure hates the dust in his feathers. Syn quickly overtakes him and flies in a completely different direction. I look over at the Guv, who indicates Syn is the one to be followed, and as one, we shift our courses, heading over the barren waste seas until a plume of thick, black smoke comes into view.

"I'm guessing this is your handiwork?" Strykr calls out to me.

"If he blew up some vrexing Drahon, good." I hear Huntr behind me.

"Let me scout first," I shout over to the Guv. "I know the place, and I know what I'm looking for."

"Take Syn with you," he replies. My annoyance must have shown on my face. "It's been a while, Jay. Take Syn. We can talk retraining when this is all over."

Syn circles me, and I know I have no option, irritating though it is not to be trusted, when I was always trusted.

But I can't say I blame the Guv for being cautious. I nod at Syn as I lift my laser rifle from my shoulder and descend towards the smoking ruin which was once the Drahon compound.

We make a circuit, and I'm ready to return fire as we swoop down low over the walls. The one closest to the shield generator is a crumbled mess, and two of the domes in the center have collapsed on themselves. There is a stench of death. And a stronger smell of something I can't put my finger on.

Having circled again, Syn heads back to the others, waiting in formation above us, and I drop back down to the compound, landing on the wall and making sure the compound is covered for the rest of the unit. I need Strykr to understand my captivity has not impaired my ability to do my job.

And I never meant to leave them all behind to face their fate.

Except, my capture meant I found my *eregri*, and I was always told that fate is never wrong.

The strange smell invades my senses again. It's at once familiar and yet not. I scan the area through the magnifying device on my rifle, looking for the source and checking that all the bodies scattered around the compound are lifeless.

A number of thumps denotes my unit landing next to me.

"Where are the Drahon?" Huntr growls.

"Dead," I reply without taking my eye from my rifle. "They should be dead."

"Huntr," Strykr says in a warning tone. "Is it safe to go down there, Jay?" he asks.

"Looks quiet, but there's no guarantee of safety." I grin back at him. "Just how you like it."

Strykr shakes his head at me. "You remain here. Cover us. Ayar, Vypr, Huntr, with me."

He's in the air and down on the compound floor in seconds, followed by the other three warriors.

As they land, I catch movement and swing my rifle over. A shadow?

The stench gets stronger. Something slithers.

"Vrex!" I'm in the air before I can alert Mylo and Syn to the danger. The Drahon had more than one Xople, and this one is an adult. Its long, stinging tentacles reach out for the others like something out of a vrexing nightmare.

In all of this moment, as I discharge my weapon at the horrific creature, Lauren springs into my head.

Pain fires through her. Pain like I've never felt in all my life because this is the pain of my mate. She appears in front of me as if the thoughtbond is made real.

"Jay." She mouths my name, her eyes clouded with agony and need.

"No!" I'm in the air, firing over and over at the Xople as the rest of the unit react to it.

Huntr charges it, leaping into its stingers.

"Vrex it!" Mylo calls out, training his laser cannon on the creature. "I need him out of the way."

I dive towards Huntr, needing to get him free so that the unit is safe, and I can get to my mate. I wrench at one wing which is clear of the squirm of limbs and beat down hard, with a slowness that is almost infinite, I pull the wriggling, snarling Gryn free, his skin streaked with multiple stings. Syn joins me, and we lift the big warrior clear just as Mylo's laser ball slams into it, and it explodes in a hail of black ooze and body parts.

"Vrex!" Strykr swears. He's dripping with innards, as are Vypr and Ayar because they were closest.

I don't have any time to explain. I have to get to Lauren.

More than anything on Ustokos, she is my priority. My unit is safe, and I let go of Huntr, my wings cutting through the air. I'm flying away from them, back to the ship, back to my mate.

I hear my name being called behind me, but I don't look back. There was a mission. I thought it was important. I thought being with my fellow warriors would complete me.

I was wrong.

Lauren is my completion. She is my *eregri*.

And I never should have left her behind.

Lauren

I can't stop myself from groaning as I swim back to the surface of consciousness. I haven't felt like this since I woke up in the Drahon compound all those weeks, maybe months, ago.

I stopped caring about time, right up until I met Jay. Time became precious. It became important. Then he left me.

And I let him. I didn't argue, I didn't make any other suggestions. I allowed him to fly away, and it looks like I'm going to regret it for the rest of my miserable life.

Opening my eyes, I see I'm still on the ship, but I'm shoved in a corner of the bridge on the floor. Yuliat and five other Drahon are shouting at each other, something about the ship not working. One of the guards spots me before I can pretend to still be out cold.

"The female is awake," he spits.

"Take her to the medical suite and lock her in. I want to check on the larvae."

I shudder at her word. Not only do I not want Yuliat touching me, the fact my translator, whatever it is, translates baby as larvae says it all about the Drahon.

Slimy, reptilian, and also, in some disgusting way, they are insectoid. I feel bile rising, and I know I'm going to be sick. All I can do is hope I manage to get some on Yuliat.

But unfortunately, I'm dragged into the corridor where I bring up my stomach contents on the boots of the Drahon guard.

"Foul human," he grumbles, shaking his feet and keeping a bruising grip on my arm. My wrist hurts like hell too, and I hold it close to my chest to stop it from being jostled.

"What's going on? Why are we still on Ustokos?" I wipe the back of my mouth with my hand as I'm dragged through the ship.

"Backward creature." He snorts. "You wouldn't understand even if I told you."

"Let me guess. The Gryn have disabled it in some way which means it won't work for you?"

His silence tells me all I need to know.

For all their muscular appearance, penchant for beating the hell out of each other, and supposed lack of knowledge about technology, the Gryn really are a force to be reckoned with.

Just because the Drahon have been able to capture single Gryn and 'train' them, whatever that means, it's led them to underestimate the species as a whole.

Which hopefully means at some point, something big, fearsome, and Gryn shaped is going to befall the Drahon.

I just have to hope it comes in the shape of my avenging angel. My sweet Jay. My feathered fury.

The ambient noise in the ship changes, and the Drahon guard grunts with pleasure.

"Say goodbye to your piece of Gryn filth," he snarls. "We'll be getting off this pathetic planet, and you will be spending the rest of your life on your back." A door next to us slides open, and I'm shoved inside. "Yuliat will be with you soon."

He bares his teeth, clearly enjoying the look of distaste on my face.

"The Gryn will come for you," I retort, curling my hands into fists, and the pain from my wrist spikes, but I don't care.

"They can try, but once they're off this planet, they are nothing. They'll stay exactly where they are, if they know what's good for them." He laughs at me, and the door slides shut.

I stare at the blank door for a while, trying to decide if I want to risk my foot with kicking it. But instead, my shoulders droop as the hum intensifies.

Yuliat is really doing this. She's taking me away from Ustokos and Jay. I'm powerless to stop her.

All my demons converge at once. Every single damn one and I'm on my knees, holding back the sobs, clutching at my chest.

I thought I wanted things in my life. A secure job, a happy relationship. I didn't have a clue what it was like to really, really want something. To want someone with your entire soul. To want Jay so much the pain from not having him is physical. It hurts even more than my sprained wrist.

What my ex did to me was despicable, but with hindsight, I should have seen it coming. He was never that interested; he always needed prompting about anything I liked and the sex, well, compared to Jay, let's say that the clit was an unknown land for Mark.

I never really missed him. My anger and tears were of anger at myself for being duped, nothing else.

But now, now what I feel in the absence of Jay is a visceral emptiness. I had gotten used to him in my head and the little thoughts which would drop in randomly, like when we were eating and he wanted me to taste something, or just as we were about to fall asleep, he'd think how much he adored my toes.

The sweetest, most perfect alien a girl could ever wish for, and I let him go.

"Excellent." Yuliat's voice rings out. "You've already adopted the correct pose for a pleasure slave. Once you've birthed the Gryn hybrid, it looks like you're going to be a natural."

I lift my head to look at her, blinking away the tears because I'm damned if I'm going to let this cold-blooded lizard have the satisfaction of my sadness.

"Don't even think for one second the Gryn are coming for you. They are backwards creatures with no knowledge of what awaits them in the galaxy, and their defense system was designed to keep things out, not in," she says happily.

She presses a hand against one wall, and it disappears, showing a blackness that can only be space, sprinkled with stars, and in the distance, a rapidly disappearing brown and tan planet.

"Say goodbye to your mate." She sneers. "It's the only goodbye you're going to get."

"Fuck you, Yuliat," I reply, my voice dull as I stare out at Ustokos.

A planet I wanted to call home, with a male I was bound to, body and soul. A fate he believed in so very much and one I was ready to dismiss.

Not anymore. It looks like fate already had plans for me, and they included ripping me away from the only male who was the other half of my heart.

Yuliat removes her hand, and the picture disappears, along with the tiny spark of hope I held onto.

"Clothes off, on the examination bed," she barks, and I comply.

Because there's nothing left in me. I've lost him, and my only way of keeping him with me is the child I apparently carry.

And the one the Drahon will take as soon as they can.

Jay.

I close my eyes as a tear trickles down my cheek in despair, and I send the thought out into the ether. He can't possibly hear me, but I imbue it with every iota of love I have for him. The male who made a broken thing fly again.

Jay

The waste seas are a shifting pile of dust and now the storm has abated. It's hard to tell if I've made it back to the area where the ship and the base were situated. Innately, I know I'm in the right place, but the absence of a large spaceship means I'm not so sure. I land on the highest point around, a dune of destruction, made up of the destroyed civilization which occupied this part of Ustokos before the Great Reckoning, when Proto took over and organics became surplus to requirements.

Some of this dust will be bones of my ancestors. Flowing over the base they built deep below before Proto. Before Gryn warriors became a commodity and before we lost everything.

Because what's worse than not being able to see the ship is the fact that the thoughtbond is silent. Lauren might have been a little mad at me for leaving her, but she can't keep me out entirely. I can't keep her out either.

So the silence is deafening, a vacuum of absence which hollows me out. There is something terribly wrong.

"Lauren!" I yell across the wastes, more because I need to hear her name out loud.

A thump behind me denotes the arrival of another Gryn. I take a look over my shoulder and see it's Syn, not the Gryn I expected to get here first, but he was the one assisting me with Huntr. He's streaked with the remnants of the Xople innards.

"The Guv?" I fire over my shoulder at him.

"Won't be happy you've left," Syn replies with a shrug. "Nor will he be happy when he finds out the Drahon took our ship."

"The one we took from them, and the one you promised me my mate would be safe on." I have him by the throat, claws digging into his flesh.

I don't care if I kill him. Syn chokes under me, claws scrabbling at my arms, wings beating as he tries to get away, but I can't stop myself. I don't want to stop.

My mate is gone. Gone. All I want is retribution. Without her, I am no longer a warrior. I am a male without a mate, and it is the end of all things.

Syn's face gets redder, and despite us being evenly matched, I'm winning. Blood roars through my veins as I crush at his neck.

Lauren is gone and something has to die.

Then I'm going to get her back.

My vision dims to a pinprick, my ears no longer hearing Syn's pleas until I'm swung backwards, spiraling in the air until instinct takes over and I unfurl my wings.

Only I can't. They're pinned and finally the fog clears to the sounds of growling, snarling, and coughing.

Syn is on his hands and knees, gasping for breath. I'm being held by both Mylo and Ayar.

And the growls and snarls are coming from me.

"Let me go, you pair of vrexers! I need to find Lauren."

"Please, Jay. Don't do this!" Mylo says in my ear. "Don't vrex off the Guv."

"I don't care about the Guv. I care about my mate." I

attempt to free myself once more, digging claws into any flesh I can find.

Ayar howls, and I have a very angry Vypr in my face.

"What the vrex, Jay?" he hisses. "This isn't you."

"This is me. This was always me, and if you both don't let me go, I will do far more damage, I promise you that." I snarl. "I want my mate, and I'm not going to stop until I find her."

"The ship has gone. The Drahon must have been able to bypass the security measures," Syn says, his voice gravel, and his chest red with blood from where my claws punctured him.

"How?" I struggle again against Ayar and Mylo. "How? You said she would be safe!"

"That was based on you having blown up the vrexing Drahon base!" he fires back with considerable ire.

I throw my head back, and it connects with Mylo who groans in pain. Ayar growls a feral growl in my ear, but I ignore him. Even when Vypr lands a punch to the side of my head, I only struggle harder against them.

"Stop!" Strykr lands heavily in between us. "Or I'll have your wings, Jay." His voice is low and even. He's using a tone which even my inner mated male has no option but to obey.

"Lyon is on his way with the other ship. If the Drahon have taken the one that Lauren is on, and it's not buried somewhere out there," he waves a wing to indicate the waste seas, "we can follow them and get both the ship and your mate back."

He places a hand on my shoulder. "We will get her back, Jay."

"I never should have let her go," I mutter, dropping my head between my shoulders.

As I relax, Mylo and Ayar release me. I walk away from my unit, past Syn, still on all fours and down the dust dune towards the crater where I'm sure the ship was last seen.

I appreciate that my life has been easy. I was liberated by

our Prime, Jyr, when I was just a youngling. I grew up in the lair, messing around with others the same age as me. We missed our families, but we found each other. When I became a warrior, Mylo and I were picked out by Ryak, the Legion's head of security for his special detail.

We became the elite.

I haven't had to deal with the horror of the camps like Vypr, or the torture of Proto like Ayar or the Guv. As for Syn and Huntr, from the look in their eyes, they've been through similar terrible experiences. Because that sort of thing never leaves you.

I want to be part of the Unit, part of a whole made up of the functional and dysfunctional. But without my mate, there is simply no point to anything anymore.

I need Lauren. If I thought my life with my unit made me whole, I was entirely and utterly wrong. She is all of me. I have to have her, to scent her, to be buried in her, or I will surely snap, like I did with Syn.

No longer an elite, no longer fit to be a warrior. Instead, my life would be in the dark because without my mate, I may as well end up a slave of the Drahon.

"Jay?" Mylo is behind me. He wing bumps me, but I turn away from him. "The Guv says we'll get your mate back."

If it's come to this, that I can't even do a simple task like protecting my mate without help from other males, what sort of a Gryn warrior am I?

"That's not up to the Guv." I curl my hands into fists.

"You can't do it alone, not if the ship's left the atmosphere," Mylo says.

If the ship's left the atmosphere.

The words send ice flowing through my veins.

I've failed the one creature who meant anything to me. The one I swore to protect, who protected me when I was vulnerable. She's in the hands of the Drahon and there is nothing I can do.

My heart goes into free fall.

I am no warrior.

Not any longer.

Lauren

Yuliat stares at me.

"You can get undressed on your own, or I can get one of my guards to do it for you. Maybe two of them. I've got a couple left who have an *interest* in warm-blooded females."

I know she'll do it too, whether the comment about the 'interest' is real or not, she'd make her guards fuck me because she's the most cold-blooded of the reptilians.

I pull off my top and trousers, the silky material sliding over my skin and making me think of Jay. Thinking of how he sometimes slid the clothes from me, kissing every inch of my skin as he exposed it. Or how he sometimes shredded the fabric in his haste to get inside me.

Everything reminds me of Jay.

"On the examination table," Yuliat says, expressionless as she picks up her tablet.

I climb up. It's set for a Drahon, and I'm having to heave myself onto it, legs kicking. I get a tiny spark of amusement Yuliat is getting the full moon, but the joy isn't long lived.

"Stay still," she says in a warning tone as a long, flat arm descends out of the ceiling over me.

I bite back a response. Is there any point in fighting them, or her, anymore?

I stare up at the arm. There's some sort of screen on it which flickers with color. I let out a long breath. I may as well take stock of the situation.

As I concentrate on the screen, the colors move, morph, and show something...odd. A flickering bean with a strange tail. I turn my head to see Yuliat studying her tablet and wonder why she's showing me a picture of what has to be a baby Drahon, or larvae, or whatever they call their young.

While I'm looking at her, something jabs me in my arm.

"What the fuck?" I clap my hand over the area just in time to see another arm withdrawing back into the table, holding a syringe. "Jesus, Yuliat, you don't have to keep doing that."

"I prefer my subjects compliant, and your pregnancy is important to me. Can't have you climbing the walls, can we, my dear?" she says in a horrible crooning voice.

Things are getting a bit fluffy around the edges, like cotton candy filling my mind. I look back up at the screen.

"That's not my baby," I say, my words slurred. "That's a weird Drahon thing."

Only as I frown at it, trying to keep it in focus, it becomes familiar. Possibly. I have spent most of my life wondering about babies but never getting close, but just maybe...

But it can't be. Jay and I have been, let's be fair, going at it like rabbits for the past five days, but there's no way I could be that pregnant. Babies are the size of pin heads or something in early gestation, surely?

"The hybrid is growing at an acceptable rate." Yuliat seems very far away. She also seems greener than normal, and I giggle until another jab in the arm stops me in my tracks.

"Stop it!" I attempt to rub my other arm, but my limbs are not really playing ball, and my hand flops around for a while as I try to find the spot.

"That will provide additional nourishment and speed things up a little."

"What do you mean?"

"Gryn young grow at an exponential rate. My understanding is they have a very short gestation. Obscenely short compared to the sensible two-year Drahon gestation." Yuliat is standing next to me, and I'm not entirely sure how or when she got there. "You'll be big and round in no time." She bares her teeth and rubs a cold hand over my abdomen. "Ready to birth and ready for sale."

I want to tell her to go fuck herself, but my eyes are drawn back to the image on the screen. A baby. One which is growing inside me. Jay's baby.

The one he wanted.

I should be crying. Everything else makes me cry, but the damn drug Yuliat has given me has robbed me of my tears. My heart strains at my ribcage. Somehow it thinks if it breaks free, it can get to him. Let him know he will be a father.

And in that moment, more than anything else, even with the drug coursing through my system, I know I have to get back to him, somehow. He has to know. He has to be a part of this because without him, I would not be having this baby.

I want this baby.

I'm laughing, the sound ringing through the room as Yuliat stares at me.

"He will come." I laugh at her. "You can't stop him."

She lifts her green, scaly head up to the ceiling as if exhorting a higher power. "The Gryn don't frighten me."

"He should, Yuliat. If I were you, I'd be really, really fucking scared."

Jay

"What do you mean, 'we can't risk another ship'?" I grind out.

Lyon arrived with the *Perlin*, as the Guv indicated he would. It meant the journey back to the eyrie was thankfully short, but then Strykr said he had to discuss matters, such as going after my mate, with the seniors.

And this means I'm standing with the rest of the unit in front of our Prime, Jyr, his Command, Fyn, and our former Guv, Ryak, in the meeting area, known as szent, at the main lair.

It's a room designed to intimidate with the massive table and chairs made up of parts of Proto's bots the seniors destroyed over the years. Everything is polished, and everything is spiked.

Jyr lounges back in his huge chair, fearsome as always. The enhancements Proto gave him make him one of the deadliest Gryn Ustokos has ever seen. Next to him, Fyn, his second-in-command bristles at my tone.

But they are both mated males, and while I shouldn't

break protocol and give them the respect they deserve, they have to understand how I feel.

Instead, I'm faced with Ryak, the lair's head of security, who stares at me as if he can read my soul.

And maybe he can, because the seniors have thoughtbond ability beyond any other Gryn. In which case, he has to know how much I have to get to Lauren.

"The Drahon have already taken one ship, given we have three at our disposal, and we don't know how they got through our security on the one they took." Ryak keeps his gaze on me. "We have to protect Ustokos, Jay. We have to protect the Gryn, and we need these ships."

"I cannot let them take my mate."

"Let us talk over the available tactical options, Jay," Jyr rumbles from his position at the head of the table. "There may be a way we can arrange things. In the meantime, you and your unit should return to the eyrie and train. Who knows what will happen in the future?"

Strykr eyes me as he turns to leave and the rest of the unit troop out of szent.

Because I'm not leaving.

"I will go to my mate. She is my reason for being, my boundless flight. You cannot keep her from me."

Fyn growls, unfolding himself from his chair next to Jyr. He's a formidable warrior, maybe more so than Jyr, and his temper is notoriously short. I don't care. None of that matters. The only thing I want is Lauren.

Fyn stalks up to me, wings held high. I brace myself, ready for the fight, because I will fight any Gryn in the lair or the eyrie in order to get a ship. I'll fight them all, over and over until I get what I want. I lift my wings and face down the legend that is Command.

He puts a hand on my shoulder. "Jay. We understand, we really do. Your mate is the most important thing in your life, now and forever. We all know, and we will get you to your female. Just give us time to work out the best plan."

I can't help the snarl rippling through me. "She doesn't have time. Yuliat is ruthless and dangerous. Lauren is alone because I left her. I will not allow her to be taken from me."

"We will make a final decision within the next half a turn. Return to your barracks, merc," Jyr says.

His dark eyes are darker than ever, and I have exhausted his patience. Mate bond or no, this is the end of my audience.

I shrug Fyn's hand from my shoulder. A gesture that under normal circumstances would have filled me with pride. Instead, I'm reduced from the elite to the rank of mere 'merc,' and I feel my Lauren slipping even farther away.

As I leave the szent room, fury courses through my veins, hot and ready. No one, not the Guv, not the seniors, are going to stop me from getting to Lauren.

"Where are you going?" Syn steps out of an alcove, one of many that dot the lair, and falls in beside me.

"Why do you care?" I fire at him.

"I'm in the mood to do something...wrong." He looks at me, eyes almost fever bright.

Under any other circumstances, I'd consider his strange behavior in the same light as Ayar's and give the warrior a wide berth, but a thought has occurred to me.

Syn's a tech warrior. He knows how to fly a ship. If he's feeling like he wants to defy something, then I can use it to my advantage.

"I'm going to the launchpad, to see if Lyon might be prepared to chase the Drahon, even if the seniors haven't sanctioned it," I say as I stride towards the exit in the side of the air, unfurling my wings and not even looking behind me.

I have an answering beat. Syn is interested, and it looks like I might just have a plan.

One I hope vrexing works this time.

The *Perlin* squats on the launch pad, next to the much sleeker Drahon ship, the one which didn't get blown up. Syn tramps down the entrance ramp.

"Lyon's not here. If you're coming, come on," he says, spinning back into the ship with a flurry of feathers.

I gaze across the launch pad at the lair in the distance. Mercs fly in and out, looking like insects. I'm about to vrex everything up with everyone I've ever respected.

And I don't care. Lauren is all I have. Without her, life isn't worth living. When fate hands you your mate, you take her and cherish her. You nest with her, and you make sure her belly is full. That is the instinct running deep inside me, in all the Gryn.

The seniors should know I won't wait for an answer, not for a minute, let alone a turn. And if they are going to ignore me, then the consequences are inevitable.

This could be the last time I see Ustokos, but I already know a planet without my mate is not my home.

Home is where the nest is, and my nest is with her.

Behind me, the entrance ramp lets out a long hiss, and I race up it. Syn wants to leave, for whatever reason, and he obviously isn't that bothered if I come or not.

"Leaving me behind, you vrexer?" I call out as I enter the bridge.

He works his way across the controls, and out of the viewing window, I see Ustokos and the eyrie disappearing below us.

"I didn't need an excuse to leave," he says, concentrated on his task.

I drum my claws on a wall, attempting to keep the anger which rolls in my stomach at bay.

I fail.

Syn is up against the console, wings flapping uselessly as my hand is around his throat.

"No one to save you here," I rasp. "Let's get one thing straight. This mission is about retrieving my mate from the hands of the Drahon. Nothing else." I put my face close to his, baring my teeth. "I don't know what you want, Syn, but I can guarantee you *will* lose a wing if you mess with me."

He stops moving. "I want to help you, Jay. I feel bad that the security protocols I put on the ship didn't work and the Drahon were able to take your mate." Something flashes across his face, a sadness of sorts. "I do want to help you get her back, and the ship too." He swallows against my hand. "I want to prove myself to the others. They hate me and…"

His voice trails away.

I want to feel sorry for him. I want to help him because I know how much being part of the Unit means to me, but only once I have my Lauren back in my arms. I release him, slowly, backing away with my hands held out to show he's no longer in danger.

"All I want is to get to my mate. Can we do that?" I ask him evenly, despite the crashing agony which swirls inside me. "Once we've got her, I'll do anything I can to make things easier for you back at home, which is unlikely to be much as I'm going to be in the gak with the Guv for probably the rest of my life."

Syn gives me a weak grin. "Not if we get the other ship back," he says. "That's what the seniors care about. Plus, although I might have vrexed up the security protocols, I think there are enough surprises on the ship for the Drahon which will give us the edge."

"Yeah?" I shake my feathers at him. "How exactly did it get past the planetary defenses?"

Syn backs away from me. "I fitted the ship with a beacon which dropped the defenses to allow it to pass," he says quietly. "That's the other reason why we need to get it back. It works both ways."

I want to rip him limb from limb. Instead, I stare at the ceiling of the bridge, studying the looping pipework as I get my temper under control.

"I trusted you. The Guv trusted you to get this right. If I had known, I never would have left Lauren on the ship, and I would have been able to properly brief the unit on the Drahon threat. If there was any possibility any of the Drahon," I close my eyes and take in a deep breath, "if Yuliat in particular, was alive, then we should never have left the ship unguarded."

"I know that now." Syn shuffles his feathers, and I can't tell if it's arrogance or attrition. If he wants the others to accept him, he's got a long way to go. "That's why I'm here, with you."

A red light blinks on the console.

"What's that?" I point to it.

"Nothing. It's just Ustokos trying to contact us."

"We are so vrexed!" I throw myself into a nearby chair and flop my head back.

We're in serious trouble all round. I have to get my mate back, and I've chosen the eyrie's most unpopular and probably most untrustworthy warrior to be undertaking this mission.

"I've got a lock on the other ship," Syn announces, as if trying to redeem himself. "It looks like it might be having some trouble."

"What?" I'm out of my chair and shouldering him aside at the console even though I don't know what I'm looking at. "What sort of trouble? Is Lauren in danger?" I fire at him, my stomach clenching with the cold fear that took me as soon as I found her missing.

"No!" Syn says, very quickly. "There's no risk to the life support systems. It's engine trouble they are having."

"Part of your surprises?"

"I rigged it for a code to be entered after a period of time or the stardrive would cut out. The Drahon are probably scratching their scaly heads at the problem right about now." Syn actually sounds happy, although the image of scaly heads causes a slight nausea to rise within me.

If it is Yuliat who has Lauren, I don't even want to imagine what the cold-blooded creature is doing to her. Because if I do, I know I will tear the *Perlin* apart.

"How long until we reach it?"

"A few more minutes." Syn looks up at me. "Then you'll be with your mate."

I'm coming for you, my mate, my eregri, my love.

I push my emotions down the thoughtbond, hoping it reaches her, despite it being empty.

She has to be alive. She has to be.

Lauren

The floaty feeling would be quite nice if I didn't also want to throw up.

And if I wasn't fucking naked. Yuliat must have left me like this after she finished prodding me, scanning me, and god knows what else before I finally passed out. Not that she'd have any concept I'd need clothes. The Drahon being cold-blooded have ramped the heating up in the ship to max, and I'm pretty sweaty.

But being nude is not a good thing, not with the Drahon guards lurking around. If Yuliat thinks she can keep them away from me, she's got a tenuous grip on reality.

Fortunately my clothes are where I left them in a pile on the floor, and I swing my legs off the chair, dropping to the floor to retrieve them.

I'm inordinately weak, limbs like jelly, and I hate to even think what Yuliat has shot me up with. I presume it won't harm the baby, and my hand goes instinctively to my belly.

My rather rounded belly. Which is...strange and concerning.

If what Yuliat says is true about Gryn babies, I have to hope this is normal. I clutch my clothes to my chest and look around at the lab area. I suppose there are things I could use as weapons, but is there much point? I'm not likely to be able to resist the Drahon for long, and all Yuliat will do is make my life even more unpleasant, but not damaging, than she already has.

And yet, something inside me wants to fight. For Jay, for his baby, for me. I want to be more than what I was on Earth. I don't want to drift anymore. I want something solid.

The door to the lab slides open, and Yuliat enters with two of her guards. She flicks a hand at me, and I'm grabbed roughly.

"Ow!" I twist in their grip, not that it makes much difference. "Do you mind? That hurts!" I add for good measure, but Yuliat ignores me.

"Take her to get cleansed, and we'll start the procedure before our contact arrives. I want her ready in good time." She levels her gaze at my captors. "We need the coin if we're going to get this piece of space junk working."

"Oh dear," I say, sarcasm dripping from my words. "Spaceship broken?"

I had noticed the ongoing hum, which I presumed was the engines of the ship, had stopped. Given that Yuliat had closed the window or screen she showed me previously, I wasn't able to determine if we had stopped moving.

But, by the sounds of things, they broke the ship. Or someone did.

My heart takes a leap into my throat. Could this be something to do with the Gryn? Could it mean that Jay is coming for me?

With a bone breaking wrench, I'm spun around in the hands of the guards and marched out of the room, my protestations only gaining me a thump in the side of my head. Yuliat must have decided that, as a vessel for a baby, I can stand some level of pain and injury.

Or she simply doesn't care because she has a buyer, and I soon won't be her problem.

Knowing Yuliat, it's probably because I'm about to be sold.

"Okay, take it easy, I'm coming!" I grumble at the guards and attempt to keep up with their pace. They might not be the same size as Jay, at least a foot shorter, but they're still bigger than me, and stronger.

I like to think I'm probably faster, but I'm not going to try it out, not at the moment.

"In here, female." One of the guards shoves me through a door where there is...nothing.

"Cleanse," the other shouts.

The door slides shut, and immediately, I'm in what can only be described as an alien washing machine. Water and foam start to sluice out from the walls, the ceiling, and *everywhere*.

"This isn't cleansing, it's drowning!" I cry out, banging on the door as the foam gets, literally, everywhere.

Followed by a sudden, hot blast of air which continues until I'm dry.

And frizzy.

The door slides open and the guards drag me out.

"Humans are always so...pink." He sneers.

"But when you are sheathed in them," the second guard grabs his crotch, "they are very hot."

"Ugh! No!" The first guard recoils, and it slightly takes the horror of being naked in the corridor away. "Put some clothes on it!" he adds.

I guess you can't please all the aliens all the time. A white shift, similar to the one I had to wear in the compound, is shoved at me, and I pull it over my head as quickly as I can.

A low 'bong' sound echoes through the ship, along with a slight shudder.

"Best get it back to Yuliat. She wants the human in stasis before handing over to the buyer." A huge hand clamps around my upper arm, and I'm being dragged along again.

"Wait! What if I don't want to go into *stasis*?" I cry out, not sure what it means, but if it involves Yuliat, it won't be good.

"Pregnant slaves don't get to choose. You've got some gestating to do, little human, and you're going to do it in relative peace so don't zarking complain and don't zark about. You don't need all your limbs functioning in order to breed."

My arm is yanked so hard it feels like the shoulder has popped out of the socket. But my heart has stilled.

Pregnant.

The word is so huge, so enormous, I don't fight them anymore. All I can think about is my big, feathered warrior, his kind, handsome face, his huge, dark eyes. The way he hungered for me, desperate to sheathe himself in me.

Desperate to fill every part of me, including my womb.

And I let him because I wanted him. I really, really wanted him in a way I hadn't wanted anything ever.

My eregri.

The words drop into my head, but I know it can't be him. We're too far from Ustokos, in the depths of space. There's no way he would be able to find me. This is simply my mind playing tricks on me because I don't deserve a male like Jay. If I'd trusted him, if I'd fought for him, said I wanted to stay with him, I know his commander would have backed down.

Instead, I'd let decisions be made against my better judgement.

And now I'm pregnant and alone, about to be sold to another alien.

"Hold on." The first guard stops suddenly. "They're docking at the wrong airlock." He looks at his comrade in alarm.

I'm here for you.

Jay

I genuinely could have given a human kiss to Syn when the ship the Drahon stole appeared on the viewing screen.

Not that I think he would have appreciated it. He doesn't strike me as a male who likes any sort of intimacy, even what is usually shared by Gryn males, including the mutual preening.

What I wouldn't give to be preened by my mate! The Drahon ship grows larger in the viewer, and I have a strange mix of trepidation and anticipation flowing through me. I'm going to rescue my mate, return with her to Ustokos and my nest.

I push my desire for her down the thoughtbond, hoping beyond hope that she can somehow feel me through the void between us.

"What's the plan?" Syn asks, interrupting me.

"Get me on board. That's the plan," I growl at him. "You can do that, can't you?"

"We can dock. They can't stop us, but we've no idea how many are on board or what sort of resistance they're going to put up," Syn says evenly.

"I'm not asking you to come with me," I reply. "It doesn't matter how many there are. The Drahon are all cowards." I pick up my laser rifle. "Get us docked, and I'll do the rest."

"I can't let you go alone," Syn says, reaching under the console for his laser pistol.

"Who the vrex is going to fly this vrexing ship if you go and get yourself killed?" I say with a shake of my head.

"Fine." Syn sounds annoyed and clips his pistol to his belt anyway. "Put on a comm link at least." He throws one of the small devices at me.

I put the comm in my ear with a wince. I might not be as bad around tech as Ayar, but I'm still not happy at having something partially inside me. Proto might be long gone, but the Gryn distaste for tech will take a lot longer to disappear.

Unless it's something which makes things explode. I think we all enjoy that sort of tech.

"Get to airlock four. I'll let you know when we're docked." Syn hands me a small vector pad which shows a schematic of the ship.

I race through the *Perlin*, stopping briefly in the well-stocked armory, silently giving thanks to Mylo and Vypr, before I end up at airlock number four.

The other ship looms in the tiny porthole, getting closer.

Jay!

Lauren's thought hits me right in my heart. She is alive! She is on the ship!

Quickly.

The bond goes dead. Blood sings in my ears.

"We'd better be docking, Syn. Right now!" I bellow through the comm.

Ahead of me, the lights run around the exterior of the airlock and change to green. I slam my hand against the opening pad, and with a huge hiss of air, it rolls away, along with the adjacent door on the other ship.

I toss through the stun explosive and hang back until the detonation occurs, and then I'm through the door and into the ship as clouds of smoke fill the corridors within. I'm gratified by the sight of two downed Drahon.

But I need at least one of them alive enough to tell me where my *eregri* is.

Which means I'm hunting.

Something that's rapidly becoming one of my favorite pastimes, along with mating and going on *dates*.

As I stalk the corridor, a laser bolt narrowly misses my arm, and I duck behind a bulkhead. Folding up my wing, I lean out to spot the sniper.

At the end of the passage, a Drahon male crouches furtively with a laser rifle. The thoughtbond which flared into life so suddenly now remains empty of my Lauren, meaning my need to get to her has intensified. I don't have long because I know she's on this ship, and every passing moment without her is killing me.

Shouldering my rifle, I leap out of my hiding place and fire off two shots before I hit the floor and roll until I reach the other side of the corridor.

The Drahon groans. Which means I got him and he's still alive.

"Where is the human female?" I stand on his chest, where a black stain rapidly spreads.

A heart shot should have killed him, which wasn't my intention, but it looks like the Drahon heart is not in the same place as a Gryn's. Or they don't have hearts, which is the other option.

"Zark off!" he fires at me, but from the look in his black eyes, he's not going to put up a fight. I push down with my foot and aim the rifle at his crotch.

I'm not interested in what the Drahon keep there, but it's

unlikely their cocks are in any other place. His whimper indicates I've found the limit of his bravery.

"The. Human. Female. Where is she?" I repeat.

"Medical." He groans. "With Yuliat," he adds, probably unnecessarily.

I don't have time to consider if he's throwing his boss to me because he knows she will not survive if she's harmed a hair on my *eregri*'s beautiful head or if he thinks the mention of Yuliat's name will stop me.

Either way, he gets a laser bolt to the head. The Drahon are scum and until I find my Lauren, every single one of them will die.

The vector pad tells me the medical suite is near the bridge. Turns out tech is helpful given my memories from being on this ship the first time are hazy at best given how tranq'ed I was.

Behind me, I hear boots, and I toss another timed explosive, one of Ayar's favorites, back down the corridor as I scramble to get as far away as I can.

The resulting explosion and cries of pain tell me it's done its job, and I allow myself a small smile at the mini victory as I run through the ship and head to the nearest port where I can climb to the next floor.

The climbing tube is incredibly tight for my wings, feathers scraping over the interior even when I hold them as close to my body as I can, and the climb seems to take forever until I reach my destination, which is unusually quiet, given the amount of explosions and laser discharges so far.

Either I've taken out all of Yuliat's guards, or there's something else going on.

"Syn?" I press the comm in my ear. "Have any of the escape pods been launched."

"Negative," he replies, crackling in my ear. *"Have you found your mate yet?"*

"I'm vrexing working on it." I heave myself out of the tube and flop out onto the floor, just as a laser bold sizzles past.

A single shot downs the Drahon, and I get to my feet.

"EREGRI!" I bellow out, because I just need to feel her in my head, in my heart, just once more.

Jay.

She is there, weak and fading but still there. I easily drop three more Drahon without breaking a stride as I race towards medical. Nothing is going to stop me reaching her.

The door is closed when I reach it, but a shot at the lock has the panels sliding open to reveal another Drahon guard too slow in drawing his weapon.

There's a medi-pod in the center of the room and no sign of Yuliat.

"Syn!" I comm him. "Definitely no pods been released from this ship?"

"Nothing has left the ship. Nothing can, not without Gryn DNA authorization," he grumbles back at me.

"Like that worked last time," I reply, pointedly.

"There was a glitch."

"Vrexing tech," I mutter and stride over to the pod. The outside is incredibly cold to the touch. I swipe at the frosted covering and peer inside.

When I see the contents, I'm immediately scrabbling to release the latch.

Lauren is in there. Completely still with her eyes closed. So pale she could almost be…

The catch releases with a hiss and I have it open. She lies, her lips a pale blue and the thoughtbond not responding.

I feel as if someone has reached down my throat and torn out my heart. I bleed, but I am not dead.

And I want to be. My mate has gone.

I was too late. I have failed once again.

Lauren

I'm not sure I've ever been this cold in my entire life. And that includes my student clubbing phase when wearing a coat wasn't cool. Shivers wrack my body, and eventually, a familiar scent tickles my nostrils.

"Who's there?" I call out. "My eyelids are frozen," I add. Of course, if it's Yuliat, she's just going to laugh.

Instead, something warm is pressed on one eye, slowly thawing the frozen tears I shed as she pushed me into this stasis pod. Then the warmth is removed and repeated on the other eye.

I open both eyes, to stare into a pair of concerned dark ones which don't leave me for a second, not even to blink. "Jay?" I ask, even though only one creature in the entire universe could have ever treated me that tenderly.

"I'm here, my *eregri*. I thought I'd lost you," he rasps, wrapping warm arms and wings around me as my body continues to shake uncontrollably. "You were so cold."

"I was cold." My teeth chatter. "I'm better now." I lean into him, making sure I feel the press of his muscular torso, inhaling the spicy biscuit scent of his feathers.

Making sure it really is him.

An emotion churns in my mind and it's not my own. It's a mixture of relief and residual terror.

The thoughtbond, the psychic link we have, it flares into life.

This is my Jay. I have him back.

"Don't ever leave me again," I say as fiercely as I can through chattering teeth. "I fucking need you, Jay. You made me need you."

"And I am lost, a feather in the wind, without you," he replies, clawed hands running through my damp hair as I delve my arms deeper in his feathers for their warmth and scent. "You are never leaving my sight again."

"That's good to hear," I say as I listen to the steady drum of his heart through his chest and allow mine to match it.

Our emotions combine to create a sense of calm and tranquility I'm not sure I've ever experienced. Deep within me, I know there is something I have to say to him.

"You did not fail," I tell him, unbidden. "You have never failed anyone, ever. And you didn't fail me. You came for me, my love, and that's all I could ever ask." I lift an arm with painful slowness to touch him on his cheek.

"It was too close. Any longer and..."

"Yuliat wasn't going to kill me. I'm..." I hesitate for a second. Maybe now isn't the time to tell Jay about the baby. "I'm valuable, apparently. Because I'm your mate," I lie instead.

"Vrexing Yuliat!" Jay fires out, but he doesn't let go of me, and I'm eternally grateful.

I'm not sure I ever want to let go of him.

He drops his mouth to mine, a slight hesitation as he stares deep in my eyes, as if he is wondering if I still want him.

I want him.

I might just have been a human popsicle, but he's heating me up from within. His kiss is tender, desperate, wanting.

And I return it, just the same. We're on this ship full of Drahon, a broken ship, with ruthless lizards, and all I can think about is just how much I want Jay.

My handsome, feathered god of gorgeousness, who swooped in to save me.

I love you. Never leave me again, my eregri.

His words flow through me, not quite spoken, not quite in my head, but with a quiet perfection which has my heart swelling, overflowing for him.

"I still have work to do," he says, withdrawing from my thoroughly kissed lips. "I'm so sorry, Lauren."

"Is there any chance your work involves beating the Drahon, doing something unpleasant to Yuliat, and taking this ship back in triumph to Ustokos?" I query, hugging him tightly. "Because if it's any of those things, you have my complete and utter permission to unleash hell." I grin up at his slightly frowning face. He doesn't get my pop reference, and I love him even more for it.

"We do need to take the ship back to Ustokos." He rubs at the back of his neck, feathers pricking slightly and with a look on his face that suggests something is up.

"The rest of the unit is here, isn't it?" I ask.

"Not quite." He gives me a worried smile. "Syn's flying the *Perlin*, that's how we got here."

"And the rest?"

"My trip wasn't exactly sanctioned by the seniors." He finds something interesting to look at on the far wall. "They wanted to wait, and I couldn't wait. I couldn't risk losing you to the Drahon." His big, dark eyes plead with me. He wants me to understand.

My feathered fury rejected everything he held dear to come after me.

Everything.

My stomach squirms. I feel nauseous. I should tell him about the baby, but it's not like we're out of danger yet, and I don't want him taking any foolish chances to 'protect' me.

"Looks like we'd better get this ship back to Ustokos, hadn't we? Make your seniors proud?" I pull his face to mine for another kiss, a long one which I can feel has an interesting effect on a warrior who is supposed to go into battle.

He's going to be taking a long, hard sword with him, and not the sort that'll be any use in a fight.

"*Eregri.*" The word is whispered with lust buried within. "I will be taking the most precious thing in the universe back with me, and it's not this vrexing ship." He kisses me harder. "Vrex this ship and vrex the seniors."

Hands delve under my dress, seeking out my skin, slipping between my legs. Tongue entwined with mine, I'm lost in my alien angel. No matter what the danger, our desires are taking over.

Until the alarm sounds, and with a considerable reluctance, he tears himself away from me, evidence of his arousal straining at his pants. He touches his ear.

"Syn, what's going on?" he asks. And waits. "Syn?" He looks at me. "Vrex it! He's not responding."

"What is that sound?" I ask.

"I don't know. Probably nothing good," Jay replies.

"Yuliat said she was meeting someone, or something, Jay. She was going to sell me and the...she was going to sell me. I don't think we should hang around."

He bristles, all his feathers pricking up as he straightens to his full seven foot height.

"I am Gryn. There is nothing in this universe I fear." He looks down at me, little me. "Save for losing my mate."

The noise of a laser bolt sizzles outside. I stare up at Jay, my mate, my soul mate apparently, if the Gryn are to be believed.

He lifts his chin, face set. Gorgeous, feathery, and stubborn, with a dirty streak a mile wide. I have to trust him. He came for me, after all.

I am a believer.

It's Jay or bust.

Jay

Every atom of my body sings now I have Lauren in my arms, back where she belongs.

Almost.

I need her on Ustokos, in my nest (which I have yet to build), and underneath me while I put a youngling in her ripe belly. Then everything will be complete. Then I can enjoy being mated.

Providing the seniors let me. And if they don't, I'll do it anyway.

But it's not good I can't raise Syn on the comm or that there are alarms blaring on this ship. Or that my mate tells me Yuliat has company coming.

Not great odds, but I've had worse and pulled through, even if I didn't know it.

My top priority has to be getting Lauren to safety and away from the vrexing Drahon. As long as they are around, she is at risk.

I can't help but be concerned that her thoughtbond is just a little guarded. Something has changed between us. Her scent is stronger; it makes me want to ravish her on the spot. But I don't know what is causing it.

"Come, my mate." I take her hand in mine, and it feels as if all the stars melt away, just her and me together against everything.

She gives me a small smile and squeezes. I tuck her behind me as we approach the door which slides open in a hail of laser bolts.

"Wait here." I duck out and back again before shouldering my rifle, and I drop to the floor, rolling out and letting fly with several targeted shots.

The laser bolts cease, and I get to my feet, dusting myself off. Lauren stares at me, jaw slack.

"Did I not tell you I am — was— the lair's best sniper in a generation," I say with a shrug.

"That was," Lauren puts her hand over her heart, "completely awesome, Jay." She runs a few steps across to me and slings her arms around me, pressing a kiss to my cheek. "Seeing you in action, it makes me all kinds of horny," she adds with a heated gaze.

"Vrex!" I mutter under my breath. I only just managed to stop myself from claiming her next to the Medi-pod.

My libido hasn't even subsided with the short battle. If anything, my cocks might be even harder. It's very distracting. She's very distracting.

"What's the plan?" Lauren lets go of me and saunters ahead, down the corridor.

"I'm going to get you back to the *Perlin*. Syn can set it on an automatic course back to Ustokos, and he can take this ship."

"On his own?" she says over her shoulder. I think she's deliberately swinging her hips at me.

"He's more than capable. There can't be that many Drahon left alive. We can easily confine the remainder."

Lauren comes to a halt next to one of the bodies, and her face blanches. My mate is a delicate little thing, and I hurry to catch up. I want to carry her, hold her to me. Make sure she doesn't see anything she shouldn't. It's only when I reach her, I see the reason for her loss of color. And it's not the dead Drahon.

"Yuliat!"

The female Drahon doesn't look too good. One side of her face is badly blackened. Her usually deep green scales are pale. The hand holding the laser pistol at Lauren's head shakes.

But it doesn't shake enough.

"The female is coming with me, Gryn."

"No!" I take a step forward, and she lets rip with a laser bolt. It lances my shoulder, and I'm pushed back with the force. The smell of burning fills the air, but I don't go down. I stand firm. "Take me, Yuliat. I'm worth more," I say, halting my progress as she levels the pistol at Lauren again.

Yuliat laughs. It sounds unhinged, like a joykill bot. No mirth, only death. She steps forward and grabs hold of Lauren, spinning her against her chest as she throws the pistol to one side.

Instead, in her hand, there's a glint of a blade, pressed up against Lauren's abdomen.

"You were worth something, Gryn. But you proved yourself untrainable in too many ways. I'm done with the Gryn. But your little mate has something worth far much more. She carries your young. A Gryn hybrid that can be molded from birth. And she's a female with more than enough time to breed in the future." Yuliat grabs Lauren's hair and yanks her head back, causing my mate to cry out in pain. "She will carry many hybrids before her days are done."

"Lauren?" I don't know what to say. I want to grab her,

but Yuliat's blade is already digging into her stomach, a bright scarlet staining her white shift.

"I'm sorry, Jay. I should have told you," she half-sobs, her eyes filled with unshed tears. "I'm pregnant. The child is yours." She whispers the words, and she may as well have shouted them from the roof of the eyrie because I am at once ecstatic and at the same time, rage fills my veins.

"Let her go, Yuliat," I say, teeth gritted against the pain in my heart, which is already outstripping that of my shoulder.

"You'll kill me if I do," she replies, black eyes glittering. "And if I have nothing for my buyer, I die too. So it doesn't matter to me either way if I kill your mate. Your *eregri*." She spits out the last word, mangling the pronunciation. "This way, at least you'll always know she's out there, her belly full of some species' young, even if it's not yours."

I meet Lauren's eyes, wide with fear.

I'm sorry.

Her despair echoes down the thoughtbond.

"So what are you going to do, Gryn?" Yuliat bares her teeth. "Your mate or your pride?"

It all caves in on me. I don't understand why Lauren didn't tell me about the youngling. She knows I want her and any young she might bear. Or even if she never bears any young. It doesn't matter either way. We haven't had much time together, but she is my *eregri* and she knows me.

Doesn't she?

An *eregri* should know everything about their mate. I'm sure, with what we have shared, our bond, our thoughts, our bodies. I feel as if I know her, every single inch, from her beautiful hair to her tiny toes. From her terror I might leave her to her delight in seeing my feathers prick. I know all of her, inside and out.

But she still didn't tell me about the young growing inside

her. Young I simply can't risk to Yuliat, who clearly will do absolutely anything for a price and to save her scaly hide.

I hold up my hands, rifle held high in my uninjured side. I back away.

"Jay?" Lauren queries, her voice rough, painful. "Don't leave. I should have…"

"Ah, he didn't know?" Yuliat's voice is nastily triumphant. "You didn't tell him?" She hisses in Lauren's ear. "Were you ashamed to be carrying a monster in your belly?"

A spike of anguish fires through me, and I recognize that it's not my own. It comes from Lauren. Does she not want my youngling? I push out through the bond, but it's blocked. Lauren stares at me, her mind closed.

"Leave us, Gryn. If you want them to live." Yuliat increases the pressure of her knife on my mate, and I have no choice but to back around the corner, out of sight.

"Vrex, vrex, vrex!" I slam my back and wings against the wall, checking over my rifle obsessively because it's the only thing I know how to do well.

My mind spins with everything. I had my mate back, in my arms. And she's gone again. She's carrying my young, but she didn't tell me.

Maybe because she didn't trust me to save her after all.

Lauren

The front of my shift runs with blood from where Yuliat dug in the knife, but the wound is only superficial. She doesn't want to risk damaging the goods.

But Jay has gone. He walked—no, backed—away from me when Yuliat mentioned monsters.

His baby is not a monster. It's our child and I want him near me. I want us to have this baby together. Instead, he did what she asked, and he retreated.

Maybe he doesn't want a child after all. My stomach fills with ice as my gullet fills with bile. That can't be right. I'm letting my insecurities get the better of me.

Jay came for me; it means he wants me. But I should have told him about the baby, and my stomach clenches painfully at my idiocy at not telling him as soon as I could.

I just wish the stupid thoughtbond wasn't dead as Yuliat pulls and drags me back through the laser scorched corridors. How come the bloody thing worked when Jay was thinking about food? Or zeroing rifle sights? And now, when it's most important. Nothing! It's a very strange thing to have between males and females if it doesn't work right all the time.

I'd even go so far to say it's just annoying.

A ringing and shuddering flows through the ship, and Yuliat looks around wildly.

Back in the compound, she was in control. Her tongue hardly ever flickered, but now, it's never in her mouth, flapping almost uselessly as she wheezes her way behind me. She is at the very edge. She might have been ruthless before, but now? She's spectacularly dangerous.

"Zarking move, female!" she fires at me, planting a spiked hand in the small of my back and pushing.

I stumble forward, trying to buy time. Jay must have a plan, of sorts. He can't possibly have turned up here and be hoping for the best. Me and baby bean need him, more than ever. It can't end like this.

We reach a part of the ship which is relatively undamaged from Jay's earlier rampage. An alarm starts, and Yuliat is momentarily distracted.

I stamp down hard on her foot, and in the half a second I have where she lets go of me, I'm running. Running as fast as I possibly can back the way I came. Hoping beyond hope I can find Jay, and we can get off this ship of hell as fast as we can.

As much as he wants to take it back to Ustokos. As much as he wants to please his seniors, I think we can safely say it's probably ruined.

I spin around a corner and straight into something hard.

And scaly.

"Fuck me sideways!" I fire out. "Can I not catch a break, just once?" I look up into the face of a Drahon guard. His long blue tongue runs over his lips, flickering over my face. He's the one who showed an 'interest' in me earlier. I'd recognize the smell of him, all cheesy, anywhere.

"I'm fed up with the Gryn getting all the nice things," he says, seizing my arm and baring his teeth. "It's my turn."

"Ah, you found her. Well done." Yuliat saunters down the corridor, and my would-be rapist pales.

"She's a feisty little one, isn't she?" the guard asks.

"Get off!" I shove at him, but he simply leers at me, spittle dripping down his scaly chin.

That earlier shudder? It comes again, only this time, more alarms blare, and both Yuliat and the guard stiffen.

"Expecting more company?" I say. At least I can revel in their discomfort.

"Give me the female," Yuliat fires at the guard. "And go see what this noise is all about."

"I expect it'll be the Gryn, coming to rip you limb from limb," I say cheerfully. "If there's any justice in the universe."

"If there is, it'll be too late for you. Your buyer is waiting, and you have an appointment to keep," Yuliat snarls.

Jay, about now would be a good time to put in an appearance!

Jay

"Vrex it! Jay! Are you there?" Syn's voice brings me back to life.

"I'm here," I reply, unable to muster more.

"I've been calling for half an hour. Have you found your mate? What's the status of the Drahon?"

"I've lost her." The words are out of my mouth before I can stop myself.

"She wasn't on board?" Syn asks.

"She was, but the Drahon, they got to her. Yuliat took her."

"My systems show no escape pods have left the ship," Syn says. *"She's still on board, Jay. You can get her back."*

"I can't," I murmur. "Not this time."

A shudder runs through the hull of the ship I'm on.

"What the vrex was that?" I push away from the wall, the fog of my despair intensifying.

"It's another ship docking. If you want to get your mate, now is the time, Jay. You're not going to get another chance," Syn bellows over the comm.

"I don't know if I can get to her and save this ship," I

comm back, my voice cracking. "If we get back to Ustokos without this ship, we'll be lucky not to spend the rest of eternity in the laundry, scrubbing gak filled maraha hide pants!"

And I'm already feeling a stint in the laundry is the least of my problems when it comes to my insubordination to the seniors.

"Then save the ship. I'm sure we can go after your mate later." Syn's voice wavers in and out over the comm, but he sounds peevish.

I know the seniors will never sanction it.

"Jay, you need to do something NOW!" Syn suddenly comes through loud and clear. *"Get to the bridge, take the ship, and we'll work something out later about your mate if the Drahon take her away again."*

If they take her away again. *If.* My mind is full of Lauren, her stunning gray eyes pleading with me as I left her with Yuliat. The feel of her lush body in my arms for just an instant

"Don't tell me what to do. My mate is vrexing pregnant, you vrexer. And the Drahon took her..." The enormity of it all, of finding my Lauren, of filling her womb, of knowing I'm going to be a father, hits me so hard my legs go from under me, and I'm on my knees.

I'm going to fail again, and this time, I'm going to fail her.

It is all there, laid out for me, as if I can walk across my nightmare.

"Are you an elite warrior, Jay? One who'll do his duty to his legion and to his mate? Who will fight to the death for what fate gives him?" Syn says with utmost clarity.

It cuts through my fog.

Because I would do anything for my Lauren. Anything. If it's my life for hers and our youngling, then she can have it.

But it doesn't need to be that way. I am a Gryn warrior, and we always prevail.

"Vrexing right I will!"

"Then vrex the unit, vrex the seniors, and go get your vrexing mate. I'll deal with the rest. And if your youngling is a male, I want him named after me!" Syn laughs, the comm crackling.

"Since when did you become such a philosopher?" I press my finger to the comm unit in my ear as the reception gets worse.

"When a certain expert sniper gave me a chance to prove myself," Syn replies. *"But you need to hurry..."* The rest of his sentence is cut off in a blaze of static.

"Vrex!" I swear. There's no time.

I have to get to Lauren.

And then we can take the ship.

I close my eyes and center myself, allowing everything to drift away. Blocking out the whine in the hull structure as it's pulled, the attempts to restart the stardrive rippling through the floor, the smell of ozone from the laser weapons. I allow it all to drift away until I feel her.

Lauren.

She is my all. She is my beginning and my end. Fate has gifted her to me. I need her to be whole. All I have to do is defeat a ship full of Drahon, outwit Yuliat, and claim my prize.

Something a Gryn warrior should be able to do in his sleep.

"Warrior?"

A familiar voice has my eyes flying open, and from my position on the floor, I see a pair of stout legs, encased in maraha hide. From there, my gaze travels upwards until I meet the craggy features of Strykr.

Oh vrex!

"Guv?"

"Any reason why I should find one of my elite groveling in a Drahon ship with his weapon holstered?" Strykr rumbles.

"Trying to locate my mate, Guv."

A laser bolt zips past his ear, and I lean to one side, letting fly a single shot which drops the Drahon to the ground. I look back up at Strykr, attempting to gauge his mood. His solemn face breaks into a grin, and he holds out his hand to me, heaving me to my feet.

"Why are you here?" I ask, "and how did you find us?"

"Syn doesn't have all the tricks, and let's just say Lyon was *not* amused when he found his ship missing."

The most tremendous explosion rings out from deeper in the ship.

"The Unit?" I query.

"Probably Ayar." Strykr groans, pressing the comm in his ear. "Ayar! You know what happens when you blow things up in space. If you do that again, you'll be on kitchen duty!"

"Sorry, Guv." Vypr's voice comes through loud and clear, meaning I can't help but grin. "I'll stop him next time."

"Dear Nisis!" Strykr rolls his eyes to the ceiling. "Why are you still here, Jay? I thought you had a mate to save?"

"Guv?"

"You didn't think we'd let you do all of this on your own, did you? We're a unit, warrior. Not a bunch of mercs. And the Drahon lost this ship once. They don't get it back." Strykr grins at me, but then a fist fires out, and I'm caught by the throat. "Just don't make a habit of disobeying the seniors, or it's my hide they'll take it out on." His dark eyes flash, and I see the fighter he is bubble below the surface.

The fighter he instilled in me over many, many hours of training.

The fighter I have become, for my Lauren.

Lauren

Yuliat isn't gentle as she kicks my legs to make me walk. I'm not going to make it easy for her, whatever she does, because I know the longer I stay on this ship, the better chance Jay has to free me.

Providing he is coming back.

It's all I can hope for. Because while I know that Jay is an 'honorable warrior,' the term he always uses, that was before I didn't tell him I was pregnant.

Literally the most important thing I could have said to him, and I thought it was the wrong time to say it.

It slams into me hard. I am a complete and utter idiot. All that shit I told myself about men being untrustworthy bastards. It was me who held myself back. Refusing to see the good out there. The good, the kind, the sweetness, and utter filthy naughtiness that is my Jay.

My *mate*. And I couldn't bring myself to tell him the one thing which meant the most to both of us.

I stumble forward, Yuliat swearing at me as chimes come from the vector pad in her hand. Her buyer is impatient. A clawed hand digs farther into my arm, and she manages to drag me back to the escape pods. The area is empty.

"Oh dear. Has he run out on you?" I snarl sarcastically. "Hope you got half up front, given you're stuck with me." I give Yuliat a shove, not expecting much to happen, given that she's a foot taller than me and considerably scalier.

To my surprise, she takes a step back. Her eyes are focused not on me but on something else, something in the shadows.

Something big, and angry, and...

Feathered.

"Jay!" My joy fills the space, breathing life back once again that this washing machine of a ride might finally be at an end.

That I might finally have my warrior in my arms, for keeps.

"Zarking Gryn!" Yuliat's voice has become shrill as Jay steps out of the darkness, rifle raised. "Why won't you just die?" She reaches for the holster on her belt and finds it empty.

Instantly, she reaches for me, her literal human shield. I jump, but I'm not quick enough, and her claws easily penetrate my skin as she drags me in front of her.

"You don't want to lose this little human, do you?" she hisses nastily at Jay, backing away from him. "Not when she carries your young in her belly."

"I'm not going to lose her, Yuliat. Lauren is mine, and she's been mine since the first day I set eyes on her." His liquid dark eyes are so deep, so full.

I don't need the thoughtbond. Jay's love radiates from him. He doesn't think any less of me for not telling him about the baby.

"Do you trust me, my *eregri*?" Jay asks me, the rifle still at his shoulder as Yuilat attempts to yank me farther in front of her.

"If you kill me, you'll have to kill her," Yuliat screams out, backing up farther, her clawed hands scrabbling at me, ripping at my skin.

His eyes don't change. He doesn't move. Not a muscle, not a feather. He is a statue in a graveyard.

"I trust you, Jay," I say. And I mean it with the whole of my heart.

The bolt from his rifle doesn't strike Yuliat, it impacts the wall behind her. As she turns, following the laser light, she releases me, and my life goes into slow motion as fury explodes around us.

Jay beats his wings once, twice. And he's reaching for me, just as Yuliat is ripped away. A blast, a deluge of searing cold hits my back, freezing the blood running down my arms as the most tremendous suction takes hold.

Only I'm in Jay's arms and he has me held so very tightly as he braces himself against the side of the ship and slams a boot against the wall. Instantly, the suction ceases, and we fall to the floor, me on top of my bundle of muscle and feathers. The ability to breathe and exist in normal time resolves itself.

"Yuliat?" I query, panting over him.

"Gone. Out the airlock." Jay raises his head from the floor and nods over my shoulder.

I turn to look. The door is closed, but through the small porthole, I see a tiny body disappearing into space, tumbling over and over.

I hated Yuliat with every atom of my being, but her death suddenly seems pointless. I bury my head in Jay's muscular chest, and he flops a wing over me, head rolling back with a groan. It's only then I see the injury to his shoulder, red raw. It's been partially cauterized. The rest has the texture of mince.

"Shit, Jay! Your shoulder." I push away from him, but a big, strong arm locks me in place.

"You'll have plenty of time to care for me again, my mate, just as soon as my unit gets here." He grins at me woozily. "And then we can care for our youngling together."

"I should have told you…"

"Ts-s-s-s." Jay puts a finger on my lips. "When would you have told me. When we were safe? Of course. I know you, Lauren." His gaze deepens, crystal sharp. "I know all of you. And I love you."

Something blooms through me, more than just the thoughtbond, more even than love. It is as if my entire being is taken to the next level of goodness. Jay has lifted me from an existence where I doubted everything to one where I can trust my one good alien angel.

"And I love you." I press my lips to his, and the entire universe collides to see us together.

I'm lost in the mere taste of him, his tongue entwined with mine, his soft lips, his scent, his everything.

His hard lengths against my thigh, pressing insistently to remind me just what a dirty alien angel Jay is. My core fires into life, throbbing at the thought of him being inside me, giving me everything he has as he groans a climax.

Not the only dirty creature on the spaceship after all.

"Vrex it!" a male voice thunders across to us. "I was promised explosions."

"Explosions are happening right here," I murmur over Jay's lips, and he snorts a laugh.

"You were told not to explode anything else, Ayar," he calls out, twisting painfully to see the scarred warrior who has his arms folded over his dirty chest.

"What's this unit coming to," he grumbles, "when a warrior can't blow things up."

"We're in vrexing space, Ayar!" Strykr strides up behind him, thumping wings. "Vypr! Get him under control, and make sure the vrexer doesn't have any explosives on him," he calls out.

"Are they all here?" I ask. "The whole unit."

"We're all here." I peer around Strykr to see Mylo grinning massively at me and Jay on the floor.

"I think we should probably get up now," I say as Jay captures my lips in another possessive kiss which leaves me panting.

"I'll get up when I'm good and ready," he growls, tilting his head back as more warriors amble into the space. "And when I know they've done their job."

Strykr's wings lift, but a smile crosses his face. "We've done our job, Jay. You and your mate can come home."

Jay

"Will you get off me?" I shove at Mylo as he fusses around my wound.

Across the med bay of the Drahon ship we've taken back, a taciturn Syn is carefully patching up Lauren, running a small device over her, thankfully superficial, injuries, and I marvel as her skin appears as good as new.

And as beautiful as ever.

My shoulder was vrexed, and Strykr insisted I get it checked out in the med bay. This has to be the one time I actually would have liked the lair medic, Orvos, to be around because it means I have to subject myself to Mylo, who claims to have medic training.

"Stay still, you vrexer." Mylo grabs hold of my wing and attempts to keep me still. "The sooner I fix this up, the sooner you're done. You're like a vrexing youngling." He ducks as I aim a wing at his ear.

"Jay, are you misbehaving over there?" Lauren gives Syn a pat on his arm and jumps off her medi-bed.

I let out a warning growl as Syn's gaze follows her.

"By the goddess!" Mylo fires out. "Okay, you're done!" He steps away from me just as Lauren approaches my bed.

"Does Ayar need any healing?" Syn asks, a mischievous look on his face.

"Nisis, no! There's not a vrexing chance I'm even attempting to heal him in here. We've got no tranq for a start, and we'd basically need to drown him in it before we could get him to stay still!" Mylo looks nervously at the doorway, just in case there's a scarred warrior in need of assistance nearby.

"Ayar looked fine to me. He and Vypr have gone to get something to eat," Lauren says, diplomatically. Her stomach rumbles, and I feel an ache to ensure she is properly cared for.

"Food," Mylo says with a sparkle in his eye. "Could do with something to eat myself after dealing with the Drahon. How long until we're back on Ustokos?" he asks Syn.

"Couple of hours, maybe half a turn. Lyon's being precious about the *Perlin*, since I stole it," Syn says with a note of annoyance in his voice.

"Come on, I'm hungry." Mylo looks directly at me, grabbing hold of Syn's wing as the warrior bristles at his touch.

"I need to speak to Jay..." Syn begins, but he's cut off as Mylo plants a boot in his rear and literally kicks him out of the med-bay.

A grinning face reappears around the doorway. "Couple of hours," Mylo says, and then he's gone.

"What was that all about?" Lauren asks me, melting farther into my arms.

"Syn thinks we're in trouble for taking the ship to come and get you."

"And are you?"

"Probably, but I don't care." I drop my head into her hair and inhale deeply. Her scent is better than ever. Her little belly already rounded with my young. I want nothing more than a nest to claim her in.

One thing I don't have.

"I care." She strokes her fingers over my hair and into my feathers. "I care about you more than anything, Jay. I should have told you about the baby."

"You should have." I nod enthusiastically as her lips purse. "I don't mean it." I smile and kiss those sweet lips. "I know you would have told me."

"I didn't want to add to all the shit going down," Lauren says, deadly serious. "Once we were safe, I was going to say something."

"Why don't we go get something to eat with the others?" I suggest. If I can't nest, I can, at least, make sure my mate is fed.

Lauren slips her hand in mine, and we head out of the med-bay, somewhere I'm pleased to leave, given it reminds me of that awful pod where I'd found her. Instead, I enjoy being next to her, all lush and full of young.

"Anyway, I would have noticed you were with young soon enough. I am the unit's deadliest sniper after all. If I hadn't seen this, I may as well have hung up my rifle." I give her a wink.

"The cheek!" Lauren gasps in mock horror, but she comes to a halt, looking down, spanning her hand over her little rounded stomach. "I can't believe I'm already showing. You don't think Yuilat did anything to me, do you? Something to harm the baby?" she asks, gray eyes glittering with unshed tears.

"Gryn females carry their babies for just under half a cycle. I think it's shorter than humans." I reach out to swipe away a tear trickling down her cheek and lick my thumb. Even her tears are sweet to me. "We can ask Strykr. He has a human mate."

"What makes you think she'll be pregnant?" Lauren hiccups wetly.

I raise my eyebrows at her, then I cup her face and slam my mouth to hers in a long, long kiss.

"Oh," she says, eyes half-lidded. "That's how." She stays completely still, my hands on her soft, warm skin.

"Yes, that's how," I murmur. Her scent is intoxicating. "And although you are already with young, I need to be sheathed in you again, so very, very much, my mate."

"I've missed you, Jay." Her breath tickles my fingers, and her hands are on my chest. "I need you too."

I drop my hand to her waist and let it drift lower as I push her up against the wall. Underneath the tiny shift, she wears nothing else, and I can let my fingers explore her thighs as she groans against me.

"Do you like having a belly full of my youngling?" I nuzzle at the crook of her neck, lapping my tongue over her skin, enjoying the way her scent invades every part of my senses. "Because I'm going to ensure you are always full of my seed and my young."

"You like me like this?" She gasps as my digits invade her channel, pumping deep inside her tight, wet hole. "Pregnant?"

"I cannot wait until you are even bigger. So delicious, so ripe. I will have you on your hands and knees in my nest and plough you from behind." I mouth in her ear, sucking on her earlobe as her body bucks against me. "But first, I will have you here and now."

I spirit her shift over her head before I release the mag catch on my pants. Lauren reaches for my cocks, stroking them both together, then separating them out in the way she knows I love. Both her hands on them, my hips jerking towards her because I can't stop myself. I dip my head to take a tight little nipple between my teeth, and it makes her squeak with pleasure.

"Here and now?" she whispers. "In this corridor? With the others not so far away?"

"I won't be kept from your sweet cunt, my mate. When I want you, I want you." I'm panting, sweat sheening my skin as I desire her, and the effort of holding back my building climax begins to bite.

Her beautiful crystalline eyes are fixed on me, even as her clever hands work at my cocks, and I feel another rush of moisture from her pussy.

"Then claim me, my warrior angel." She barely has to say the words and I'm buried in her.

"Oh, I'm going to claim you. Thoroughly, until you are hoarse with screaming my name."

Lauren

Jay fills me in one quick movement. And when I say fills, I'm stretched to my very limit. Both cocks inside me are incredible, the combined ridges and nodes hitting all the right spots. I wrap my legs around his waist as he holds me easily up against the wall, one huge hand cupping my buttocks, the other gently tweaking a nipple, while his mouth meets mine in a kiss which could set the ship on fire.

"By Nisis, you are tight." He moans. My pussy flutters over him, and it elicits a further grunt of satisfaction as he withdraws and thrusts back again. "Wet and needy mate," he whispers in my ear. "Can you call for me?"

"But..."

"I want everyone to know what we are doing. I want everyone to know I am filling you, mating you hard and long. So call for me, mate. Let me hear my name on your lips."

Jay circles his hips and drives deeper inside me, the largest node on his main cock hitting my g-spot perfectly so everything goes red, and I can't even stop myself from groaning his name.

"Louder." He plucks at a nipple as his cocks pump into

me. "Louder, my mate. I want them to know just how I got you with young."

I can't stop myself. I can't hold back the orgasm which threatened the moment he slid inside me. I needed my alien predator as much as he needed me.

"Jay!" I holler. "Fuck!" He withdraws and slams back into me as I convulse over him, soaking his cocks, soaking him.

The ship spins as if we're in free fall, and I love falling with him. I love the way he makes me feel, wanted and protected.

I love that he wants our child. I love it that I've lost my fear of rejection.

And, oh god, I love how he makes me come apart, bringing me down to his dirty, filthy level.

"Jay!" I moan again, loudly as he pants and pants, trying to hold back from his own orgasm, desperate to keep plundering me, but I know him as surely as he knows me. "Mate me, Jay! Claim me!" I redouble my breathless cries of pleasure, and his thrusts grow irregular.

"Mate, you make me spill me seed when I don't want." His chest heaves, his dark eyes drilling into mine. "You make me paint your channel and swell when I..." His head tips back as he grinds against my clit, sending me spiraling again, pussy clamping onto him, sucking at his cocks, eating them up as he explodes, literally explodes inside me.

I feel the pumping of his hot cum. It gushes into me as the pain of his swelling secondary cock reaches my brain, and I gasp until it pops inside, just far enough, and we are locked.

Bound.

Unbreakable.

"Vrex!" Jay pants out. "Vrex, that was good." He puts his forehead on mine, sweet breath covering my face before he drops his lips to the skin on my neck. "Vrex it, my Lauren, you will be the death of me, making my cocks do such things. And in public too." His sharp canines raking my skin raise goosebumps even though I've just had one of the best orgasms of my life.

"I think you'll find you started the whole public sex thing." I wriggle against him, but it's no use, we are stuck.

"I could get used to it. I like to mate you like this. So sweet and dirty," he mouths over my breast, thrusting up inside me with his still hard cocks and letting out a groan. "I could mate you like this all the time."

I can't help but laugh, not at him, but because I'm so deliriously happy to be with Jay. The swift, naughty intimacy we've just shared is unlike anything I've ever done before because I couldn't trust anyone before.

I bury my head in his warm skin, inhaling his gorgeous musky, spicy scent and relax over him, enjoying the fullness his swollen cocks provide, enjoying being here, being bad, with my alien angel and his dirty ways, most of them introduced to him by me and which he has rapidly made his own.

In the distance, we hear voices, and I freeze.

"Jay!"

"I know," he moans, his mouth covering mine for a kiss which would sink a battleship. "Looks like we're going to get caught in the act."

"You are shameless!" I slap him on his leathery shoulders, knowing he'll hardly notice.

He studies my face for long, long seconds. "It's you, Lauren. You make me what I am. You are everything, everything I could ever want. The fact you are carrying my young makes me want to shout from the top of the lair, the top of the eyrie, the top of Ustokos that you are mine, and I have claimed you."

Jay pulls out of me, and I'm gently lowered to the floor on jelly legs as he takes my face between two massive, clawed hands, his dark, beautiful eyes never leaving mine.

"Jay, you make me whole," I reply, closing my hands over

his. "You made a broken thing take flight again. I finally have the family I never thought I would have."

His handsome face breaks into a smile of epic proportions.

"Oh, my *eregri*, you don't know what flying is, not yet. I have so much you have yet to experience once we return to Ustokos. You will have the best nest, the best coverings, the finest furs. And you will fly with me, properly, to see your new home."

He hands me my shift, and I pull it over my head just as Strykr and Syn appear down the corridor. Jay surreptitiously tucks himself back in his pants, and we both attempt to look like we are out for a stroll.

"I hope this is you on your way to the canteen to make sure your mate is well fed," Strykr says to Jay. "We are summoned to szent once we land. I have made arrangements for my mate to meet us to settle Lauren into the eyrie while you meet with the seniors."

I look up at Jay, and he squares his shoulders, feathers rattling.

"What I did for my *eregri*, I would do time and again. I will meet with the seniors and tell them so," he says.

He's absolutely done it. Not only am I pregnant with his baby, but this massive, feathery warrior, all sweetness and filth, has stolen my heart and has it fully entwined with his own.

"Are you sure you're okay to stay with Kat?" Jay asks me for what must be the hundredth time.

I look over at the other human female, the only one I've seen since I was abducted god knows how long ago. She's definitely pregnant. There's no hiding her rounded stomach, and given the way Strykr embraces her, his hand on her abdomen, he couldn't be happier.

"I won't be long, then I can make our nest," he adds, dark eyes full of worry for me.

"I'll be fine, Jay. I'm on Ustokos, surrounded by Gryn warriors, and you won't be far away. I'm not going to give birth in the next few hours. Go and do what you need to do."

Jay's mind is full of a gray fog. He's desperate to start nesting again. It's like an itch he can't scratch. He has no desire to go to this meeting, but it's more of a summons which cannot be refused. All these conflicting emotions are making for one anxious warrior.

The least I can do is keep him calm because now we're back on Ustokos, my stomach is in knots.

This is my new world. My home. With Jay.

And he has to leave me because his Legion demands it.

Strange new world.

"Hi! I'm Kat Bolton." Kat interrupts us slightly shyly and holds out her hand. Her accent is North London which sort of takes me by surprise.

"I'm Lauren Ellis, and you're British!"

"We all are," Kat says with a smile. "By we, I mean the human women on Ustokos. I was as surprised as you are."

"Are we starting some sort of trend, or have aliens gotten sick of abducting Americans?" I ask, taking her hand, and she grins at me.

"We're definitely the cool ones."

"Sub zero."

"Hi, Jay," Kat says to my anxious mate. "Strykr's asked me to help set Lauren up with clothes and so on, while you're at your..." she gives me a slightly worried look "...meeting. Is that okay?"

Jay makes a concerned noise, wings flared. "My mate is pregnant, like you. She should be treated with great care, especially after everything the Drahon have done to her."

"Jay!" Strykr calls out from across the landing pad.

"Szent." He springs into the air, and Jay embraces me once more.

"I have to go. I will be back." He nudges his head into my hair like he always does when he wants to center himself.

"I know you will," I reply, attempting to use the thoughtbond to give him all my love because he needs it, and I mean it.

Jay takes a couple of paces away from me and unfurls his wings. He looks truly magnificent, and when he fires himself from the ground, I gasp out loud, watching him climb easily into the air to follow Stryker and Syn.

A cheer comes from the rest of his unit, who are continuing to unload from the *Perlin*. Lyon, the grumpy ship's captain, watches them with his arms folded. He really wasn't amused his ship had been stolen.

"I'm not sure I've made the best impression," I venture to Kat.

"Oh, don't worry too much," she says. "They are mostly bluster, these males. And once there is a female involved, normally everything is fine." Kat puts her hand on my arm. "All the seniors have human females as mates. Jay won't be in that much trouble."

"Not as much as me, or you," I say, patting my stomach.

"Woah! How long have you been, er." Kat hesitates. "Friends?" she ventures.

"Not that long, but apparently, Gryn have a shorter pregnancy?" I say. Suddenly, my worry has ramped up hugely, and I clamp down on the thoughtbond so as not to let Jay know.

"Five months, but you look a month gone at least! And in human to Gryn terms, that's about three months. Is that what Jay meant about the Drahon?"

"They were impatient," I say, darkly. "But maybe this is normal?"

"Let's get you something to wear that doesn't flash every male in the eyrie," Kat says, eyeing my tiny shift with undisguised horror. "And we can go see the lair's healer, Orvos. He can check you over, and I'm sure it'll be fine."

After everything she's said, I'm feeling more worried than ever. And the one creature who grounds me? He's just flown away.

Jay

"This is vrexing gak," Syn grumbles as we leave szent. "Just because you have a mate, you don't get punished."

Jyr was not a happy Prime. I think Fyn an even less happy Command. Our deliberate disobedience, despite the recapture of the ship and the half a dozen Drahon males who managed not to be blown to atoms by Vypr and Ayar, has not exactly endeared our unit to the seniors.

We were lucky Ryak was prepared to stick up for his former team. Very lucky. I suspect if Fyn had his way, we'd be back in his barracks and doing mostly laundry duty with the occasional light maraha gak cleaning session. Probably for the rest of eternity.

I'm excluded from the next mission, and I'm expected to help Lyon with the *Perlin* for the foreseeable future, which should be fun given how vrexing unhappy he was at Syn and me, but Syn got the brunt of the punishment.

"Kyt won't need you for long at the other lair, I'm sure."

"He drives me mad. Once he's away from his mate, he's a nightmare," Syn grumbles. "Constantly pining. It's hard to believe he once used to party every night." He references the lair quartermaster's former occupation as lair party coordinator.

"What can I say? Mating makes you see things differently." I shrug.

"Good thing it does." Mylo sidles up to me, and I turn to see the rest of the unit, including Huntr who leans against the crumbling wall of the lair, a thunderous expression on his face, as if he doesn't want to be here, even though I didn't invite him. "Because you need to get your mate to take your band."

"Wait, what?" I feel my legs give a little. "She won't want my band, not yet."

Huntr snorts unhappily. "Females don't know what they want."

"Ignore him." Mylo slings an arm around my shoulder and turns me away. "She's your *eregri*, isn't she?"

"Vrexing right!"

"And you've already filled her belly, haven't you?" Mylo wing bumps me with a wink. "Then the next thing you must do is give her your band."

"You just want a vrexing party." Vypr intervenes, shoving Mylo away from me. "Ignore him," he tells me. "You do what you want, Jay."

He's always protected all of us, especially Ayar. From each other as much as anything. And I know his relationship with Ayar runs far deeper. Even so, I appreciate his gesture.

"No," I say. "Mylo's right. Lauren is my mate, and while I might have claimed her, I want her to take my band."

I look round at my brother warriors. Mylo grins cockily. Ayar broods just behind Vypr, and our newest members, Syn who is still unhappy at his lot, and Huntr, the dark one who looks like he might explode at any time.

I want them all to share in my happiness as a mated male. To see the joy to be had in the new world we are building.

Because although we are strong together, our strength comes from deep inside.

My Lauren taught me this lesson; she didn't have to accept me. An alien being to her, where other aliens had held her as a slave. She showed me how to be the Gryn warrior the goddess wants us to be.

She has taken this warrior to a place he never thought he would go, from male to mated male. I adore her for it.

"It's time we had a vrexing party!"

"Finally, Jay!" Mylo is grinning from ear-to-ear, and I'm surrounded by my team, exchanging wing bumps.

"You'll need to get your bands from Myk as soon as possible," Vypr tells me.

"I'll get the var beer ordered from the brewery." Mylo smacks his lips. "When are you going to ask her?"

"I think you should ask her now," Ayar adds with unusual excitement for him. "Taking a mate and having a youngling is, well, amazing." He looks over his shoulder at Vypr.

"I can't exactly spring it on her, can I?" I say to the group of charged males. "We've just gotten back to the eyrie, and I have my nest to build."

"I'd do it as soon as possible, before she changes her mind," Huntr grumbles from across the room. He spins on his heel and walks out.

"Ignore him," Vypr says. "When the Guv rescued him and the human females, he was with one, but it seems she's not so sure now. Or he is. It's hard to tell with that vrexer. He's worse than this one." Vypr slips an arm around Ayar's waist and gazes at him.

"That's saying something," I say with a grin at Ayar. One he returns with his usual, slightly unhinged glint.

"Ustokos would be boring if we were all the same," he says.

"I'd prefer some of my life to be boring than exploded, which seems to be your forte," Strykr rumbles from behind us.

"Guv!" I attempt to look like I've not just been planning a celebration. From the look on his face, I've failed.

"I'm pleased to hear one of my unit is settling down with a mate." He glares around at us before his gaze softens. "And I'll try to keep the banding celebrations from the seniors who have strictly forbidden the eyrie to have any parties ever again."

Mylo and Ayar look stricken at this news.

"Well, maybe not ever." Strykr grins before returning to somber with a look back at the now empty szent chamber. "Maybe just for a few months. Anyway, Jay, you had better speak to Myk about your bands and go to your mate. She's with Orvos."

"With the healer? Why?" Ice forms in my stomach. "Is she unwell. Is the youngling unwell?"

"She's fine. Kat thought it was best she went to see Orvos, for something she calls a 'check up,'" Strykr says, but his words are already fading as I race out into the main atrium and leap into the air, spiraling down as fast as I can to complete my mission.

To claim my mate.

Lauren

The walk over from the landing pad to the lair was interesting. But I couldn't help worrying about Jay. He's convinced me the Gryn are honorable, but this meeting is a big deal, and I'm worried he's going to be punished for coming to get me.

And now I'm also worried about the baby and what Yuliat might have done to me. But I'm not about to give in to the tears threatening, and I attempt to concentrate on my surroundings, rather than my worries and the closed off thoughtbond stretched to its very limit between Jay and me.

"Is this entire planet in ruins?" I ask Kat as she strolls next to me.

"How much of it have you seen?"

"Not much. Where I was being kept by the Drahon was somewhere Jay called the 'waste seas.'"

"Charming!" Kat laughs. "I presume he told you about the war with Proto and how the planet was decimated, the organic life killed or captured?"

"The AI robot thing? Yeah, he mentioned it. I'd have said it was something out of a science fiction movie except…" I wave my hand at my surroundings, all destroyed, crumbling buildings and the occasional winged male zipping over us. "But being pregnant with alien spawn..."

"I resemble that remark," Kat says, very seriously.

"Shit! Sorry!"

She frowns but can't hold. Her face splits into a smile, and she laughs merrily. "I was kidding, Lauren. It's a lot to take in. You'll feel better once you've met the others and their super cute kids."

"Do they all have, you know?" I make a flapping motion with my hands.

"Wings? Yes, all of them. I guess the Gryn genes are strong."

"That'll make babysitting interesting."

"Oh, you don't need to worry about things like that. If your mate isn't able to help out, and these males are *very* hands-on in the childcare department, then there are always other males wanting to help out. The older warriors love younglings."

I think of how Jay messed around with his unit back when we were underground. They had an easy way with each other which spoke volumes about why they came to help him find me.

"What happened to all their females?" I ask Kat quietly as we climb a set of crumbling steps into the bowels of the imposing 'lair.'

"Gone. No one knows where. Maybe the Drahon do. Maybe we'll get some answers now." She shrugs, leading me into a huge atrium spiraling up many, many floors. We begin to walk up a ramp which circles the large open space.

I'm beginning to wish I could grow wings by the time we reach a level where Kat breaks off and turns down a short corridor, leading me through a set of double doors.

"Another one?" a deep voice rumbles out as we arrive into

a room lined with beds jutting out of the walls. A couple are occupied by unconscious warriors.

"Hi, Orvos," Kat says brightly to the large, bulky Gryn who sits behind a desk, strewn with papers. His hair is grizzled, and he has scruff covering his chin, looking much older than the other warriors I've met. "This is Lauren. She's mated to Jay, and she's pregnant."

If Orvos is surprised in the least by this revelation, he doesn't show it. Instead, he unfolds himself from behind his desk and reveals he is just as large as all the other warriors, big, dark wings rustling.

"That, young female, is what happens when you mate with a Gryn," he intones.

I'm slightly lost for words at being called 'young,' so much so the term 'female' hardly penetrates.

"She was held by the Drahon and is worried they might have done something to harm the baby. Isn't that right, Lauren?" Kat speaks for me, helpfully.

"I can't be this pregnant, this soon." I span my hands over my stomach, feeling hugely self-conscious and wishing Jay was with me.

Orvos snorts dismissively. He clearly has an excellent bedside manner. Not.

"Go and lie on that ledge, there." He points to an unoccupied one and bustles off.

"He's an acquired taste," Kat says. "Like most of the Gryn."

"Oh, I don't know." I walk over to the bed he indicated. "Jay's unit seems okay."

Kat breaks into an indulgent smile. I had almost forgotten she's with Strykr, Jay's imposing commander. "They're adorable, aren't they?" she gushes. "I'm so pleased Jay found a mate, too."

I sit and look at the occupant of the next bed, nearly

jumping up again when I see it's the still, pale form of another human woman. Kat walks past me and over to the bed. She strokes over the forehead of the woman, and her eyes flicker open.

"Hi, Robin, how are you feeling?" she asks, sitting down on the edge of the bed. "This is Lauren. She just got here."

The pale face turns towards me, bright, almost feverish blue eyes stare out from under a mass of blonde hair.

"Hi?" I say uncertainly.

"I'm getting better." Robin tries to push herself up, and it's then I see she has an arm in a sling. Lauren helps her sit, and she seems to be struggling to breathe.

"Robin, Diana, and Jen were also taken by the Drahon. Strykr and his team rescued them in the same mission Jay went missing," Lauren says, and I see a look of pain cross her face. "Poor Robin was injured when the Drahon tried to blow up their ship."

"I think I was on that ship, too, but I didn't know there were other humans on board." I shake my head. "It was all a bit hazy for a while."

"Lucky you." Robin winces. "That feathered bastard keeps trying to sedate me." She nods over at the back of Orvos. "He seems to think if I'm asleep I'm not in pain."

"Well, are you?"

Robin lets out a harsh laugh. "I suppose not. I'd still rather not be asleep," she says darkly. "Not when I'm stuck on an alien planet with a bunch of alien males."

"The Gryn won't hurt you, Robin. I've told you..."

Robin flaps a tired hand at Kat. "I know, they care for females. Whatever." She closes her eyes and leans her head back against the wall.

Kat gives me a concerned look as a rustling denotes Orvos returning.

"Lie back," he orders me, holding something that looks like a cross between a trumpet and a stethoscope.

Kat nods encouragingly.

"I don't know about this, Kat. I think Jay should be here," I say.

"Does he not know you are with me?" Orvos's expression doesn't change, but he backs away a couple of paces.

There is an impressive commotion just outside the double doors which draws his attention, and he sighs.

"Looks like he's found out anyway."

Lauren!

The thoughtbond blares with my name, with Jay's terror and his love, just as the big warrior bursts through the doors, feathers flying. He's followed, at approximately the same speed, by the rest of his unit, minus Mylo.

He races across to me, and I'm in his arms before I can even blink.

"Are you okay?" He nuzzles at me, hands roving over my body. "When I heard you were here, I..." He can't even complete the sentence.

"I'm fine, Jay. I just want to be sure Yuliat didn't harm the baby. Kat suggested I come here." I kiss him gently on his jaw, and he molds to my body.

"Yes, and I'd like to complete my examination, but not with an audience." Orvos gives the rest of the unit a death glare which doesn't seem to bother them at all. "Get out!" he adds forcefully.

Unfortunately, at that moment, Mylo chooses to put in a noisy appearance, shouldering his way through to the front.

"This is a surgery!" Orvos growls. "Leave now, or I will inform the Prime, and I know you are already in enough trouble."

They still don't seem in a hurry to leave, even when faced

with the grumpy medic. Grins are exchanged. Mylo sidles up to Jay and wing bumps him.

"Good hunting, brother," he says cryptically. "I'll make the arrangements."

"I mean it." Orvos is snarling. "Out!" He points at the two remaining warriors, Ayar and Vypr.

Ayar has his eyes fixed on something in the room. As Vypr pulls at a wing, he huffs out an angry breath. I follow his gaze and see it's on Robin. She stares right back, unblinking, as if mesmerized.

Orvos stamps his foot in an action I'd find funny if he wasn't so big and angry. Vypr whispers something in Ayar's ear and, lips brushing his skin, and he runs a hand over Ayar's wing. Finally, the scarred warrior shifts, and the pair of them troop out, but not before Vypr looks back over his shoulder.

"Come," Orvos says. "We will have some privacy." He beckons us both. Jay swings me into his arms and despite my protests, carries me as we follow Orvos through to a back room which has the one thing I hoped never to see again.

The chair of nightmares, the one from the ship.

Jay

My mate at least looks well which is an incredible relief. However, the bands Mylo slipped into my pocket sit heavy.

All of this is happening so fast for my mate, her thought-bond is a riot of emotions, and I don't want to overwhelm her.

But I do want her to take my band. I've seen the human mates of the seniors wearing their bands, and I long to see mine on Lauren. As well as wearing one proudly on my arm next to the gold of the elite unit.

As we walk through to the back of the surgery, she freezes in my arms, becoming stiff.

"What is it?" I ask.

"I'm not going in that thing," she says, and I spot the medi-pod. It's similar to the one on the ship, the one where I found her.

"You don't have to do anything you don't want to do," I say fiercely, setting up a growl at Orvos.

"I'm not putting a pregnant female in the pod." Orvos sighs. "For a start, it's set up for vrexing useless Gryn warriors who injure themselves vrexing about drunk or fighting."

He walks around the machine, and I gently lower Lauren to the ground. We both peer around it to see Orvos fussing with something next to an ordinary ledge.

Immediately, I feel her mind calm, even though the concern for our youngling is still there.

"Come! I haven't got all day," Orvos calls out.

"Is he the only doctor you have?" Lauren hisses under her breath. "Because he could use a crash course in manners."

"Orvos is Orvos. He does have to deal with 'vrexing useless Gryn warriors' all day," I say in what I hope is a passable imitation of our grumpy medic. Lauren giggles, covering her mouth as she eyes him.

"Now I've seen your unit in action, I think I know what he means." She strolls across the room and takes a seat on the bed next to Orvos.

I'm next to her in a flash, my instinct wanting to protect my mate from the elder male, despite him not being a threat of any kind.

"The lair's had so many younglings in recent cycles, since the humans arrived, Kyt finally helped me repurpose this scanner to assist me." Orvos holds up something that looks like a cross between a smart phone and a metal detector. "For some reason, all you mated pairs want to know is how your younglings are progressing," he grumbles. "Instead of letting nature take its course."

"I think I like you," Lauren says with a smile.

"Lie down," he orders. "I will not be touching your mate," he snaps at me as I let out a low growl. "Look at that screen there, and you will see your youngling inside her," he adds, in a slightly softer tone.

He moves the scanner over her abdomen slowly. Lauren keeps her eyes fixed on me as I watch the screen. It starts off dark, but suddenly light fills it, and an image resolves into focus.

The perfect, tiny image of a youngling. Hardly there, I can see the outline of a head, tiny arms, tiny nodes on its back where wings will form.

"Lauren." I'm whispering because I'm so awed. "Look what we made."

She slowly turns her head until she can see the screen too. Her breath stutters.

"Is he okay?" she asks Orvos, the words catching in her throat. "Is this normal? Jay and I haven't been together more than a few weeks."

"Gryn fetal development varies. You are a little further along than I would expect, but so much depends on the male." He looks up at me. "And you have a very good male."

"Jay?" Lauren's eyes are back on me. Her cheeks are slightly flushed, and tears make her eyes sparkle.

She is surely the most beautiful creature in the entire universe.

And she is all mine.

"My *eregri*, I have two things I must do. I must build you a nest worthy of you, and seniors be vrexed, I must do it immediately." I brush my lips over hers.

With Orvos in attendance, I have to show her exactly what I want to do to her in our nest down the thoughtbond, which causes her flush to deepen and the scent of her arousal to fill my nostrils.

A pregnant mate is most definitely the best and dirtiest mate a Gryn could have.

"And the other thing?" she rasps, because I've just filled her mind with all the panting, grinding, and thrusting I can muster.

I dig into my pocket, not hesitating for a second.

"Lauren, you are my beginning and my end. My fated mate, my boundless flight. You fill my heart. I would fly to the moons for you and to the end of time. Please take my band and let me claim you."

I hold out the metal circle. It glints perfectly in the light, etchings over its surface echoing how her gray eyes glitter like crystals. I marvel at how Myk has made these bands in such a short time and met my exacting criteria.

"You want to marry me?" Lauren's eyes are wide now, tears spilling down her cheeks.

"That's what humans call taking a band," Orvos says helpfully.

We both stare at him.

"I've got work to do," he grumbles and, switching off the scanner, huffs as he rises and rustles out of the room in a fury of feathers.

Finally, I'm alone with my *eregri*. She takes the band from my fingers and turns it over in her beautiful, clawless hands.

"You don't have to do this, Jay. You don't have to marry me just because I'm pregnant," she says, her eyes not meeting mine.

"I'm not doing this for any reason other than the fact I love you and you are mine." I sweep an arm around her expanding form, slamming my lips to hers and kissing her in a way she should know is a claiming.

Lauren laughs as I release her. Such a simple sound which fills my soul and the thoughtbond with life.

"You are something else entirely, Jay." She rubs her hands over my chest and up onto my shoulders. "You've proved to me one thing."

"And what's that?"

"Love is being in the heart and mind of a dirty alien angel. You've made me something I never thought I could be. Happy." She tilts her head back, the little shift she wears allowing me to look right down at her creamy breasts, ones I will most definitely be paying a lot of attention to later, once I've nested.

"Jay!" she exclaims. "You do know I heard all of those thoughts, don't you?"

"Of course, my *eregri*. I wanted you to know just how much I desired you." I trace a finger over the soft skin at the base of her neck. "Now, will you take my band or no?"

"Like you even have to ask." She holds it out to me, and I take it from her, gently slipping it over her hand and up her arm until it settles on her skin, the psychic metal molding to her.

"My turn." She raises her eyebrows. "You have to have one too. I don't want any other designing women taking my Jay from me."

"Like I could even look at another female when I have you," I snort, but pull out my band, a darker gray that matches my wings.

Lauren takes it from me and slips it up my arm, slowly, her fingers grazing me and her gaze lingering on my chest and arm. She settles it under the gold of my Unit and traces the tips of her fingers over it, gently biting her lip.

"It is done," she whispers.

"And now, all I have to do is claim you until you scream." I toss her into my arms.

"I think you'll find you're the one who'll be doing the screaming." She wraps her arms around my neck. "Because there's a whole lot more about mating you've yet to discover."

"I look forward to every single second, my sweet *eregri*."

Epilogue

Lauren

The atrium in the eyrie is lit by thousands of pinpricks of light. I've no idea what they are, but it's incredibly pretty.

While the main lair of the Gryn is imposing, the eyrie seems more intimate somehow. It houses Jay's unit and an influx of warriors they received when the planet was liberated from the sentient AI called Proto. Apparently, fights are frequent, but the slightly less stifling atmosphere is helping them adjust to their new lives, where they can do what they want, when they want.

The Gryn like to fight and fly and, as I've discovered over the last week, these males love to party.

Our banding ceremony has taken up all of our time, other than when Jay has me in our nest, which is situated near the top of the eyrie, neatly tucked away. He spent a long time making it, and when he did the big reveal, I couldn't have been happier.

Although, providing he hadn't just torn up strips of bedding, anything could have done. However, he had procured two rooms, one with a sanitary area containing a large pool, like the one back in the Drahon compound. The other held an enormous bed, covered in pelts and furs of all kinds. The ceiling, he adorned in soft cream fabric which ripples like silk. It's like a huge tent, and I immediately felt at home, given it reminded me of my time spent out on digs in the wilderness.

And the best part—it's what Jay wanted for me.

Tonight is all about the party, apparently, and we have some very excitable males present. Some scuffles have already broken out, but having been with all of the Gryn for a week, I know this is just par for the course.

"Have I told you how beautiful you look?" Jay says as he takes a step back from me and admires the long silk gown which is the deepest of blues.

"Oh, only about a hundred times." I spin back into him. "But you can say it again if you like."

"I hope this night never ends." He presses a kiss to my cheek and, taking my hand, he strides out into the center of the atrium.

On cue, Syn lifts into the air. It's his last night in the eyrie, and by the way he's been getting stuck into the barrels of beer that have been brought in, you'd think it was his last night on Ustokos.

"ALL HAIL JAY AND LAUREN!" he bellows as he circles the atrium.

"I think you'll find that's my prerogative." Strykr drops down from above as a hush falls over the atrium. "As Jay's commander."

"Guv?" Jay queries, his hand in mine.

"Your mate has taken your band?" he says solemnly.

He extends a wing, and Kat joins him, her pregnancy emphasized by the scarlet dress she wears, all floaty and light.

"Lauren has accepted my band, Guv," Jay says holding me tightly, almost as if Strykr would spirit me away.

"And Jay has taken your band?" He addresses me.

"He has," I reply, resting my head against Jay's chest so I can hear his heart beating.

"Then, by the goddess, you are bound. For now and for eternity." He raises his voice. "So let's get on with this vrexing party!"

The assembled warriors erupt with cheers so loud I nearly clap my hands over my ears.

"IS THIS AN UNSANCTIONED GATHERING?" The voice penetrates even the cheering of the warriors, and that dies away as an enormous Gryn spins around the atrium and lands in front of Jay with a thump that seems to shake the gathering.

"Prime, I..." Strykr takes a step towards the huge warrior.

He holds up a clawed hand.

"Did I not decree this unit was to have all privileges taken away until the mercs learned to obey their seniors?" Jyr says, gazing directly at Jay.

"You did." Jay doesn't move, doesn't flinch under this imposing Gryn's glare.

"And what is this?"

"It is the celebration of my banding with my mate." Jay holds me tighter. "Nothing is more important than her, nor will it ever be."

Jyr stares at us both, dark eyes giving away nothing, but his hands curl into fists, and I can almost feel the warring of emotions within him. Not as strong as with Jay, but they are there nonetheless.

"You are banded, my dear?" Jyr asks me directly.

"With all my heart," I reply. "And all my soul. Jay saved me, not just from Drahon, but in so many ways."

"And you are with young, yes?" Jyr's eyes glitter.

"She is," Jay says proudly, his hand spanning my stomach.

"Then what are we vrexing waiting for?" Jyr roars out,

grinning from ear to ear. "Where's my beer and who's organizing the games?" He throws an arm around Jay's shoulders, dragging him from me. "You're going to get so vrexing drunk you won't know what way is up!"

"I really don't think so." I fold my arms, staring up at the huge warrior.

For the first time, Jyr hesitates. "It's a tradition?" he ventures.

"It is not!" a female voice rings out through the open space.

Behind him, a gaggle of women appear. Kat leaves Strykr's side to embrace them. An utterly devastatingly beautiful woman, her long, tawny hair flowing down her back and her stomach rounded in late stage pregnancy steps into the light. She reaches Jyr, and he bends to kiss her with a tenderness and intensity which is equally as beautiful.

"Let Jay celebrate how he wishes, Jyr," she says. "I'm sure there are plenty of mercs who will happily play your games tonight."

"Although," Jay ventures, "if we're flying, I'll join in." The thoughtbond rings with delight. I already know he'll win whatever he enters.

"Then get me a beer and we'll get started," Jyr growls.

My Jay could not be happier. He's here, with me and with the seniors in attendance. I am banded and I am his.

I am truly home.

Book 3: CHAOS: A Sci-Fi Alien Romance releases in

August 2022. Read on for a taster of Ayar, Vypr and Robin's story!

Sign up to my newsletter for a free bonus scene which has the aftermath of Jay and Lauren's banding party. You'll also get sneak peaks, cover reveals, exclusive content and giveaways.

So if you want all of the above, sign up HERE

You can also sign up on my website www.hattiejacks.com

And you can follow me on Bookbub, Amazon or even join my Facebook group - Hattie's Hotties!

CHAOS
A Sci-Fi Alien Romance

Robin

If I had a watch, I could set it by the comings and goings in the surgery.

It's the only place on this whole alien planet I've seen so far with its crumbling concrete walls and the scent of antiseptic and sedatives. But I have seen some of what lives on this planet. They're big. They're most definitely male. They have huge wings, dark eyes and long, sharp claws.

I don't know how many of them there are, or anything else about this place. All I know is I was abducted in a space ship by a huge lizard with stinking breath who found me huddled in my car at the deserted car park. I understand everything the aliens say because they did something to my brain, and I got blown up when the flying aliens rescued me from the lizard aliens.

My luck knows no bounds.

I start to count down under my breath, the surgery's first visitor should be coming through the double doors right about...now.

One door slams open and through it stagger three aliens, young ones, by the pale color to their wings. One droops between the other two. The ruler of this little kingdom within a kingdom, Orvos, medic for the Legion of the Gryn, rises from his desk. Naked from the waist up, like they all are, probably due to the wings, his imposing, craggy features twist into a grimace.

"What now?" He fires out.

He's not got the best bedside manner.

"Drink, drugs or fight?" He spits.

Or temper.

"Um, flight competition." The upright one says. The other, dangling in his arms, eyes rolling in his head, says nothing.

"Vrexing mercs." Orvos clucks. "Put him over there." He points to a ledge which, similar to mine, doubles as a bed and juts out from the concrete wall.

It has a crude mattress, covered with a fluid resistant material. I know from experience he'll get one blanket.

I pull my two blankets over me a little further. Hard fought for and I'm not letting them go. They're all I have in this world.

Orvos bustles around the young warrior he referred to as a 'mercs', which I think denotes they are the bottom most rank in this legion. The hapless male is quickly sedated, and his wounds treated. If he's lucky he'll get a couple of hours rest before Orvos kicks him out, still drowsy, feathers slicked down, with an exhortation not to come back, ringing in his ears.

He's just one in a long line of minor injuries which will troop through the doors over the next hours.

"How's my little human today?" Orvos, having finished with the merc, bustles over to me.

"Great!" I smile up at him. "I'm feeling great! Maybe I can get out of here?"

"Sit up." Orvos says.

Bastard.

"I'm fine just here, thanks." I smile warmly at him, hoping he'll leave me alone and let me out of the surgery, too. Some hope.

"Up you get." He reaches in, hooking his arms under mine and lifting me into a sitting position. Unable to help myself, I let out a little cry at the pain in my ribs and arm.

"You're not going anywhere, little human." Orvos gazes at me, his dark eyes impenetrable. "Not for a while."

Fuck. Fuck. Fuck. I can't stay here any longer. I'll surely go mad!

I try a different tack.

"But I'm so bored! The other humans will look after me. At least I'd have someone to talk to." I plead with him.

I could always talk the hind legs off a donkey. It was part of my charm. Part of my job. That's what my former boss said.

Former boss as in, the boss I left behind on Earth. Former boss because I'll never have to let him touch me again. Because I've been abducted by aliens, not because I could have escaped his clutches any other way.

I give Orvos the benefit of my best, most impressive, most 'please discharge me' smile.

It doesn't work.

"Human females in my surgery are my responsibility." He rumbles. "Jyr would have my hide if anything happened to you. Your little body took a real pounding and until you heal, you stay here."

He's referring to the blast which broke numerous ribs, my left arm, and my right ankle. We were in the process of being rescued by the Gryn when the space ship we on which were captives decided to explode.

I seem to have gone from the frying pan and into the fire as far as aliens go.

From the disgusting confines of a ship full of scaly lizard

aliens who prodded us around like cattle to being at the mercy of a parade of huge, muscled warriors, most of whom are unhappy and injured, or occasionally drunk and the constant smell which seems to be designed to remind me of the one man I should forget.

The man who took my pride, my self-belief, and more. Even the thought of him makes me swallow hard and shrink back under my blankets. It doesn't help that the Gryn have no females, other than the handful of found humans they have taken into their care. The only females I see are the ones I know from my captivity and who didn't get as damaged as me.

"You are to rest. Your breakfast will be here shortly." Orvos doesn't smile, but the tone in his voice has changed.

I don't think he likes much, but I've become some sort of mascot for him, I've been here so long. Not that he likes the visits from the other humans any more than he likes having his surgery 'cluttered up with mercs'.

Other than that, he doesn't talk much.

I wish my stupid useless body would heal. Diana and Jen have told me about life outside of these four walls, and as much as it sounds alien strange and terrifying, at least I could see it. See something else, other than Orvos and the endless parade of 'vrexing mercs'. Curiosity about my new home burns at me.

Hopefully Diana will come today. Maybe bring Kat, the human who was with the team of Gryn warriors who rescued us and scraped me up off the ground. She has the cutest little robot. I could spend hours with it. I don't see much of Jen these days, but then she was a bit of an enigma, preferring to spend time with the hulking, dark and dangerous Gryn we first met when we were all captives of the lizard creatures called the Drahon.

My breakfast arrives and Orvos carefully places the tray on my lap. For a male his size and his temper, he can be nice when he wants to be. Maybe like the father I always longed for. A dad I could look up to, rather than run away from.

"Hey you!" I wake from a light doze to see Diana sitting down on the edge of my bed.

"Hi!" I attempt to push myself upright but fail. "Any chance of a breakout today?" I hiss conspiratorially.

Diana appraises me cooly and looks over her shoulder at Orvos, who is sitting at his desk pretending to ignore us.

"When you can sit up on your own I will petition that great hulk, Jyr, to let you out. But until then, you're best off here, hun." She gives me a hesitant smile.

Diana is a strong lady. She's a Londoner through and through, while I was an incomer, drawn to the city from my rural roots in Yorkshire. Leaving behind the stone walls and emerald, green fields for the big smoke. Leaving behind my disaster area of a family and dropping myself into something else entirely. But I loved to hear her stories. She was some sort of antiquities dealer and has tales from her travels which raised the hair on your arms. Although nothing quite beats alien abduction.

And she didn't take any shit either, not from the Drahon and not from the Gryn either, it seems.

Given I've seen the Prime, Jyr, the leader of all these enormous males, once, he's not one I'd challenge. He visited me along with his human mate Viv, a beautiful woman who was very kind and understanding. She made sure I had the extra blanket. Despite his formidable appearance, I'm pretty sure I could've talked Jyr round given half the chance. I can talk my way out of most things. That's what made me valuable to my former employer. But actually stand up to one of these big aliens? I learnt a long time ago not to do anything rash. Not where men are concerned.

"I'm so bored." I complain to Diana.

"I know, hun. But until you're well enough to deal with

these males, you have to stay here. They mean well, honestly, but they're rough around the edges, and sometimes don't know their own strength."

Her words send a shiver through me. I've seen some of what she says in the males who come in with fight injuries, their naked torsos streaked with blood.

To distract myself, I curl my hand around hers. "Have you heard anything about your sister?" I ask.

Diana's eyes go cold for an instant. "Nothing. The Gryn have promised to look for her, and I know she's here on Ustokos. I just know it." She bunches her hand into a fist, but I don't let go.

My life might be boring, and painful at the moment, but at least I have no one to miss and no one to miss me.

"I'm sure they'll find her." I say, attempting to be strong for Diana.

After all, I can't be strong for me. I lost that ability a long time before I was abducted. I may as well try to do some good for someone else.

Vypr

"The weapons store is somewhere around here." Syn checks his vectorpad again, then he turns it the other way up, while I sigh in frustration.

To my left, Ayar kicks a rock and eyes the vectorpad with suspicion, but at least his weapon remains slung over his shoulder.

I look around at the ruined buildings. We're in the neighboring city, or what's left of it, to Kos, where our lair and eyrie are situated. Not that any city on Ustokos is unscathed. The great reckoning between organic life and the sentient AI, Proto, which sought to destroy it all did for virtually all our cities and most of our technology.

What tech was left, was untouchable. Proto was in it all and when it found you, it was death or capture. And if you were captured, you'd most likely long for death. It doesn't bear thinking about, not anymore.

Since the Gryn finally managed to destroy Proto and regain control of our planet, we're starting to rebuild little by little as our numbers are small. We're also discovering tech which has lain dormant for a long time. Our forefathers were once as sophisticated as we are backward.

Today, we're trying to locate a weapons dump Syn claims to have identified. Because this is a low level mission, only half of our Elite unit has been sent out, consisting of me, Ayar and Syn. Syn because he knows tech.

Ayar because he can't be trusted on his own, anywhere.

I growl at Syn, wanting to hurry him up. We are exposed out here, and although the threat of killer bots is long gone, I don't like being this exposed. I glance at Ayar again. He shakes out his feathers a little, his skin sheens because I made him have a bath and a preen earlier. He is a magnificent male, and my heart beats a little faster for him.

He is my mate. I knew he was the first time I saw him, trapped in the terrible machine. They say you always know your mate when you see them, and for me, it was Ayar. My beautiful, troubled warrior. The male I saved and now I love.

And protect, constantly. Mostly from himself.

"Got a lock!" Syn says, triumphantly.

"About time." Ayar grumbles. "I was promised explosions." He levels his gaze at me, and it's one I recognize of old. He's in the mood to fight.

"No blowing anything up today, you vrexer." Syn retorts. "We need these weapons. Especially after we got the last cohort through. The Guv's desperate for more laser pistols and rifles." He references our Commander, Strykr, who has been given the unenviable task of marshaling some of the newer Gryn warriors into units like ours.

Maybe not quite like ours. We are the original Elite. Formed by Ryak, the lair head of security and who moved us all the eyrie a cycle ago. Any other units will be a poor imitation.

With Strykr busy setting everything up, I'm hoping a command position might open for me. Maybe then Ayar and I might get a small barrack room to ourselves, rather than having to share with the others.

All of which means, I could do with this mission going well and not turning into a vrexing shambles.

"We know how important the weapons are, Syn. Any chance you could tell us where they are, and we can get on with our jobs?" I fire out at him.

Syn has had a downer on Ayar since he joined the unit. Most of the time it doesn't bother Ayar. A lot of social interactions seem to go straight over his head. But it bothers me. Right now, Ayar stares into the sky, probably thinking about blasting something.

"That building, over there." Syn points north and springs into the air.

Ayar and I unfurl our wings and follow him as he rises over the shattered remains of the Gryn civilization and swoops low over the one building in the area which still possesses a roof.

When we land, I see why. It's more like a bunker, thick walls and roof have protected it from the original bombardment which reduced this place to rubble many hundreds of cycles ago.

"How do we get in?" I ask.

Both Ayar and Syn turn to look at me. Ayar looking particularly baleful.

"Vrex the pair of you." I get busy with the various explosives I've become an expert in since Proto fell.

Before, when the skies were full of bots and laser weapons were out of bounds due to the tech contained in them, we used swords, daggers and crossbows. Even now, I probably prefer this type of weapon for combat, if given the choice. But I seem to have found a new calling when it comes to explosives.

Having carefully rigged everything to blow the corner off

the bunker, I indicate to the others to get back and let rip with the charge.

A huge cheer comes from Ayar as the thing blows. He loves a good explosion, which is why I have to keep his contact to my stash of ordinance minimal, or quite a lot of Kos would be in even more ruins.

Given we're trying to rebuild, it wouldn't go down well with the senior Gryn if he did start damaging more things.

Dust settles and reveals a warrior sized hole in the side of the bunker. Before I can stop him, Ayar is inside, whooping loudly like a youngling.

Syn stares at where his feathers disappear, slithering down the hole. He looks at me, and I run my hand through my hair in exasperation.

I love my mate, but even I have to admit he's a liability.

Howls of delight echo from the hole as Syn makes ready to drop in, and I follow.

Maybe, just maybe, for once this is a mission which will go right for a change.

READY FOR AYAR'S POINT OF VIEW? PRE ORDER Chaos now!

Also by Hattie Jacks

Elite Rogue Alien Warriors Series

STORM

FURY

CHAOS

REBEL (Coming soon)

WRATH (Coming soon)

Rogue Alien Warriors Series

Fierce

Fear

Fire

Fallen

Forever

Sci-fi romance Anthology

Claimed Among The Stars includes:

Fated: A Rogue Alien Warriors Novella

Haalux Empire Series

Taken: Alien Commander's Captive

Crave: Alien General's Obsession
Havoc: Alien Captain's Alliance
Bane: Alien Warrior's Redemption
Traitor: Alien Hunter's Mate

Just who is this Hattie Jacks anyway?

I've been a passionate sci-fi fan since I was a little girl, brought up on a diet of Douglas Adams, Issac Asimov, Star Trek, Star Wars, Doctor Who, Red Dwarf and The Adventure Game.

What? You don't know about The Adventure Game? It's probably a British thing and dates me horribly! Google it. Even better search for it on YouTube. In my defence, there were only three channels back then.

I'm also a sucker for great characters and situations as well as grand romance, because who doesn't like a grand romantic gesture?

So, when I'm not writing steamy stories about smouldering alien males and women with something to prove, you'll find me battling my garden (less English country garden, more The Good Life) or zooming around the countryside on my motorbike.

Check out my website at www.hattiejacks.com!

Printed in Great Britain
by Amazon